Royal
CRUSH

ROYAL CRUSH
Copyright 2024 © Rich Amooi
http://www.richamooi.com

To Paul Cardenas.
The funniest guy I know.
You should write a book.
Really.

Chapter One

PRINCE OLIVER

"I'm going to sabotage my wedding," I said to my friend Dante, who also happened to be my personal assistant.

His eyes went wide and both of his brows shot up toward his hairline in typical Dante fashion.

Admittedly, it probably sounded absurd for the royal prince of Verdana to want to sabotage his own wedding. On the other hand, someone had the audacity of naming a sans-serif font after my country, so who was really the crazy one here?

"Are you sure you have thought this through completely?" Dante asked.

"Believe me—it's the perfect plan," I said, glancing out the window of the palace billiard room. "Veronica knows about it."

"And she approves?" he said.

I grimaced. "She's on the fence. Veronica doesn't want

to get married, but she also wonders if we can really get out of it."

As for the proposed wedding, any man would count his lucky stars to have the opportunity to marry someone as delightful as Princess Veronica of Kastonia, but I would not be one of them. She was more like a close cousin to me than a future spouse. We knew each other well, yet neither of us had ever harbored a single ounce of romantic feelings for the other.

This arranged marriage felt more like a cruel joke.

I glanced over at the gaudy painting on the wall next to the dartboard that depicted a dashing knight professing his undying love for a swooning maiden. If only real life worked out so idyllically. Perhaps I could pull off such a dramatic declaration of love if the occasion called for it. But I would not settle for a pre-chosen woman to be my wife, not even for my beloved country.

I ran my fingers along the emerald-green felt of the full-sized pool table as the Tiffany glass chandelier cast a warm glow across the top of my hand. "Pool or darts?"

"Darts," Dante said without hesitation. "Ready for a thrashing?"

I took a pull from the beer in my frosty mug, set it down on the mahogany bar, then reached for the three darts. "I'm ready for you to eat those words."

Stepping up to the line, I plucked one of the three darts from my palm. I held it thirty centimeters from my nose, closed one eye to focus, then twirled the dart dramatically between my fingers.

Without fail, this always irritated Dante.

"Please," he said, right on cue. "Any time this century would be lovely, *Your Highness.*"

With my mind obsessed with thoughts of a wedding I did not want, I stared at the red bull's-eye far longer than necessary before letting the dart fly. Unfortunately, the results were less than pleasing. The dart missed the board entirely, instead hitting the aforementioned painting and, like a dagger, stabbing the dashing knight right in his gallant heart.

"Aha, a metaphor!" I said.

"My goodness—the prince is in rare form this evening," Veronica said with a delicate laugh as she entered the billiard room. "It's a good thing we don't need to rely on your dart-throwing skills to get us out of this predicament." She shook her head in amusement.

"Clearly I'm not fit to be anyone's husband yet," I said.

I frustratedly took a deep breath and set the other two darts down on the cocktail table. Hurling sharp, pointy objects when one was not concentrating fully was not the wisest course of action.

"Perhaps, instead of sabotaging the wedding, you could simply develop a sudden allergy to people," Dante said. "That would surely be a valid reason to postpone the wedding."

"I'm afraid I am going to have to disagree with you," Veronica said. "Queen Annabelle would then force us to get married in a plastic bubble. Nothing stops her when she wants something."

"We need a realistic, full-proof plan to extract ourselves from this extremely inconvenient and ill-advised situation we've found ourselves in," I said. "Let's revisit my idea."

"Queen Annabelle would have our heads if she found out we sabotaged the wedding," Veronica said.

"Then she can't find out," I said. "But we both know she would never allow us to go through with the wedding if there were signs of problems."

Mother was possibly the most superstitious person in all of Europe. Any inauspicious events during the wedding planning would be considered a sign to her that the impending marriage would be doomed, and she would put a halt to it. With a little strategic planning, we could end this farce without yours truly having to run away from home like a petulant child.

"With all due respect, that does not solve the food-supply problem, which was the primary reason for your union," Dante said. "Queen Annabelle may be strict, but she only wants what's best for the kingdom."

"Good point," I said. "But that doesn't mean it is good for either of us in the long run. We should be free to choose our own lifelong partners."

Mount Verdana had erupted a little over a year ago, blanketing our country's fertile farmlands on the west side of the island in volcanic debris, and rendering them useless. Luckily, there are still many beautiful parts of the country, but since then, the kingdom had temporarily relied on Veronica's country for over seventy percent of essential food imports like wheat and rice. Mother believed our marriage was critical to cement an alliance that would ensure vital grain shipments continued to sustain Verdana for decades to come.

"If anyone can solve the problem, it's Veronica," I said, hoping she would put to good use her master of science in agriculture from the University of Copenhagen. "One step at a time. We need to focus on getting out of the wedding first."

"And how do you expect us to do that?" Veronica asked.

"We'll leave that to Miss DuPont," I said, hoping the royal wedding planner would understand the bind we were in and help us. "Send her a text and tell her we need to meet at once. Miss DuPont owes me a favor or two—she won't let me down."

Dante nodded, pulled out his phone, and tapped. "Done."

"Do you really think Miss DuPont would go against the queen's wishes?" Veronica asked doubtfully.

"Technically, she won't have to if there are a couple of unexplained mishaps," I replied confidently. "Besides, she will understand that my happiness is on the line. Trust me, once Miss DuPont makes things magically fall apart, this arranged marriage will be history."

"She's just outside in the courtyard. She's on her way," Dante informed me, glancing at his phone before sliding it back into his pocket.

A minute later, there was a polite knock on the door, and in walked Miss DuPont.

"Good afternoon, Your Highness, Princess Veronica."

She greeted us with a curtsy, then gave a nod to Dante. Her eyes flicked between Veronica and me, as if sensing the urgency in our expressions. "You wished to see me?"

"Miss DuPont, we have a . . . delicate matter to discuss with you," I began cautiously, glancing at Veronica for support. "Please, have a seat." I gestured to the leather chair opposite Veronica.

As I settled into the other chair, she leaned forward with an air of professionalism, pulling out her pen and notepad. "How may I be of service?"

I took a deep breath, steeling myself for what I was about to propose. "I need your help in sabotaging our wedding."

Miss DuPont's eyes widened in shock, her pen slipping from her fingers and clattering onto the floor. "Your Highness, I . . . I don't understand."

"We cannot go through with this arranged marriage," I said. "It goes against everything we believe in. I need you to make it impossible for the wedding to proceed."

"Prince Oliver . . ." Miss DuPont reached down to pick up her pen from the floor, then hesitated before answering, clearly weighing her options. "While I empathize with your predicament, I'm afraid I cannot assist you in this endeavor. My reputation and livelihood depend on my ability to plan and execute flawless events for the royal family, as well as for the fine people of our country. To do as you ask would be tantamount to professional suicide."

"Miss DuPont, please," I implored, noting the desperation seeping into my voice. "You understand that I am not asking this lightly. I am trapped, *we* are trapped." I gestured to Veronica, then back to myself. "You're the only person who can help us. Nobody will know you are behind the problems, and you would be compensated generously for your work."

"Your Highness," she replied, her tone firm, "I'm sorry for the position you find yourself in, but my duty is to the Crown and to the successful execution of this wedding. I cannot, in good conscience, take part in any form of sabotage. Besides, nobody would ever believe that I made a mistake."

Even under the dire circumstances, that made me smile. "Once a perfectionist, always a perfectionist."

"It's a curse I have to live with," Miss DuPont said with a slight smile. "I guess it would have made your life easier if I were a disaster like that American wedding planner who went viral."

I hesitated, confused. "I'm sorry—I don't understand."

"Grace . . . her last name escapes me at the moment," Miss DuPont said. "She has become rather infamous for her calamitous events."

"How so?" Dante asked.

Miss DuPont slid to the edge of her chair. "This woman has the opposite of the Midas Touch. Everything she touches turns into a calamity. She plans high-profile weddings in Beverly Hills. Well, she used to. Word is, her phone stopped ringing after several videos went viral, then some tabloid labeled her as the worst wedding planner on the planet. The poor thing."

"I found her—her name is Grace Fullerton," Dante said, his eyes glued to his phone. "Wow."

"What is it?" Veronica asked, peeking over Dante's shoulder.

Dante winced, then winced again. "One of her wedding cakes collapsed, then there's another video of wedding guests running right past her in the pouring rain."

"Let me see," I said, then shook my head. "They're blaming the rain on the wedding planner? That is the most ridiculous thing I have ever heard."

"Apparently, there was no back-up plan in case of inclement weather," Miss DuPont pointed out. "That would be on the wedding planner for not suggesting it or having a back-up plan."

I continued watching more videos, including one of a bride approaching the altar to get married, then tripping into the officiant. They both lost their balance and fell into the swimming pool. And another video of Grace making the national news.

"Apparently, Grace caused the break-up of a bride and groom before their actual wedding day," I said. "She gave unsolicited advice to the groom, and then he called off the wedding."

"And that bride is now suing her," Miss DuPont said. "Everybody at the International Society of Wedding Planners has been talking about it."

I nodded, thinking about it, then glanced over at Veronica and smiled.

"You smile at her misfortune?" she asked.

"No," I said. "I smile at our good luck. Grace is the answer to our problems."

"No!" Dante pointed at me, his mouth hanging open. "You want to hire Grace to be your wedding planner?"

I nodded. "Absolutely."

Veronica laughed. "First of all, she's over six thousand miles away. And secondly, what are you going to say to her exactly? Hello, Grace. I'm Prince Oliver from Verdana. Would you be interested in sabotaging my wedding?" She shook her head, clearly amused. "She's not going to agree to anything that would get her into even more hot water, or end up landing her in jail."

"That's just it," I said. "She doesn't have to do anything illegal or immoral. She just needs to be herself, nothing more. Then we will sit back and watch as nature takes its course and she ruins everything."

"Your highness," Dante said, then gestured to Miss DuPont. "You already have a wedding planner, and I seriously doubt Miss DuPont would want to work with someone of that low caliber. Plus, the queen would never approve of this."

"The queen is out of town," I pointed out.

Miss DuPont stiffened and nodded. "If you're still seriously entertaining this idea of sabotaging your own wedding, I regret that I would have to resign as the royal wedding planner. People would talk, there's no doubt. Wonder why I walked away from the opportunity of a lifetime. Although walking away is far better than me being connected to a failed event. That cannot happen."

"Okay—let me think about this for a second," I said, standing, then walking to the window, hoping to find some inspiration in the view.

The vast lawn that stretched out before me was meticulously maintained, spanning the length of an entire football field. In the distance, I could see the palace gardeners busily tending to the vibrant flower beds, their bright colors a stark contrast to the dull feeling in my gut if I didn't come up with something good.

Luckily, inspiration struck when I glanced at the yellow roses.

I flipped around and snapped my fingers. "Miss DuPont, do you still have relatives in France?"

She nodded. "I do. I even have a great-grandfather who will be celebrating his one hundredth birthday soon."

"That is amazing," I said. "When was the last time you saw him?"

Miss DuPont thought about it, then sighed. "It has been far too long. Almost seven years ago."

"Well, have I got a proposition for you then," I said with a grin. "Would you consider taking a leave of absence? To attend his party?"

Miss DuPont studied me. "He's not having a—"

"Yes. He is," I said. "In fact, it will be the grandest birthday party France has ever seen, because I will pay for it, and *you* will plan it. You will travel first class, all expenses paid, of course. That would give me time to contact this Grace person and hire her, without raising my mother's suspicions."

Miss DuPont considered this, then a smile slowly grew on her face. "I suppose I could arrange a brief sabbatical. It sounds quite wonderful, but I do also have the charity event to tend to."

"I'll take care of that as well," I said. "With my mother conveniently out of the country and you in France, I can bring Grace in swiftly and quietly."

"*If* she accepts your offer of employment," Dante said.

I grinned. "Since when have you known me to fail when I put my mind to something?"

Dante gestured to the painting with the dart still stuck in the dashing knight's heart. "Since about five minutes ago?"

I chuckled. "Trust me. This is going to work."

"Very well, Your Highness," Miss DuPont conceded with a sigh as she stood to leave. "I don't approve of deception, but I understand matters of the heart cannot be reasoned with, especially when you and Princess Veronica feel the same way. And it would be a thrill to see my relatives again."

"Thank you, Miss DuPont. I'll arrange for your travel after I secure Grace's services." I smiled, feeling the first rays of hope in days. "Oh, and I would appreciate your discretion."

She nodded. "Of course, Your Highness. But please be aware that if I am questioned directly by Queen Annabelle about this matter, I will be forced to tell the truth."

"I would expect nothing less from you," I said. "And if it comes to that, I will take full responsibility. You have my word."

"I appreciate that, Your Highness," she said.

After Miss DuPont left the room, Veronica turned to me. "Is this really what we're resorting to?"

"Desperate times, Veronica," I replied. "I just need to find Grace's contact information."

"Already found it and texted it to you," Dante said.

"Good man," I said, pulling out my phone and glancing at Grace's website and phone number. "Okay, wish me luck."

I wasted no time dialing the number.

"Grace's Wedding Wonders," answered a hesitant voice on the other end of the line.

"Good day," I began, doing my best to sound casual despite the weight of my future happiness resting on this conversation. "Is this Grace?"

"Who is calling, please?' she replied, her tone guarded.

"Prince Oliver," I said.

"Yeah—and I'm Cinderella," she scoffed before she ended the call.

I pulled away the phone from my ear and blinked, then turned to face Veronica and Dante. "She hung up on me."

"Give it another shot, Oliver," Veronica suggested, the corners of her mouth twitching with amusement. "Start off with something that will get her attention, like that you would like to acquire her services. Money talks, as they say."

"Very well," I sighed, redialing the number and mentally preparing myself for another round of hostility.

"What?!" she answered.

"Please don't hang up on me—I require your services for my wedding," I said.

There was silence.

"Hello? Grace? Are you there?" My voice cracked in an unusual fashion.

"Who are you now?" she asked. "Kermit the Frog?"

I hesitated. "You can't possibly believe that. Kermit's voice is high-pitched and raspy, and he shifts his tone to convey different emotions. My voice is more monotone."

"I would say it's more monotonous," Grace said. "Now, if you'll excuse me, the Queen of Hearts is about to chop off my head. I regret I must bid you adieu!" Just like that, she was gone.

"Unbelievable," I fumed, pacing the room once more. "She just hung up on me again."

This time, Veronica laughed. "You gave it a valiant effort. Let's come up with another option."

I huffed. "Absolutely not. If she thinks I'm giving up so easily, she's in for a rude awakening."

"Then at least put it on speakerphone, so we can all be entertained," she said.

I dialed her number again and tapped the speakerphone as she answered on the first ring.

"Listen, you creeper—I don't know who you are, but stop calling here and yanking my chain!" Grace snapped, her patience clearly wearing thin. "I don't need this from you, I don't need this from anyone! It's not funny."

"Grace, I assure you, I am indeed Prince Oliver of Verdana, and I am quite serious about hiring you," I insisted, feeling my frustration mount. "Please hear me out."

She sighed in my ear. "Just leave me alone . . . please." Her voice was cracking as she spoke this time.

Wait, was she going to cry?

"Just answer this," I said. "Are you taking on new clients?"

"I know what you're doing," Grace said. "You saw videos of me online, and you called to have a little fun. Well, I'm sorry to tell you that you're not being original. You're the third person to call today for the sole purpose of being cruel. If you have any heart at all, leave me alone. Please."

"You've got me all wrong—hang on," I said, taking a selfie with my phone and texting it to her. "Check your phone. I just took a picture of myself, so you can see that it's really me."

"Big deal—I can text you a picture of Taylor Swift and tell you it's me," Grace said. "This proves nothing."

"Fair enough," I said as Veronica and Dante watched me with curiosity on their faces. "I suppose my word alone isn't sufficient proof for a total stranger. Let me provide you with a photo known only to the inner royal circle." I rapidly searched my phone before continuing. "There. I just sent you a rather embarrassing snapshot of myself learning to cook homemade macaroni and cheese with our palace chef. As you'll see, I'm an absolute mess with melted cheese covering my apron. Now surely even you can admit such an undignified image would never be leaked to the public. If my mother, the queen, knew this photo existed, she'd be horrified, and I'd likely face banishment to muck out the royal stables for a month. Now, do you believe it's me?"

Veronica and Dante exchanged amused glances as we all waited for Grace to say something, anything, really.

There was silence on the other end of the call.

"Hello? Grace?" I said.

She was laughing.

Hysterically.

I looked up at Veronica and Dante, but they both shrugged, clearly as confused as I was.

"Okay, I see you're amused by the photo, but I wouldn't say that it's funny. Slightly entertaining? Yes. Interesting? Sure."

Grace tried to speak while continuing to laugh. "I didn't see any macaroni. You sent me the 'Macarena.' Or I should say, a video of you attempting to do the dance. Holy smokes! Are you wearing a coconut bra?" More laughter from her.

"What?!" I said, tapping back to my text messages, my eyes going wide. "Good heavens. That was a video from our Christmas party. It shouldn't even exist anymore. I command you to delete that at once."

"I shall not!" Grace shot back defiantly, still laughing. "You look like a drunk octopus who lost control of his tentacles."

Veronica and Dante were now howling with laughter.

I placed my index finger over my mouth to quiet them down, then shot them both an indignant glare. That made

Veronica laugh harder, covering her mouth as she snorted and giggled. Dante slapped his knee, wheezing with breathless laughter at my embarrassment.

"Thank you," Grace said. "I really needed a good laugh. Especially today. Is there somebody there with you?"

I wasn't expecting that question.

"Just the television," I lied. "Please . . . let's get back to the reason for my call. I want to hire you to plan my wedding."

"Why me?" she asked.

Another question I wasn't expecting.

"Because—I've seen what's happening to you on social media and in the news," I said. "People deserve second chances, don't you think?"

More silence from her end of the call.

"Grace?" I said.

"I'm here."

"Does ten thousand dollars for one month sound reasonable?" I asked. "All expenses paid, of course. First class flight, all meals, anything extra that you need, consider it done."

Grace hesitated. "Ten thousand dollars?"

"Make it twenty," I said, hoping to ride the momentum since it felt like she was coming around. "And any other expenses you may have, clothes, shoes."

"I can meet with you in person to discuss, but I make no promises," Grace said. "Tomorrow at three in the afternoon. It's the only opening I have this week."

I found that very hard to believe. She knew I was in

Europe and that I would have to drop everything and leave immediately if I wanted that appointment.

Grace was trying to get rid of me again.

Or she was trying to complicate my life.

"Verdana is over six-thousand miles away," I said.

"Well then, you'd better get going," Grace said, hanging up on me again for the third time.

"That woman has quite possibly lost her mind," I said.

I shook my head in disbelief, then took another big gulp of my beer before I glanced out the window again.

"It was a good effort on your part," Dante said. "Back to square one, then?"

"On the contrary . . ." I turned to him, ready to take the biggest gamble of my life. "Get the plane ready. We're going to California."

Chapter Two

GRACE

The Next Day . . .

My once lively office now felt like a ghost town, littered with broken dreams, unpaid bills, and an empty canister of See's Candies Almond Royal chocolate bites. The only thing missing was tumbleweeds, but knowing my luck, they would blow through the front door at any moment now.

I sat at my desk, staring at the almost-empty inbox on my laptop screen. I hadn't received a new email in three days, unless I counted the free dessert offer for my birthday from California Pizza Kitchen or the message in my spam folder from a very generous Nigerian prince.

Two prince imposters in twenty-four hours.

How did I go from being the most sought-after wedding planner in Southern California to rock bottom in fewer than three months? I really needed to stop dwelling on what happened and focus on drumming up new business.

My best friend Cristina would tell me to forget about the past, to chin up, and to manifest my future by visualizing what I really wanted. She's the champion of pep talks, which I try to absorb as best as I can to keep myself from slipping into the pit of despair.

"Knock, knock!" Cristina beamed as she entered my office.

"Hey," I said. "What are you up to?"

"I just happened to be in the area and thought I'd pop in to say hi."

Cristina "just happened" to be in the area every single day this week, though I knew she was simply checking up on me. I honestly don't know what I'd have done without her support. We'd always been there for each other. Like last year, when I had done the same for her during her ugly divorce. That's what friends were for, to help us pick up the pieces when living our lives felt more like a losing round of Jenga.

Cristina plopped down on the edge of my desk, then leaned over to glance at my laptop. "What are you working on?"

I sighed. "Today's the day I beg catering directors for potential clients." I gestured to the list of names and phone numbers I had laid out. "I need to call these wedding venues."

"I still think you should call back that prince," Cristina said. "He could be your fairy godfather!"

"He's nothing but a scam," I replied. "European royalty would not call to request my disaster-magnet services after seeing those viral videos online."

She refused to accept my response. "Prince Oliver believes in second chances, remember? He obviously wants to help make the world a better place. And you just are the lucky recipient of his kindness and compassion!"

I couldn't help smiling. "I can't believe how gullible you are."

"I prefer to think of myself as a dreamer," Cristina said.

"Okay, I'll give you that one."

"How about lunch?" she asked. "I'm starving."

"Thanks, but I already ate," I said, gesturing to the empty See's Candies container, then reaching over and tossing it in the trash can.

"And you don't think that's cosmic direction that you ate something called Almond *Royal* the day after talking to a prince?" Cristina asked.

"Fake prince," I corrected. "And sorry for being such a downer. I just need one new client to save this sinking ship, to get my life going in the right direction. I don't need any further surprises or fake princes. I stopped believing in fairy tales."

"Chin up—you can do it," she said, right on cue. "I have a feeling the tides are shifting for you. I can feel it." She gave my shoulder a supportive squeeze. "Your happily ever after is right around the corner, in your career, in your love life, in everything you set your mind to. Your next big opportunity could walk through that door at any minute."

She gestured to the door, as if she were expecting someone.

Like magic, there was a knock.

Cristina's mouth fell open as she jumped back. "See?" She clapped excitedly. "Maybe it's Prince Charming now! Kick off one of your shoes and pretend you lost it."

"You really need to get your fairy tales straight," I said, rolling my eyes as I opened the door. My heart sank when I saw the property manager standing there.

Tommy Tightwad.

Okay, his real name was Tommy Tighter, but Tightwad was a much better fit. The man never smiled, didn't know the meaning of the word flexible, and we only saw him when he was looking for money. *My* money.

"I've been trying to reach you about your late rent payment," he said, his tone cold and unsympathetic. "It's the third month in a row. This is unacceptable. Pay up now or you're out."

"Look, I know I'm behind, but I just need a little more time," I pleaded, feeling the weight of my world collapsing in on me. "I'm just about to get a new client."

"You brought this on yourself," Tommy replied firmly, slapping an eviction notice down on my desk. "Be out of here by Friday, or I'll send someone over to help you pack." He turned and stormed out the door without saying another word.

Was that even allowed? Didn't he have to give me notice? It looked like I was going to have to add getting legal advice to my list of things to do.

I snatched up the eviction notice and rushed after him outside. "Please don't do this."

"It's done," Tommy said.

Cristina came out and stepped closer to him. "You know what she's been through. Do you even have a soul?"

"I have something much more important than that," he said. "A boss who pays me to get rid of the deadweight." He turned to leave, then stopped and placed his hands on his hips when two black Mercedes Benz SUVs pulled up in front of the office on the street. "Who the hell is this hotshot?"

The vehicles had tinted windows, making it impossible to see who was inside. Two men wearing all black and dark sunglasses got out of the first SUV, glancing around the perimeter.

They looked like security.

An impeccably dressed driver wearing dark sunglasses got out of the second SUV, looked around, then opened the back door. A dashing man stepped out, wearing all black, glancing in our direction.

Cristina gasped, then leaned closer to whisper, "Grace, I think that's your prince!"

"Prince Oliver?" I whispered back. "That's impossible."

But even as I said it, I knew I was wrong.

The prince was there in the flesh.

The one I'd hung up on multiple times.

Prince Oliver sauntered over with effortless confidence, with another man who got out after him in the second SUV trailing slightly behind him. He really looked like royalty.

"Wow, he's even more handsome in person," Cristina swooned, not at all hiding her admiration. "What a shame the man is getting married. He's just your type. And my type. And every woman's type. Tall. Dark. Handsome. And look at that swagger. Good golly, Miss Molly."

"Keep it down," I whispered, trying to compose myself as I did my best to not notice the confidence in his stride.

He'd flown over twelve hours to see me.

This made no sense.

"Grace," Prince Oliver simply said as he approached us with a charming smile.

"Y-yes, I'm Grace," I stuttered, then blurted out, "I thought you were a prank caller." I attempted a curtsy, but my high heel got caught in a crack in the sidewalk. I stumbled forward, my arms windmilling as I face planted directly into the prince's chest with a loud THWACK.

Prince Oliver blinked in surprise. "Are you hurt?"

I just shook my head and mumbled, "Only my pride" into his chest.

Of all the clumsy, bumbling ways to meet a real life prince, I had to trip right into his arms—literally.

My face burned hot as I imagined what he must think of me now. Did he assume I was always this much of a walking disaster? I would imagine so, since he had seen the viral videos of my wedding mishaps. Little did he know that none of those fiascos were my fault.

Prince Oliver glanced at Tommy, who was still lurking nearby. "Have I arrived at an inconvenient time?"

"My business is done here," Tommy replied, eyeing the

prince up and down. "And who exactly are you? You look familiar." He snapped his fingers. "You're that famous actor. What's his name? That guy who played *Spider-Man*?"

"I'm Prince Oliver of Verdana," he said, then gestured to the tall man with sunglasses directly behind him. "This is my assistant, Dante."

"I'm Tommy Tighter," he said, puffing out his chest like he was the actual prince. "I'm the property manager. How can I help you folks?"

Prince Oliver gave a courteous nod. "I've come to speak with Grace about a business proposal."

"She doesn't do business here anymore," Tommy informed him smugly. "She's being evicted for failure to pay rent."

My jaw dropped. "I'm just a teensy bit late on the rent this month." I shook the eviction notice at him. "This isn't fair."

"I'm sure Grace has a logical explanation," Prince Oliver said calmly. "How much is the monthly rent, if you don't mind my asking?"

"Two grand," Tommy blurted without thinking.

The prince did a double take and glanced over my shoulder. "Per month? For this closet-sized office? How do you justify such astronomical prices?"

Tommy puffed out his chest again. "Welcome to California, buddy."

The prince surveyed the vacancies surrounding my office. "With so many empty offices, I'd think you'd be more lenient with a tenant like Grace."

Tommy scoffed. "Being nice isn't in my job description. I manage this property and collect rent. When rent isn't paid, people pay the piper."

Prince Oliver gestured to the eviction notice. "May I see that?"

I nodded and handed it to him.

The prince scanned it briefly, then glanced over his shoulder at his assistant. "Dante, how long do tenants legally have to vacate after being served an eviction notice in this country?"

"I believe it would vary state by state, Your Highness, but I'm confident we are talking a minimum of thirty days," Dante replied. "I'd be happy to research the matter for you." He pulled out his cell phone.

Prince Oliver shook his head. "Unnecessary. I had the same suspicions myself." He handed the piece of paper to Tommy. "Perhaps this notice would be more useful lining a rabbit cage?"

"That's not funny," Tommy said.

"Good," Prince Oliver said. "Because I wasn't joking." He eyed the "For Sale" sign on the lawn near the street. "I've been thinking of expanding my real estate portfolio. Perhaps I'll simply buy the building and then relieve you of your services for having not one ounce of compassion. Dante, please note the phone number on that sign. Remind me to make an offer on the property."

"As you wish, Your Highness," Dante said, tapping on his phone.

Was he serious? Would he really buy the entire building

just to keep me from getting evicted? He was obviously bluffing.

Tommy sputtered in protest. "Whoa, whoa, slow your roll, amigo. No need to get your royal panties in a bunch. I'll give you seventy-two hours, Grace." And with that, he scurried away.

The prince turned to me, his eyes twinkling with humor. "Where were we?"

"Are you really going to buy the building?" I asked, still skeptical about this entire situation.

"I'll keep it in my back pocket as an option," Prince Oliver replied casually. "Now, about my wedding . . ."

I held up a hand to stop him right there. "Okay look, as flattered as I am by this bizarre business proposal, I'm kinda in career-crisis mode at the moment. I'm fresh off a lawsuit, my reputation is trashed, and I just narrowly dodged eviction. Forgive me for finding this entire thing just a little farfetched."

"Grace, put aside your suspicions and let's get down to business," Prince Oliver said. "I will pay your next three months of rent if you plan my wedding. That is not your salary. Consider it a signing bonus. I mentioned my proposed salary for your services on the phone, which would be approximately one month of your time."

"Twenty thousand dollars?" Cristina said.

"Exactly." Prince Oliver gave me a big smile.

"Done!" Cristina blurted out.

"Not done!" I said, shocked that Cristina had suddenly

become my agent, and that Prince Oliver had actually agreed to that much money with zero hesitation.

"Look—I'm offering you not only a chance to resuscitate your career but also an all-expenses-paid trip to Verdana." Prince Oliver winked, his charm impossible to ignore. "There are five people on your wedding planning team. They all have their assignments and duties. All you have to do is manage them. Instead of what people in your business call a day-of coordinator, consider yourself a month-of coordinator. Most of the big items for the wedding day were set in place long ago. Your job would be to oversee the entire wedding process in the final month, confirm that everything is set, and ensure that the day goes off without a hitch. Surely, you can handle that. And *I* will handle the legal fees of your pending legal battles here and any other issues that arise. Think of it as a one-month European vacation with everything covered. Travel, accommodations, food, and wardrobe." He glanced down at my feet. "That includes shoes."

I was so shocked, I didn't know what to say.

"What kind of shoes are we talking about here?" Cristina jumped in and asked.

"Whatever Grace's heart desires," Prince Oliver said.

Cristina's eyes went wide. "Gucci, Valentino, Versace, Prada? Louboutins? Anything at all?"

He nodded. "All the above, if that's what she wants."

"Grace could definitely use some new shoes," she said. "I mean, look at these things." She grabbed my foot and lifted my leg in the direction of the prince.

"Hey!" I said, latching on to her shoulder to keep myself from falling into him again. "No deal!"

"Excuse us, Your Highness," Cristina chimed in, dropping my leg, then grabbing my arm this time. "I need to have a little chat with my friend."

Prince Oliver nodded. "Of course."

Before I could object, she dragged me inside my office and closed the door behind us.

"What exactly are you doing?" I asked.

"Um, hello?" Cristina said. "I was going to ask you the same thing. A real-life prince is asking for your help and offering you the world to boot! You'd be crazy not to take this opportunity."

I glanced out the window at Prince Oliver and Dante, both chatting, but staring in my direction. I quickly closed the blinds, then turned back to Cristina.

"Something doesn't feel right about this," I said. "It can't possibly be legit. "

"Grace—this is real," she said firmly, grasping my hand. "You've got this. You're talented, passionate, and you deserve this opportunity. Plus, it's a chance to work closely with an incredibly handsome prince. And who knows? Maybe he's got some handsome, single prince friends. What's not to love about this? You really have nothing to lose."

"No?" I said. "What if I ruin his wedding and destroy any hope of rebuilding my reputation? This could be the biggest break of my life or the final nail in my career's coffin. People seem to take joy in watching others fail, and I'm really getting tired of it."

"Life is full of risks," Cristina reminded me. "If you don't take chances, you'll never know what you're capable of. And who knows? Maybe this is exactly what you need to find your way back to the top. If not, you pivot and try something new. Either way, you're taking action to get your life back on track. He is trusting you. Why don't you trust yourself? The Universe is giving you this golden opportunity. Take it."

I would've loved nothing more than to face my fears and prove everyone wrong, but planning the prince's wedding was a jump off a cliff, and I preferred baby steps.

A knock on the door startled me.

Cristina took it upon herself to walk over to open the door. Then the prince stepped inside my office, looking around.

"Excuse the mess," I said.

Oddly enough, he glanced inside my garbage can before waving it off. "Your untidy surroundings reflect an imaginative mind that is too busy creating and exploring new ideas to be confined by strict organization."

"Are you speaking from experience?" I asked.

He chuckled. "Our offices are very similar, actually."

"I seriously doubt that," I said. "Your office must be pristine, thanks to a cleaning staff, plus I would imagine it's the size of a football field."

"Not quite, but it overlooks one," Prince Oliver said. "Look, I don't want to be a pest, but I think you are passing up the opportunity of a lifetime. Meet me for dinner and we can discuss this further. No strings attached."

"Dinner?" I said, not expecting that.

Prince Oliver nodded. "I'm staying at the Beverly Hills Hotel, but I've heard about a restaurant called Fixins Soul Kitchen that I must try."

I blinked twice. "You're kidding."

"Never stand between a man and his macaroni and cheese," he said. "Have dinner with me. Strictly business, of course. I'm an engaged man."

"I'm still trying to wrap my head around the fact that you eat mac and cheese," I said.

"Well, I do need to also try their chicken and waffles," Prince Oliver said. "And the fried green tomatoes, of course."

I was speechless.

"Are you aware that your mouth is open, but nothing is coming out?" he asked. "Why are you staring at me that way?"

"This is definitely a scam," I said. "I've never heard of a prince who eats soul food. You should be eating escargot and tuna tartare, and drinking tea with your pinkie extended."

"I assure you that my pinkie is always pressed firmly against my other fingers whenever I drink tea," he said with an infectious grin. "Life's too short not to enjoy the simple pleasures of other cultures, is it not? Will you join me for dinner?"

"What if I said no?" I asked.

Prince Oliver shrugged. "Then I would ask again."

"Do you ever take no for an answer?"

He held my gaze. "No."

Biting my lip, I thought about it. I felt a mix of emotions all swirling together inside of me.

Anticipation.

Dread.

Hope.

Was this really the break I needed? Was Cristina right? Did I really have nothing to lose? I doubted a dinner with the prince would change my mind about planning his royal wedding, but I could at least extend a courtesy and hear him out.

I finally conceded. "All right, Your Highness. I'll have dinner with you tonight to hear more details about your wedding, but I'm making no promises beyond that."

His eyes lit up in triumphant delight. "Perfect."

I had to admit, the idea of an all-expenses paid trip to Europe was awfully tempting. Still, as I watched him saunter away, confidence in every step, I couldn't ignore the nervous feeling stirring in my gut.

Something about this situation felt off.

It seemed too good to be true.

And that was exactly what scared me the most.

Chapter Three

PRINCE OLIVER

I followed Dante through the side door of Fixins Soul Kitchen in Los Angeles, keeping my head down low beneath the brim of my baseball cap to avoid detection.

So far, so good.

No one seemed to pay attention to me.

Maybe Dante was right about the new outfit helping me fit in. He had stopped by a popular American store called T.J. Maxx earlier in the day. He'd picked up everything I needed to go incognito and transform myself into a common tourist for my clandestine meeting with Grace.

My new wardrobe consisted of:

1) Hawaiian board shorts.

2) Flip flops.

3) A blue Santa Monica T-shirt.

4) A pair of dark sunglasses.

5) An "I Love LA" baseball cap.

I felt ridiculous.

Be that as it may, the last thing I wanted was to be spotted by the paparazzi, since not a single soul knew I had left Verdana. Maybe we were being overly cautious, but better safe than sorry.

We had arrived fifteen minutes early to the restaurant. Luckily, I was able to secure a table tucked behind a wooden partition that shielded me from many of the patrons.

Dante sat facing me at the table directly next to mine—to be on alert for any suspicious-looking people or activity, although he seemed to be obsessed with giving me worrisome looks over the top of his menu. He wanted to say something but had been biting his tongue.

"What is it?" I asked. "There's something on your mind."

Dante leaned closer. "I'm feeling a tad paranoid, if I'm being honest, Your Highness. This plan could have dire consequences and seriously backfire on you."

I winced and looked around, then whispered, "Please refrain from addressing me in that manner inside the restaurant. And regarding my pending marital-status change, it's not like I have any other options."

Dante nodded. "True, but the queen—"

"Relax," I said. "Everything will work out to perfection."

"I want nothing more," he said. "But I would advise to remove your sunglasses indoors. I do feel you will attract more attention with them on."

He was right.

I slid my sunglasses to the back of my head, then glanced around the bustling restaurant, taking comfort in the cheerful chatter and the mouthwatering aroma of fried chicken wafting through the air. What a delightful location to dine while remaining incognito among the urban populace.

A middle-aged server happily sauntered over with an electronic tablet in hand, flashing me a brilliant smile. She wore a black T-shirt with FIXINS splashed across her chest in large letters.

"Welcome to Fixins," she said. "I'm Sadie. How are you doin', sweetie?"

Dante cranked his head in my direction with surprise, clearly not expecting such a casual greeting from someone who had never made my acquaintance.

I'd seen this strange phenomenon in movies, the use of informal language and endearing terms with complete strangers. I'd heard it was common in Southern culture and a sign of friendliness, warm hospitality, and respect. We were in a restaurant that served Southern cuisine, therefore it made sense.

The logical thing to do was to play along.

I did my best to act naturally. I was just a normal customer. Nobody would know that a prince sat among them in such a casual eating establishment.

"I'm absolutely wonderful, darlin'," I said.

Dante looked flabbergasted, mouth agape like a codfish.

"Now, that's what I like to hear!" Sadie said with a wink. "Can I start you off with something to drink?"

"A sweet tea, if you don't mind," I said.

"Don't mind at all." She smiled again, tapping my drink order on her tablet, then gesturing to the menu in my hands. "Do you need more time to decide on food?"

"Not at all," I said, glancing down at the menu.

Grace had texted me to let me know she was running late, and that I could order the food. When I inquired what she desired, she simply said that everything looked good on the menu, and to surprise her.

Challenge accepted.

"I'd like the deviled eggs, fried green tomatoes, and the fried okra," I said.

"Three of my favorites," Sadie said, tapping my order into her tablet. "Anything else?"

"Oh, yes—I'm just getting started," I said. "I'd also love to try the chicken and waffles, mac and cheese, catfish nuggets, collard greens, potato salad, and black-eyed peas."

Sadie looked up from her tablet, eying my physique. "Please tell me you're expecting someone else to join you."

"Indeed, I am," I said. "She's running late."

She pretended to wipe perspiration from her forehead. "Phewww! You scared me there for a second. Still, unless you love to have leftovers to go, that is a lot of food for two people. You do know that, right?"

"I'm aware that it's more than we could possibly eat," I said. "But this is our first time eating together and I don't have a clue what she likes, so—"

"You thought you'd just order a variety to make her happy," she said.

I hesitated, surprised she knew that. "Yes, actually."

"You're just as sweet as our peach cobbler," Sadie said. "She's a lucky girl if you're so thoughtful this early in your relationship."

I shook my head. "Oh, we're not—"

Sadie waved it off. "I don't need to know all the juicy details. I'm not one to pry, but I would recommend *two* sweet teas, since you'll have company."

"Excellent recommendation," I said. "And please add an order of buttermilk biscuits and cornbread."

Sadie smiled as she took my menu. "A meal fit for a king."

"A prince, actually," Dante said.

I froze.

Dante's hand flew up to cover his mouth.

Sadie turned and eyed him. "Pardon me?"

"Sorry to interrupt." Dante quickly pointed at the ceiling. "I, uh, asked if that was *Prince* playing on your sound system?"

Sadie studied Dante intently, then glanced up at the speakers on the ceiling. "That's Bruno Mars, hun."

"Ha, of course, silly me! What was I thinking?" Dante babbled nervously. "It shouldn't be a surprise. I once mistakenly thought Hilary Swank was Jennifer Garner. Can you imagine?"

"I made the same mistake! What a coincidence," I said, trying to cover for Dante.

Fortunately, Sadie didn't look suspicious at all.

After she took Dante's order and walked away, the two

of us discussed my agenda for the week as we waited for Grace. Luckily, with the lively ambiance of the restaurant and the music, nobody could hear our conversation.

Fifteen minutes later, with perfect timing, Sadie set the plates of food down and left, just as Grace breezed into the restaurant.

Dante waved her over, and with purposeful strides, she wove between the crowded tables in our direction.

Her eyes widened at the sheer amount of food spread across our tables, then widened even further when she saw what I was wearing.

"Looks like someone had a head-on collision with a souvenir shop," Grace said wryly.

I stood and said in a low voice, "I'm just trying to fit in. A necessary precaution to avoid the paparazzi."

Grace glanced around the crowded restaurant. "Somehow, I doubt they're stalking casual soul food joints. They're probably all down in Hollywood or Beverly Hills."

"You may be right, but all it would take is a simple phone call from one person to have them swarming around here like locusts," I said, gesturing to the space across from me in the booth. "Please. Have a seat."

"Don't mind if I do." Grace slid in, eyes roving over the heaping platters of food that crowded our table. "Hungry?"

"Famished," I replied, sitting back down. "I took the liberty of ordering a sweet tea for you as well as a variety of their most popular dishes. I hope there's something here that looks appealing to you."

Grace surveyed the table. "Pretty much all of it." She reached for her sweet tea.

"Good," I said. "Let's eat, darlin'."

Grace choked on her sweet tea.

"My goodness," I said. "Are you all right?"

She nodded adamantly. "What did you call me?"

My stab at Southern charm was a complete failure.

"What did I call you *when*?" I said, giving my best effort at stupidity.

"Just now!" she said. "Did you call me *darlin'*?"

"There is a lot of noise in here, isn't there?" I asked, trying to change the subject. "Let's eat." I tucked a napkin into the collar of my T-shirt and smoothed it over my chest.

Grace shook her head. "Uh-uh . . . Nix the napkin. That *is not* fitting in, unless you're eating crab legs or barbecued ribs."

I glanced around at the other diners, none of them with napkins tucked into their shirts, then removed mine. "Good to know."

Grace dove into the feast, piling her plate precariously high with fried chicken, collard greens, mac and cheese, and biscuits, for starters.

I watched in amusement as she took her first bite of fried chicken and let out an indecent moan of delight, before following it up with a bite of a buttermilk biscuit.

"The food is to your satisfaction, I take it?" I chuckled.

With her mouth full, Grace nodded enthusiastically.

She ripped off a piece of buttermilk biscuit and held it in front of my mouth. "Mmm, you've got to try this. Open up."

Hand-feeding the prince biscuits in public?

Scandalous.

I blinked, then glanced over at Dante, who paused his eating, appearing just as surprised. I wasn't accustomed to someone hand-feeding me food. Well, not since I had been a baby. I had to admit I was a little perplexed at the moment, almost paralyzed, as I decided my next course of action.

Grace waggled the biscuit insistently under my nose. "Come on. You're going to love it."

It had been far too long since I'd enjoyed a truly satisfying meal among regular people. The constraints of royal dining—multiple courses, countless pieces of cutlery, an army of hovering staff—often made eating feel more like a chore than a pleasure.

"I'm getting a cramp in my arm," Grace said. "Live a little."

I glanced around the bustling restaurant. Friends and families laughed over heaping plates, licking their fingers, and savoring every morsel. What must it be like to live so freely?

No scrutiny, no expectations, no pressure.

Just joy, apparently.

Grace frowned, then leaned closer and whispered, "You're not allowed to act like a normal person or touch food with your hands and get your mouth dirty? Is this one of those royal protocol things?"

She was about to retract the piece of buttermilk biscuit away from my mouth, but I reached for her wrist to stop her.

Grace's eyebrows shot up in surprise.

I honestly found it refreshing that she talked to me like I was someone asking for directions. No titles. No pretenses.

Just two people having a bite to eat.

I leaned forward and bit the piece of buttermilk biscuit from her hand, chewing, nodding. "You're right. That is fantastic."

"See?" she said, smiling proudly, then reaching for a piece of chicken. "You need to loosen up."

Maybe I did.

Diving into the food, I had launched myself into heaven as we ate in silence for a few minutes. Everything I sampled was delectable.

Grace watched me and shook her head in what appeared to be astonishment. "I never imagined a prince chugging sweet tea and chomping on fried chicken."

"I'd hardly call that chomping," I said, then whispered, "And I may be royalty, but I'm still a man who enjoys the simple pleasures in life."

"Clearly," she muttered, watching with raised eyebrows as I took a bite of the perfectly seasoned collard greens with smoked turkey.

They were so good I took several more bites, never having tasted something like this in my entire life.

Dante froze, then his eyes went wide as he tapped his mouth.

I blinked at his strange behavior, but then realized it was possible I had something on my face? Maybe some cheese from the macaroni on my nose? I grabbed my napkin and gave it a good wipe.

Dante continued to give me an awkward glance.

Then he subtly gestured to his teeth.

I started manically prodding each tooth with my tongue, desperately trying to dislodge whatever was there with what must have been an odd display of tongue acrobatics. I nodded to Grace when she looked over and pointed to my mouth to acknowledge I was fully aware of my public oral emergency and was in the process of rectifying the situation in a timely manner. But Grace must have wrongly interpreted the sign because she suddenly stuck out her tongue and probed her own teeth like a large brush at one of those American drive-thru car washes.

Was that what I looked like?

I shook my head vigorously and pointed at myself, signaling it was my issue, not hers. But Grace misinterpreted again, looking even more mortified as she felt her face for imaginary food particles. She brushed her fingers under her nose as if checking for bats in the cave, then she started swiping at her face, signaling with her hands like a catcher at a major league American baseball game.

Utterly confused, I continued to search around again with my tongue, surreptitiously making weird sucking noises as I went quadrant by quadrant searching for the runaway particle. Luckily, I finally found the leafy culprit and extracted it.

I shook my head in embarrassment. "I was trying to tell you I had something stuck in my teeth. It wasn't you."

"Why didn't you just tell me with words?" Grace said.

I shrugged. "Then you would see what was stuck in my teeth."

"There's nothing wrong with using a toothpick, you know," she said. "Unless that goes against your proper royal protocol."

I cocked my head to the side. "What is it with you and your obsession with royal protocol? Don't tell me—you learned it all from films and television?"

"Correct," Grace said. "I don't often meet princes for dinner."

"Well then, you are really missing out," I joked. "And I hate to be the bearer of bad news, but royal life is much different from how they portray it on the big screen. Especially *my* royal life. You'll see. When you're in Verdana."

"*If* I'm in Verdana," Grace said. "I haven't said yes yet."

That was true, but I was quite certain she would say yes to my job offer and accompany me back to Verdana.

Grace dabbed the side of her mouth, then looked over. "Tell me about your bride-to-be."

I supposed I needed to convince Grace I was head-over-heels in love, which would not be easy.

"Veronica is . . . quite lovely," I began unconvincingly.

Grace gave me a look that was difficult to decipher. "Lovely? If I were your fiancée and that was all you said about me, I would break off the engagement. Try again. What do you love most about her?"

"Ah! Right . . ." I drummed my fingers on the table, quickly concocting a list of admirable qualities. "She's poised, elegant, well-educated, patient, and kind." I nodded, satisfied with myself.

"Uh-huh," Grace said, clearly not buying it. She pulled a notepad and pen from her bag. "How did you know she was the one?"

I froze with a forkful of mac and cheese halfway to my mouth. "Oh, well, you know, it just felt right."

Grace tilted her head. "Forgive me, but you don't seem over the moon. Most of the grooms I have met couldn't stop gushing about their brides, but you seem to be more excited about the fried catfish. What's going on with you? You're not getting cold feet, are you?"

I found it fascinating that she could pry into someone's private life without knowing an ounce about the person. Maybe this was all part of the getting-to-know-you, allowing her to customize the wedding based on our likes and dislikes. Still, I thought it was best to tell her the truth. At least, about one part.

Sadie returned and pointed to the table. "Looks like you made quite a dent in the food. I'm impressed."

"Everything is absolutely fabulous," I said.

Sadie smiled. "I'm happy to hear that." She turned to Grace. "And you are one lucky girl, the way he's spoiling you like a princess."

You have no idea.

"Not bad for a first date," Sadie added.

"Oh—this is not a date," Grace corrected.

Sadie nodded. "That's right—these days, people say they're grabbing a bite and hanging out." She winked at me, but before I could respond, she said, "I'm guessing you will not have room for our world-famous peach cobbler."

"Nonsense—we have to try it," I said.

"You got it," Sadie said. "And I will bring you some boxes to take the leftovers with you."

After she walked away, I sat down my fork and leaned forward. "Where were we?" I snapped my fingers. "That's right. You asked me if I had cold feet regarding the marriage. Can I be frank with you?"

"Of course," Grace replied.

"I mislead you," I said. "This is an arranged marriage orchestrated by my mother, Queen Annabelle, and Princess Veronica's parents. This wedding is my duty. Our duty."

Grace blinked in surprise. "That has got to be the most unromantic thing I have heard in my entire life."

I nodded. "Welcome to my world."

"So . . . you're not in love," she said.

I shook my head. "Not even a little. She and I are more like cousins, so excuse me if the entire thing feels absurd."

"Then why go through with the charade?" Grace asked.

"It's complicated," I said with a sigh. "Let's just say it's expected of me as the heir apparent, and according to my mother, it's what is best for my country. Now, it doesn't need to be an emotional wedding. The priority is throwing a lavish, opulent affair befitting royalty. I want you to pull out all the stops. Spare no expense. Will that be a problem?"

Grace chewed her lip thoughtfully. "I still haven't said yes, Your Highness. I usually plan weddings for people who are truly in love."

I held up a hand. "Please, call me Oliver."

Grace smiled warmly. "Sounds good, *Oliver.*"

"What will it take?" I asked. "Name it."

She set down her fork. "My life is in complete disarray. Going to Europe for a month feels wrong. Like I'm running away. That's not something I've ever done before, even when things were at their worst."

"I paid your rent for three months," I said. "I also offered to pay your legal fees for the bride suing you, plus I will compensate you very well for your services. Your life will only get better by accepting the job. It gives you breathing room to turn everything around. I'm offering you a lifeline. Take it and don't look back. This is an opportunity for redemption and positive publicity for your company."

Grace sighed, then glanced over at Dante. "You've been mighty quiet. What do you think about all this?"

Dante wiped his mouth. "Well—"

"It's not his wedding," I said.

"I'd like to hear what he has to say," Grace said. "Unless you don't allow your employees to speak their mind."

"Dante has never had a problem with expressing his thoughts." I chuckled and turned toward him. "Very well. Dante, my good man, what are your thoughts on Grace planning my wedding? Do you think what I am offering is fair?"

Dante hesitated. "The offer is very generous, indeed."

I held up my hand before he addressed me formally. "That is all we need to know."

A woman walked by and did a double-take in our direction.

"Not good," I mumbled.

"What is it?" Grace said.

I kept my voice low. "I can't be certain, but there is a distinct possibility that the woman who just passed our table knows who I am."

Grace eyed my clothes. "With that outfit? I doubt it."

"Actually, I got the same feeling—she looked suspicious," Dante said, watching the woman walk outside, then turn to glance at us through the window. "It would behoove you to take care of the check."

"I think you're right." I pulled out my credit card and waved Sadie over.

"Something else, darlin'?" she asked.

"Would you be so kind as to wrap up this food up to go, along with that peach cobbler?"

"My pleasure," she said, taking the credit card from me and walking away.

I turned back to Grace. "Does this mean you'll plan my wedding?"

She took a deep breath and nodded. "I accept your offer on one condition."

"Name it," I said.

"If I'm going to pull off a royal wedding in just one month, I'll need complete creative freedom."

I grinned. "You shall have it. I trust your vision wholeheartedly."

And hopefully, her creative choices would lead to

complete and utter chaos, as they had heretofore proven to do, making me a free man.

"Wonderful," Grace said.

A few minutes later, Sadie returned with the check for me to sign as she and another employee boxed up our food.

With no sign of the paparazzi, we were able to chat for another fifteen minutes, mostly about food and other cultures.

"I forgot to ask," Grace said. "When shall we leave for Verdana?"

"The jet will be fueled and ready to depart tomorrow morning at ten sharp," I said. "Pack light, as you'll have your pick of any wardrobe items once we arrive."

Grace's eyes lit up, as if she were starting to finally loosen up to the idea. "Sounds good."

Just then, the front door of the restaurant burst open with a BANG. Suddenly it was chaos, a swarm of paparazzi flooding the restaurant like a tidal wave, cameras flashing so rapidly it looked like strobe lights at a nightclub.

"I knew it," I said, turning to Dante. "We need to get out of here. Now. Grab the food."

Grace's eyes widened in panic, then she popped up to her feet, and scurried to the backdoor, knocking over a chair in her haste.

Before I could even make a move, the reporters surged right past us, cameras clicking furiously, not even glancing in our direction.

It was as if Dante and I were invisible.

My mouth dropped open. "Wait a minute—they were

after Grace?"

Dante nodded. "It appears so."

That was unexpected.

"Let's make sure she's okay." I grabbed the bags of food and headed out the back door with Dante. We stopped near the back of our idling SUV as Grace and the paparazzi disappeared.

The realization hit me like a punch in the gut; they hadn't been looking for me at all. I wasn't the story here. Somehow, despite all my efforts to keep our visit under wraps, the vultures had gotten wind that Grace was involved. And now they were chasing her through the streets while I stood there uselessly.

I needed to go after her.

"We need to get out of here." Dante opened the back-door of the SUV. "I'm sure Grace will be fine. You can call her."

I quickly slid into the SUV, with Dante right behind me, closing the door. The driver took off, the tires screeching.

"Everything was going so well," I said. "I hope she doesn't change her mind. She's my only hope for escaping this dreadful, arranged marriage."

"Don't worry," Dante said. "Grace already agreed to being your wedding planner. The seeds are planted in her mind about turning her life around. You have nothing to worry about. She won't change her mind."

I sighed and stared out the window as the boulevard lights passed by in a blur. "I hope you're right. My entire future depends on it."

Chapter Four

PRINCE OLIVER

The Next Morning . . .

I peered out the jet window from my seat, watching the activity on the Burbank Airport tarmac. The sun glinted off the sleek white jet, almost blinding me. I shielded my eyes with one hand, desperately searching for any sign of Grace's arrival.

Nothing.

Dante sat across from me, his stoic expression showing no emotion. "She'll be here soon, Your Highness." His voice was resolute and reassuring as he scrolled through his phone. "Put your mind at ease."

Despite his confidence, I couldn't shake the nagging feeling that the paparazzi might have scared off Grace for good.

What if she didn't show up?

What if she decided it wasn't worth the risk?

What if I had to resort to Plan B?

That was the problem . . .

I had no Plan B.

My entire scheme rested on her bumbling help. Without Grace, I was doomed to marry someone I should not be marrying.

As I reluctantly settled back into my seat, I caught sight of a figure emerging from the executive terminal. My breath hitched in my throat as I recognized Grace's brown hair shining in the sunlight. Directly behind her was a porter, lugging her overstuffed floral suitcase on a cart toward the tail of the jet.

"There she is!" I practically shouted, then jumped to my feet as joy and relief surged through me at the sight of her.

"Indeed," Dante said, like he'd expected it all along.

Grace's cheeks flushed as she stepped onto the jet and locked gazes with me, her eyes darting around the luxurious interior of plush leather seats and polished wood accents.

"I'm sorry I kept you waiting," she said sheepishly, tucking a loose strand of hair behind her ear. "I had second thoughts."

"What happened to change your mind?" I couldn't help asking.

"Well . . ." Grace appeared to mull over the question. "When a person is at rock bottom, they really have nothing to lose. The only direction is up. Plus, going to Verdana is a chance for me to escape the chaos in Los Angeles."

"Well, I'm certainly glad you're here," I said.

"Welcome aboard," Dante said.

"Thank you," she said with a smile.

I gestured to the seat across from me. "Please make yourself comfortable. We'll be on our way to Verdana shortly."

She nodded and strapped herself in as her eyes glittered in wonder and amazement. "I've never flown private before. Or first class. Or anything remotely close to comfortable. This is really something." She gently ran her fingers across the buttery-soft, white leather seats.

"Anything you need, just let us know," I said.

"Thanks." Grace sank into her seat with a happy sigh. "I'm grateful for this opportunity. It couldn't have come at a better time."

I raised my hand to signal Jill, the lead flight attendant.

She approached us with a tray of drinks, her smile warm and genuine. "Mimosas for the prince and our lovely guest." She handed each of us a glass.

Grace accepted hers eagerly. "Wow—thank you. I'm Grace, by the way."

"I'm Jill—such a pleasure to make your acquaintance," she said, before returning to her station.

"To new adventures," I said, raising my glass in her direction.

"And to second chances," Grace added, a soft look in her eyes.

We clinked our glasses.

Grace took a long sip, then leaned back against the headrest.

Jill returned a moment later with a tray of freshly baked croissants and pastries, leaning closer with the mouth-watering offerings.

Grace gasped, clearly delighted. "This is amazing—thank you." She grabbed one of the chocolate croissants from the tray. "I'm used to Diet Coke and peanuts when I fly, so this is a slight step up." She laughed and took a bite of the croissant. "I could get used to this royal treatment."

"Just wait until you see the palace," I said proudly, then reached for a pastry with raspberry filling. "It has the most beautiful gardens you've ever seen, and the view from the terrace of the apartment where you'll be staying is unparalleled."

"I'm looking forward to it," Grace said enthusiastically. "All of it."

"Welcome aboard Your Highness, and his esteemed guest, Miss Grace Fullerton," the captain announced over the intercom. "Please ensure your seatbelts are securely fastened as we prepare for takeoff. We're second in line on the runway and will be airborne shortly, beginning our journey to Verdana. Sit back, relax, and enjoy the flight."

Once in the air, Grace glanced over at Dante, then back to me. "How long have you two known each other? You seem very close."

"Too close," I joked. "I can't get rid of the man."

"We used to get into a lot of trouble together as children," Dante said with a chuckle and a shake of the head.

"Remember when we raided the kitchen and stole those fresh tarts?" I asked.

"How could I forget?" he said. "We must've been ten years old, maybe eleven, lured in by the heavenly aroma."

"I can still picture those flawless, golden tarts cooling on the rack," I recalled. "As soon as Chef Sherman left, we swooped in and gobbled every one of them in record time."

"I don't think anything had ever tasted so sublime," Dante said.

"Pure delight," I agreed. "Until Chef Sherman caught us red-handed, since we had left a crumb trail all the way back to my room. She marched us straight to my mother, who informed us those tarts were supposed to be for the visiting King and Queen of Sweden."

"Oh, no!" Grace gasped and covered her mouth.

"Oh, yes," I said. "I thought smoke was going to billow out of her ears like she was a cartoon. We had ruined their afternoon tea. Mother was so angry she confined me to my room, except for music lessons and official events. Never get between royalty and their sweets!"

We laughed, though Dante and I shared a nostalgic look, silently agreeing those tarts had been worth it.

After a couple of hours of delightful conversation between the three of us, there was still one question Grace had not answered completely when I had asked earlier.

"So, tell me what happened to you last night," I said. "When the paparazzi chased you down the street? I called and texted you, but you never responded."

Grace grimaced. "Sorry about that. I've gotten in the

habit of turning off my phone after work since I still get prank calls at all hours of the night. Anyway, I ended up diving behind a dumpster to catch my breath and nearly did a face-plant into a stack of wooden pallets! I could hear the paparazzi around the corner yelling, 'Where did she go?' Luckily, they disappeared after a few minutes, then I snuck back to my car and hightailed it out of there without further incident or embarrassing photos."

I nodded. "I'm glad to hear that."

"And I must say that dinner last night was the best," Grace said. "But I never got to try the peach cobbler."

I grinned. "You never know what the future holds."

"True," Grace said, then wiggled her nose and inhaled deeply. "It's funny. Now that we're talking about that wonderful food, it smells like the restaurant in here."

"You have a wild imagination," I said.

"No—I'm serious!" she said, inhaling again. "Too bad we had to leave in such a hurry. I bet they just tossed our leftovers. What a waste!"

I tried my best to keep my face free of emotion. "Whatever gave you that idea?"

Right on cue, Jill wheeled a cart down the aisle and smiled. "Lunch is served." She uncovered platters revealing the leftover fried chicken, mac and cheese, catfish nuggets, and cornbread.

Grace's eyes grew wider and her mouth fell open. "The leftovers."

I chuckled. "Indeed. I'm a big fan of leftovers."

"Me, too!"

"It drives Mother absolutely insane," I added, then gestured at the food. "Let's eat."

Between the three of us, we devoured every morsel on the cart.

"There is one small piece of business I would like to discuss with you, if you don't mind," I said, glancing over at Dante, who handed me the paperwork.

"After that wonderful surprise, we can discuss whatever you wish," Grace said, wiping her mouth with her napkin.

"A contract," I announced, handing her a copy and a pen. "You have everything we discussed in writing. I just need your signature on the second page, and you have a guarantee. Not even my mother can oust you from your position."

Grace was glancing the first page of the contract, but then glanced at me. "Why would your mother want to get rid of me?"

I shifted in my seat. "Well, you see, I hired you without my mother's consent. She doesn't even know I replaced the official wedding planner with you."

"What!?" Grace said, practically jumping out of her seat. "Why would you do such a thing?"

"It's just, when she finds out I hired you, she may try to fire you," I said. "That's just what she does. This contract guarantees you will benefit from our arrangement. You are under my hire, and that she can't do a thing about it. That's all."

"That's all? Are you kidding me?" Grace exclaimed. "You want me to sign something that makes me directly at odds with the Queen of Verdana? No way!" She stood up abruptly. "Get me off this plane. Now."

My eyes widened. "You want to exit the aircraft? At thirty-five-thousand feet?"

"Yes! Get me a parachute," Grace demanded, crossing her arms. "I want no part of this."

"Grace, please relax," I said reassuringly. "This is just a formality. My mother is away visiting the Spanish royal family right now in Madrid. When she gets back, I will tell her the wedding planner left, and I was solving a problem by bringing you in to take over the duties. I will convince her I cannot have a wedding without you. I promise. You have nothing to worry about. Besides, the contract is between me and you, so technically, she should not be able to fire you."

Grace bit her lip, uncertainty flickering across her face. "I don't know. I already have enough drama in my life."

"Let's not assume the worst." I stood and took her hands in mine, giving them a gentle squeeze. "Please. I can't do this without you."

Grace searched my eyes, then sighed. "Okay. I'll sign, since she's away. But you better keep me far from the queen until you break the news."

I grinned as she scrawled her signature, securing our partnership.

Grace handed me the signed contract and pen. "Is there

anything else you need to tell me or warn me about? I don't like surprises."

I nodded. "Just one more thing . . ."

She sighed. "I don't care if you're a prince—don't make me hurt you."

I chuckled. "I promise—you'll like this surprise." I signaled to Jill, who returned with slices of peach cobbler for the three of us.

Grace's expression softened as she sat back down. "Okay, you're right. This is a good surprise."

After dessert, we chatted about movies, books, vacations, and life in the palace. A few hours later, the gentle hum of the jet's engines seemed to lull Grace into a state of drowsiness. Her eyelids grew heavy, and soon enough, she drifted off to sleep, her head resting against the plush seat.

I couldn't help but steal glances at her as she slept, her face a picture of tranquility. There was an angelic quality to her appearance, with her brown hair framing her face like a halo. I found myself entranced by her peaceful slumber, marveling at how easy she was to talk to, even when we disagreed.

Dante caught me staring and gave me a knowing look.

I quickly buried my nose back in my book.

As the jet began its descent toward the airport runway in Verdana, Grace stirred from her slumber, rubbing her eyes and giving us a disoriented smile. She yawned and stretched, trying to wake herself up.

"How long was I sleeping?" she asked.

"A couple of days," I joked.

"We're here?" Grace's eyes widened as she looked out the window at the approaching coastline. "Oh, wow . . ."

The brilliant azure of the Mediterranean sparkled below us. White stucco buildings with terracotta roofs were nestled along the shoreline, backed by gently rolling green hills.

As we touched down at Verdana's small private airport, Grace was glued to the window, taking it all in. "It's beautiful. Like a postcard come to life."

I grinned, pleased with her reaction. "I'll give you a proper tour later."

This surprised Grace. "You actually go out in public?"

I nodded. "Another thing my mother dislikes with a passion."

Once the jet came to a halt, Jill came by to help us collect our things. We disembarked and found a sleek black SUV waiting on the tarmac for us. Our driver, Marco, greeted us cheerfully as he loaded the luggage into the back, then whisked us away to the palace.

Grace let out a gasp as we drove along the scenic Mediterranean coast, the sea stretching out to the horizon. "This is paradise. I can't believe how blue the water is." She had her face pressed against the car window for practically the entire drive.

Ten minutes later, we passed through the sprawling gates of the palace.

"Your Highness, welcome," Henri said when we got out of the SUV, offering a respectful bow.

"Thank you," I replied. "Grace, this is Henri Bonnet, our head steward who oversees the day-to-day responsibilities of the palace. Anything you need, just ask him and he will deliver."

Grace gave a slight bow, which made me smile. "Nice to meet you."

"The pleasure is all mine," Henri said, bowing right back.

"Could you please make sure Grace gets settled in nicely into the apartment in the south wing?" I asked.

"With pleasure, Your Highness," Henri said, reaching for her suitcase, then pausing when my brother and sister approached.

"Where have you been?" Theo immediately asked, hands on hips. "You just disappeared."

"I had to run a little errand," I said, then turned to Grace. "Allow me to introduce you to my brother, Prince Theodore, and my sister Princess Adriana."

"Hi!" Grace said cheerfully, extending her hand to Prince Theodore for a handshake. He hesitated for a moment, clearly baffled by her informality, before shaking her hand with a bemused smile.

"A pleasure to make your acquaintance," he said politely.

"Likewise," Grace responded, now offering her hand to my sister, who was equally perplexed by Grace's informal manner.

"Was that wrong to shake your hand?" Grace laughed nervously, realizing her faux pas and segueing into a half-bob, half-curtsy, nearly falling all over herself with embarrassment. "Sorry, I'm not used to meeting royalty, and I have no clue what is appropriate. I'm messing this up big time, aren't I?"

"Please, don't worry about it," Adriana said. "We're not so formal at home, especially when Mother is not around." She reassured Grace with a kind smile.

"I wasn't aware we were expecting company," Theo said, his gaze jumping back and forth between me and Grace.

"Grace has assumed responsibility as our wedding planner and will stay with us for the next month," I said.

"What happened to Miss DuPont?" Theo asked.

"She took a leave of absence to visit family in France," I said. "Apparently, her great-grandfather will turn one hundred years old this month."

Just then, Dante approached us, his face tight with concern. "Your Highness, there's something you should know." He glanced at Grace and lowered his voice. "Queen Annabelle is returning early from Spain. She will join you for dinner this evening."

"What?!" Grace and I said simultaneously.

Mother was supposed to be away for at least a week, which would have given me plenty of time to ease Grace into the inner royal circle. I felt a knot forming in the pit of my stomach as I considered the inevitable confrontation that awaited us. My mind raced with ways to soften the blow when revealing our new wedding planner to my mother.

"You two look like you have seen a ghost." Theo's gaze once again bounced back and forth between me and Grace.

"Why would it be a problem that Mother is returning early?"

"Who said it was a problem?" I gave a valiant effort to play off the shock reverberating through my body before saying, "It's no problem at all."

Which was a flagrant fabrication.

This was a problem of epic proportions.

Chapter Five

GRACE

I felt all the energy drain from my body.

Queen Annabelle was already returning home.

Today.

Panic settled in like an unwelcome guest as I recalled Oliver's reassurances that I'd have at least a week of wedding planning before the queen found out about the change in personnel. My mind raced with wild and absurd possibilities of what she might do to me when she discovered the truth. I only hoped the contract would protect me before she thought about having me killed.

"Miss Fullerton, allow me to show you to your chambers," Henri said, guiding me through the opulent halls of Verdana Palace.

Lining the walls were oil paintings and tapestries dating back centuries, and classical statues of Greco-Roman busts. Everything dripped with luxury and history.

I stopped in front of a display case that featured an ornate jeweled egg. "Is that what I think it is?"

Henri stopped, glanced at the end, then nodded. "Fabergé." He continued to lead me down the hall. "If there is anything you require during your stay, please do not hesitate to ask." His voice was calm but firm, the perfect antidote to my spiraling thoughts.

"Thank you, Henri," I choked out, since my nerves were still frayed like a worn-out rope.

"Indeed, it is my pleasure," he said as he opened the door to my bedroom and rolled my suitcase over next to the bed, placing it on top of a rack. "I'd be happy to unpack your suitcase for you."

"That's not necessary, but thank you," I said.

"Very well," Henri said. "Dinner will be served in one hour. And I recommend you take a moment to enjoy the view from your terrace and from the tower. They both are quite spectacular, if I may say so myself."

"This room has a tower?" I asked, confused.

Henri walked over to the door in the bedroom's corner and opened it, revealing a spiral staircase. "Right through here. Please watch your step and hold on to the handrail as you ascend and descend." He smiled before leaving me to settle into my luxurious new home for the next month, or until the queen killed me, whichever came first.

I sank onto the edge of the massive four-poster bed, its plush duvet puffing up around me. I imagined the queen bursting into the room, her hair flying as she shouted and pointed one long, manicured finger toward the door. A burly guard would grab me by the collar and drag me down the stairs, my head bumping on each stone step, until he tossed me out of the palace on my butt.

Unless . . .

Was beheading legal in Verdana?

I shook the negative thoughts out of my head. I had dealt with my fair share of Bridezillas in the past. The queen couldn't possibly be any worse.

I decided to video-call Cristina for some moral support, but when her groggy face appeared on the screen, I winced, forgetting the time difference and that she usually sleeps in.

"Grace?" she mumbled, rubbing her eyes. "Are you okay? Did something happen?"

"I'm so sorry! No, nothing happened," I said. "I didn't remember you were in a different time zone until after I dialed your number."

"It's fine," Cristina said. "It looks like you're already at the palace. How are the accommodations?"

"This place is outrageous," I said, flipping the camera around to show the expansive space. "Look at this bedroom! It could fit our entire apartment in it."

"Show me the bathroom!" Cristina said.

"Okay, hang on . . . I haven't seen it yet." I carried the phone into the bathroom, the marble counters and gold faucets gleaming. "The bathtub can fit five people!"

"Party time!" Cristina laughed. "What I wouldn't give to be royal for a day. We're going to have to connect every night so I can live vicariously through you!"

I smiled. "It's kind of surreal, really, but I have one big

problem. The queen does not know that Prince Oliver hired me to replace the royal wedding planner *she* approved. She's going to flip her royal lid, or I should say *her crown*, when she finds out."

"Why didn't he tell her?" Cristina asked.

"I'm not sure, but he's afraid she might get rid of me, so he put a stipulation in the contract saying she can't touch me. " The thought of meeting her still weighed heavily on my mind. "The queen wasn't supposed to be here for at least another week. I don't know what I'm going to do. What if she poisons me so they don't have to pay the money? That's what royalty used to do, even to their own family members."

"Grace, you've got this. Just take a deep breath and remember who you are. You're a fantastic wedding planner who has just had a little rough patch. They're lucky to have you. And regarding the poison, you can drink little bits of it every day until you build up an immunity."

I laughed, feeling more grounded. "Thanks—I needed that."

Cristina was the best friend a person could ask for. She was always so positive and supportive.

"I need to get ready for dinner, but let's check out the view from the terrace before I let you go," I said. As I opened the terrace door and stepped outside, the magnificent vista before me made me stop in my tracks.

I gasped. "Oh. My. Word."

Below me sprawled a vast expanse of vibrant green grass, the royal lawn stretching out for what seemed like miles. Intricately trimmed hedges bordered the edges, dividing the lawn from splendid gardens filled with bursts of colorful flowers, roses, tulips, hydrangeas, and more. Graceful willow trees dotted the landscape, their long branches swaying lightly in the breeze. Marble statuary and bubbling fountains added an air of elegance.

"Let me see!" Cristina shouted eagerly over the phone. I flipped the camera around to give her a view of the majestic grounds that unfurled below.

"Okay—here you go," I said.

"Holy cow!" she exclaimed. "Their back yard is like Central Park in New York, but even more colorful and gorgeous!"

I nodded in agreement, still trying to take it all in. I had never seen anything so grand or beautiful in my life. It was like gazing upon a royal palace from a fairy tale. I stood there transfixed, feeling both awed and humbled by the magnificent view before me.

"I could enjoy looking at this for hours, but I need to unpack and then take a shower," I said. "Talk to you tomorrow?"

"Of course! Good luck, and fill me in whenever you can, but make sure you know the time here in California first!" Cristina said before we said our goodbyes.

I started rifling through my suitcase, hanging up items as I tried to decide what to wear to dinner. My pants suit seemed too stuffy and the sequined gown too formal. Perhaps I was being too picky and needed to relax. A shower would help, especially after such a long flight.

As soon as I turned on the water in the enormous walk-in shower, I was met with a torrential downpour of water and pressure that felt like Niagara Falls. It was such a dramatic change from the weak drip, drip, drip of the shower back in my LA apartment.

I stood frozen, eyes closed, letting the water cascade over me.

I have no idea how long I stayed in there, but it was so incredibly rejuvenating that I lost all track of time. It was like getting a full body massage. I felt pounds of stress wash away down the drain along with the lavender-scented shampoo suds. When I finally emerged, I felt utterly refreshed, hydrated, and relaxed. Ready for whatever was to come.

After drying off, I slipped into the simple black cocktail dress I had picked out, then did my hair and applied some make-up. I appraised myself in the full-length mirror. I had to admit the dress hugged my curves perfectly.

"You've got this," I told myself in the mirror, hoping I sounded more assured than I felt. Tonight, I would make my first impression on the queen. I couldn't afford any missteps. But no matter what happened, I knew I had to stay true to myself, just as Cristina had told me.

A gentle knock on the door startled me from my thoughts. I took a deep breath and opened it to find Oliver standing there, his brown hair perfectly styled and a warm smile on his face. He wore what I suspected to be an Italian suit, without a tie, and the top two buttons on his white shirt unbuttoned. That relaxed me, knowing he wasn't dressed so formally.

"Wow, Grace, you look . . . stunning," he complimented, his eyes sweeping over me appreciatively.

"Thank you," I said. "You look quite dashing yourself."

"Thank you," Oliver said. "Ready for dinner? I thought I would accompany you, if you don't mind."

"Don't mind at all," I said as we began our descent down the grand staircase.

"Before we get there, I thought I'd share some tips on navigating dinner with my mother," Oliver whispered, his voice low.

"I'll take all the help I can get."

"She can be a bit . . . intimidating," he said. "Just remember to address her as 'Your Majesty' and follow her lead, or anybody else's, for etiquette at the dinner table. If you're unsure about something, just watch what she does and mimic it. I'll lead the conversation and you won't have to speak much. Relax and try to enjoy the meal."

"Thank you, Your Highness. I appreciate the advice," I said, my nerves tingling with anticipation.

"Call me Oliver in private," he said. "In public or in the presence of my mother, call me Your Highness, or her left eye will twitch."

I laughed, but then stopped when he wasn't laughing with me. "Oh, you're serious?"

Oliver nodded. "She's a little too formal for my taste, but she is the Queen of Verdana, and the legacy of our kingdom flows within her veins."

We approached two grand wooden doors, which the footmen opened into the dining hall. An enormous crystal chandelier hung over a long mahogany table set with fine china.

My stomach churned with both excitement and dread. Prince Theodore and Princess Adriana were already seated at the table. If I were to guess, I would say they both were most likely in their mid-twenties. They looked so incredibly regal and poised that I felt a surge of insecurity wash over me, but then I had to remind myself that Oliver was dressed in a more casual manner.

We said our hellos again, then took our seats when I noticed Prince Theodore was watching me like a hawk.

What was with him?

Was he the rebel child looking to cause problems?

Something told me I needed to watch out.

I forced a smile as I fidgeted with my napkin, trying not to appear as anxious as I felt. Then a beautiful blonde woman swept into the room. She had an air of dignity and sophistication about her.

This must be Princess Veronica.

"Grace!" she exclaimed, making me jump in my seat. "I've heard so much about you. It's nice to finally put a face to the name."

"Thank you, Your Highness," I replied nervously, sliding out of my seat to shake her hand, then wincing. "Whoops. I did it again." I gave another clumsy curtsy.

"Please, call me Veronica, and there's no need to be so

formal," she insisted, her eyes sparkling with genuine warmth.

"Thank you, Veronica," I uttered, marveling at how comfortable she made me feel.

Oliver was one lucky man, even if it was an arranged marriage.

As for Prince Theodore, he appeared to have a chip on his shoulder because he was still glaring at me.

Veronica gracefully took her seat on the other side of the table next to Princess Adriana, and I wondered why she wouldn't want to sit next to her fiancé.

As we took our seats again, I leaned closer to Oliver and whispered, "Where's your mother? Sharpening her sword?"

"Relax," he chuckled. "She hasn't beheaded anyone in over a month."

I narrowed my eyes at him.

"Just breathe, Grace. You're doing great."

My hands played idly with the intricate silverware as I contemplated the complex rules of etiquette that accompanied these formal dinners.

I felt like a fish out of water.

Just as a servant appeared to pour wine, the double doors swept open. An elegant woman entered, clad in a midnight blue satin gown accented with intricate silver embroidery that glimmered under the lights. Her gaze immediately locked onto mine like a radar, and I froze.

Queen Annabelle.

I stood up hastily, nearly knocking over my chair, as

everyone else remained seated. The Queen appeared to glide over to the table with an inscrutable expression.

"You must be Miss Fullerton," she said coolly. "The wedding planner."

Wait. How did she know?

I turned to Oliver, who whispered, "I had to tell her. Relax."

"Uh, yes, Your Majesty," I stammered, then dropped into an awkward double-curtsy, which I am sure looked more like I was having a seizure.

The Queen grimaced and waved her hand at me.

Seriously? Again?

I nodded and gave her another curtsy.

Her eyes went wide, then she shook her head.

Still not satisfied?

Tough crowd!

I gave one more curtsy, and if she didn't like it this time, she could stuff it.

Queen Annabelle blew out a breath. "Please take a seat, Miss Fullerton."

I glanced down at my chair and swallowed hard. "Oh . . ." I slid into my chair and avoided eye contact.

Queen Annabelle took her place at the head of the table. An uncomfortable silence settled over the room as they served us the first course. I had no idea what to say. She was even more intimidating than I had imagined.

"You must know I did not approve of this change, and I don't know if I will," Queen Annabelle said. "I find it quite odd and unsettling that Miss DuPont departed so abruptly, and without advising me. Do you have letters of recommendation from other kingdoms validating your taste and discretion?"

My mouth fell open. "Well, uh, no, I—"

"Then what qualifies you to plan the royal wedding?" She narrowed her eyes at me, then glanced at the top half of my cocktail dress that was visible.

This felt like an impromptu interview that I was in no way prepared for, and the way she was scrutinizing me, it was as if she knew I bought my dress off the clearance rack at Macy's. My mind went blank. I frantically tried to recall my resume as I met her piercing gaze.

"Well, uh . . ." *Think!* "I have over ten years of experience planning events of all sizes and budgets."

"And you have experience planning large-scale, high-profile events, such as a royal wedding?" Queen Annabelle asked. "One thousand people. Dignitaries, royals, celebrities. News outlets, magazines, and newspapers from around the world documenting every moment?"

"Well, not a royal wedding specifically," I hedged. "I did a bar mitzvah for the Horowitz family at the Beverly Wilshire Hotel. Six hundred guests, including two members of the Backstreet Boys and a world-renowned German cellist."

Queen Annabelle blinked.

I cleared my throat. "I have also handled large celebrity weddings, which require similar attention to detail, discretion, and grandeur to a royal wedding."

Her lips were pursed in a thin line.

"Let's hope so," Queen Annabelle remarked dryly. "I would expect nothing less than perfection and stellar reviews. Are you telling me you have achieved that level of service and client satisfaction?"

Just then, Oliver jumped in. "People can't stop talking about Grace, Mother."

That could be taken a lot of ways, especially since the way they had been talking about me hadn't been favorable in the least.

"Her creative vision will bring a fresh, modern perspective that I think we'll all enjoy," Oliver added. "I wouldn't have hired her without doing my research and verifying my sources. Trust me, Mother, because nobody is more invested in this wedding than I am, except Veronica, of course. Now, are we going to eat before it gets cold? Grace, you simply must try the roasted chicken our chef has prepared. It's superb."

That was smooth.

Shooting him a grateful look, I said, "It smells amazing."

I glanced down at the array of forks, knives, and spoons that surrounded my plate. Nine in all.

One fork was in the wrong place.

It was bugging me.

A lot.

I glanced over at Oliver's place setting.

His fork was also in the wrong spot.

Oliver leaned closer. "Is everything all right?"

I whispered, "Somebody messed up the place setting.

The dessert fork should be where the salad fork is." I reached up to swap them.

Oliver leaned closer again. "I would advise against that."

I froze, then dropped my hand back down to my lap.

How did he know?

He was probably right. It was better to just eat and mind my own business, but before I could take a bite, I was interrupted again.

"What inspired you to become a wedding planner?" Queen Annabelle said out of nowhere, her piercing eyes focused on me like a hawk zeroing in on a rat.

Didn't she want to talk to anybody else at the table?

Couldn't she tell I was starving?

I put my fork down and hesitated, desperately searching for the right words while under her intense gaze. "Well, ever since I was a little girl, weddings have fascinated me. There's just something magical about being able to bring two people together and create a day full of love and joy."

"I see," she said, slicing the leg of her roasted chicken with her death stare on me, most likely imagining it was one of my limbs instead.

Across from us, Veronica was making polite small talk with Princess Adriana, while Prince Theodore continued to shoot me dirty looks.

What was his problem? We'd just met, and he acted like I was his worst enemy. Or was he always like this?

"You look like you're sitting on a cactus," Oliver teased under his breath. "Try to relax."

I snuck another glance at the imposing monarch seated sternly at the head of the table. She looked about as friendly as a gargoyle.

"Easy for you to say," I whispered back. "You're not the one being judged by the Queen of Verdana."

"On the contrary—she has judged me every single day of my life," Oliver said. "Just do as I do. Think of her as a cuddly kitten."

I raised my eyebrows doubtfully. "More like a hungry lioness sizing up her prey."

Oliver chuckled. "I promise—I'll protect you from her claws."

I could barely stifle a very unladylike snort at that comment. Oliver surprised me with his kindness and sense of humor. Maybe enduring this royal dinner wouldn't be pure torture after all, not with him lightening the mood.

I raised the fork to my mouth and—

"Miss Fullerton," Queen Annabelle said in a tone that made it sound like she was regurgitating my name. "I don't know how they do things in America, but I hope you are prepared for the demands of this position here."

I nodded, setting my fork down, and wondering if I would ever eat again.

"I am, Your Majesty," I said.

"Well, I guess we'll find out soon enough with the charity event," she said.

I blinked twice. "Uh . . . what charity event is that?"

Queen Annabelle glowered at me. "Miss Dupont was in charge of our annual Royal Children's Hospital fundraiser gala. Obviously, you are taking over all of her responsibilities, are you not?"

"I . . . um . . ." Clueless, I glanced at Oliver for help.

"Mother," Oliver interjected. "Grace only arrived a few hours ago. Perhaps we should give her time to settle in before we overwhelm her with more details. I'd be more than happy to get her up to speed on everything tomorrow."

"Very well . . ." Queen Annabelle's eyes narrowed. "Being in charge of the gala will be an excellent test. If you can handle that, I will relax and feel confident you are up to planning a royal wedding."

"Of course, Your Majesty. I can handle it," I said with more confidence than I actually felt. "When is this gala?" I reached for my wine, needing more liquid courage than food at that moment.

"The fundraiser is this Saturday," Queen Annabelle said.

I almost choked on my wine.

A charity event.

In three days.

That I knew nothing about.

How was I going to pull this off on top of planning the most anticipated royal wedding in decades? One misstep could spell disaster, not just for the royal family, but for the children, and my entire career.

"You can handle it," Oliver said, as his mother's steely gaze remained locked on me, waiting to see if I would crack under the pressure.

Taking a deep breath, I met her scrutinizing stare head-on with a forced smile. "I look forward to the opportunity to prove myself, Your Majesty. Consider the gala handled."

My false bravado seemed to catch her off guard.

Oliver gave me an approving nod.

Queen Annabelle pursed her lips. "We shall see about that."

Her thinly veiled threat hung in the air.

The gauntlet had been thrown down.

The next seventy-two hours would make or break my entire future. The weight of it all pressed down on me, almost forcing the air from my lungs.

No pressure at all.

The only thing I had to do was pull off a miracle.

Chapter Six

PRINCE OLIVER

The rhythmic pounding of our feet on the side-by-side treadmills filled the royal palace gym as I tried to keep up with Dante's steady pace. Twice a week, we held our meetings during our workouts, since most of the royal business we needed to discuss was monotonous and tended to bore me. I really needed to dedicate more time to something I was passionate about.

What that was, I did not know.

Presently, it felt as if I were just going through the motions in life, the same old routine, instead of living it to the fullest.

"How did it go with Grace last night at dinner?" Dante asked.

"As expected—it was painful to watch," I said. "I knew hiring her would ruffle Mother's feathers, but I didn't expect an outright insurgency on their first meeting. I do have to give Grace credit, though. She braved her first storm, and came out mostly unscathed, from what I could tell."

"And was there another storm this morning at breakfast?" Dante questioned with concern etched on his face.

"Grace wisely skipped breakfast today," I said. "Probably hiding from Mother's wrath, which is not such a bad idea at all." I chuckled and slowed the speed of the treadmill since we were almost finished. "Actually, Marco drove her to the hospital to chat with the directors about their fundraising goals and how she could better serve them. She also wanted to get up to speed on the event, and see if she could make any changes to improve the outcome."

Dante pressed the stop button on his treadmill and furrowed his brow, worry creeping into his eyes. "Is it wise to let her change something that the queen has already approved? You know how particular your mother can be."

"True," I admitted. "But maybe—"

"Oliver!" Mother's voice echoed through the gym, startling both Dante and me.

"Yes, Mother," I said, then tapped the stop button, stepped off the treadmill, grabbed my towel, and wiped the sweat from my face and neck. "I just finished. The machine is all yours."

She glanced at the machine and grimaced. "You know very well that I would never use such a contraption."

I knew that.

One of these days, her sense of humor would return. She'd had one before my father died, but it has not made an appearance since.

"What brings you here, then?" I asked, even though I was confident that it had something to do with the American staying with us.

"Grace brings me here!" she hissed, her gaze unwavering. "I have it on good authority that she went to the hospital this morning without consulting me. I don't trust that woman with our affairs. You hired her, and it's your responsibility to supervise her. You must go there at once and make sure she doesn't make a mockery of our fundraiser."

"A mockery? How would she do that?" I asked.

"Good heavens—how would I know?" she said. "But she's asking an exorbitant number of questions. Those people have jobs, you know."

"Grace is just doing her due diligence," I said. "She didn't even know the event existed until last night. Give her the benefit of the doubt. Wouldn't it make sense that she learns as much as possible, in order to better perform her duties to the best of her capabilities?"

Mother scoffed. "We cannot have this American flitting about, changing plans on a whim. Need I remind you that the reputation of the crown is at stake?"

It was always at stake.

"Go deal with her at once!" Mother ordered.

"As you wish," I said, preferring not to get into it again with her. Especially since she seemed more off than usual these days. "I'll just get cleaned up and I will be on my way."

After showering, Marco drove Dante and me to the hospital, a short fifteen-minute drive from the royal palace.

We entered the pediatric ward and walked directly toward the sound of laughter that filled the air. We stopped in front of the window of the brightly colored, child-friendly play room. It was stocked with toys, games, art supplies, books and more to provide fun distractions and social engagement for young patients at the hospital. Two child-life specialists stood nearby, monitoring their activities, smiling.

In the middle of the room, however, was Grace, talking animatedly with a group of children. She knelt down to their level, her eyes sparkling with genuine interest, and her laughter joined theirs as she handed out cookies. She showed a remarkable patience with a young child who repeatedly escaped the attendants to drive a small dump truck up Grace's backside.

"Thank you!" a young girl said, tugging on her top.

"You are quite welcome," Grace said.

The sight was unexpected—both endearing and sincere.

"Look at that, Your Highness," Dante said, nudging me gently. "She's quite good with the children, isn't she?"

"Surprisingly so," I murmured, finding myself captivated by the scene before me. Grace seemed so at ease with her new environment, so natural, that I couldn't imagine what my mother was so concerned about. She was supposed to be working and fulfilling her duties, but she appeared to be having fun. How was that possible? I was jealous for a moment, actually. I didn't have that ability for enjoyment with something so simple.

My gaze shifted to the table of cookies, most of them shaped like stars. "Where do you suppose those cookies came from?" I asked.

"I'm not sure," Dante said.

Marco approached, standing to my right. "Miss Grace bought them from the Verdana Bakery, Your Highness." There seemed to be a hint of admiration in his voice. "She asked me to stop on the way here. And please pardon the intrusion. I just came up because you left this in the car." He handed me my phone.

"Thank you." I nodded and slipped the phone in my pocket. "The cookies were charged to the royal account, I take it?"

"No, Your Highness," Marco said. "She insisted on using her own money, a credit card."

"Really?" I said, glancing back at her. "Why on earth would she do that?"

I couldn't hide my surprise, especially considering how strapped she was for cash. It made little sense since I had been clear that I would pay for all of her expenses while she was here.

Grace clapped her hands together, gathering the children's attention. "Okay, I have an exciting idea I want to run by you all. As you know, there's a big charity gala coming up to raise money for the hospital this weekend. How would you all feel about being part of the event? We could have some of you share your talents. Maybe you can play a musical instrument, or can sing or dance. I think it would mean a lot to the guests to see and hear directly from you all. You're amazing, and I'm sure every one of you has some form of talent! Let it shine! What do you think?"

The children cheered, their faces lighting up.

"Great!" Grace said. "Then *we* are going to do it! If you want to take part, raise your hand and say yes!"

Every single hand flew into the air as they all shouted, "Yes! Yes!"

"The queen's worst nightmare has just unfolded right before our eyes, Your Highness," Dante muttered.

"It has," I said. "Although, to her credit, I think what Grace is proposing is an absolutely brilliant idea. It will inspire people to donate more once they see what these kids can do. I would have never come up with such an idea."

The fundraiser was an adult event, aimed at spoiling the wealthiest citizens of Verdana with dinner and drinks and entertainment, hopefully in exchange for their generous donations. Since Hotel Verdana was directly next door, the logistics could not be any easier to add Grace's idea of including the children in a small part. Why should the adults have all the fun? These kids were going through so much with their health issues, it made sense to give them a chance to let loose and be seen.

A young boy spoke up shyly. "I can show my drawings."

A cute girl with pigtails chimed in, wavering her hands frantically to get Grace's attention. "Ooh, and I can sing!"

"I can play the flute!" a boy said.

Grace beamed. "Amazing! This is going to be so much fun. We'll make it a true celebration for you kids."

"Can I wear a dress?" a little girl asked. "I'm a ballerina!"

"I don't see why not," Grace answered. "I think I'll wear a dress, too! Now, do you have any other ideas for what you'd like to see at the gala? Things that would make it more fun for you?"

The kids shouted out suggestions—face painting, juggling, balloon animals, and of course, lots of snacks. Grace jotted down their ideas, promising they'd make it the best party ever. She made each child feel included, listening thoughtfully, even when they spoke over each other in their excitement.

I had visited this section of the children's hospital more than a few times over the years and I can honestly say I had never seen so many smiles on their faces before. For a few moments, they seemed to have forgotten why they were in the hospital. The innocence and joy of these children was infectious. I couldn't help smiling as well.

Grace glanced over in my direction, a smile forming on her face when she saw me. "Hey, Prince Oliver is here! Would you like him to join us?" She waved us over to the group.

"Yes!" the kids all screamed.

"So much for being discreet," I said, entering the room with Dante right by my side. "Why, hello everyone! There seems to be a cookie party going on here!"

A young girl approached me and tugged on my sport

coat. "Do you have a special talent, Prince Oliver? Besides being a prince?"

I chuckled. "I have two. For starters, most people don't know that I paint."

"Really?" Grace said, tilting her head to the side.

I turned to her. "Does that seem surprising to you?"

She shrugged. "I don't know. I suppose it does. I've never heard of a prince who paints, that's all."

"Do you paint with your fingers?" a boy innocently asked.

"I'm afraid not," I said. "I use good, old-fashioned paint brushes, like most people."

"Do you paint houses like my uncle?" another boy asked.

I shook my head. "Unfortunately, I don't know how to do that. I like to paint portraits of people. And sunrises over the Mediterranean."

"Doesn't that get boring?" a boy asked.

I shook my head. "Not at all. No two sunrises are the same."

"And what is your other special talent?" Grace asked.

I leaned closer. "Okay, don't tell anyone, but I am also a magician."

"I want to see!" a young girl said. "Do a trick for us!"

"Great thinking, Beatrice!" Grace encouraged, surprising me she knew her name. "I want to see, too!"

I nodded. "Very well . . . I will just need a cookie to perform my trick. Does anyone know where I could find one?"

All the children pointed to the cookies on the table. "There!"

Grace shot me a playful glance as she reached over and handed me a cookie. "Here you go, Prince Oliver."

"Okay, watch carefully as I make the cookie disappear," I said, waving the cookie in front of my face, left, right, up, down. "Now you see it, and now you don't!" I theatrically made the cookie vanish into my mouth.

The children laughed and pointed at me.

"You ate it!"

"It's in your mouth!"

I threw my palms up, pretending I didn't know what they were talking about, then tried to chew the cookie and swallow it without laughing, which was quite a laborious task.

"I think we all know that trick!" Grace said, laughing with the kids. "Let's show Prince Oliver we can do it even better than him!"

Everybody rushed to Grace and grappled for a cookie. A minute later, the boxes were empty, as they all continued to perform the disappearing cookie trick.

As we prepared to leave, I pulled Grace aside. "You were really wonderful with the children."

She looked surprised. "Oh, thank you. You weren't so bad yourself, Mr. Cookie Monster. I just want them to have some fun."

"It's more than that," I said. "You really connected with them. Few people can do that, especially with kids who have health issues."

Grace smiled modestly. "Well, they make it easy. Their spirits are so resilient, and I think sometimes they just want to feel like children, not patients."

I nodded. "I never thought about it that way, but it makes sense."

One worker asked if she could take a photo of Grace and me with the children. Grace and I stood close together, and I caught the scent of her lovely floral perfume, with a hint of chocolate chip.

"Hmm, is it lavender you're wearing?" I guessed.

"It is not," Grace said, opting to not tell me any more than that.

We said our goodbyes and headed to the car. On the drive back, I continued trying to identify Grace's scent, playfully quizzing her.

"Orange blossom?" I said, wiggling my nose.

She smirked and shook her head.

"Rose?" I tried.

"Sorry—not even close," Grace said, clearly enjoying that I was wrong so many times.

"Your Highness—how long will Princess Veronica be staying on her visit?" Dante asked, clearly trying to pull me away from my conversation with Grace since he already knew the answer to the question.

"She will be here a week before she needs to return to Kastonia," I said, wondering if he thought I was flirting with Grace.

That wasn't flirting.

Call me curious.

I was simply being conversational.

Dante nodded. "A week is plenty of time to catch up on the wedding preparations, I would imagine."

"You would imagine correctly," I said.

"I'd like to go over Miss DuPont's files for the wedding," Grace said. "Can you and Princess Veronica meet me after lunch to discuss the next steps in the planning process?"

"Of course," I said. "We are at your disposal. Dante, please make sure Grace has access to Miss DuPont's wedding planning files, and that she is aware of our availability for the next week."

"Will do, Your Highness." Dante tapped a note into his phone, then leaned forward in the seat as we pulled up to the front of the palace. "The queen appears to be awaiting our arrival."

"Does this car have an *eject* button?" Grace asked.

I couldn't help but laugh. "You'll be fine. Just remember that most people let her have her way because she's the queen. If you strongly believe in something, let it be known. She may not show it, but she will respect you for your conviction."

Grace nodded. "I'm not looking for respect. Right now, the most important thing is for me to stay alive. Can you confirm the guillotine has been outlawed in your country?"

"Yes." I chuckled. "I can confirm that."

As we exited the car, Mother stepped closer to Grace, then snapped at her. "Just what did you think you were doing at the hospital? Inviting children to the event was not part of the plan. Some of them are gravely ill. Did you even know that?"

It wasn't a surprise that mother already knew of Grace's plans. The royal family had eyes and ears all across Verdana, informing us of anything and everything.

Grace met my mother's icy glare steadily. "Of course I knew they were ill. That's precisely why I extended the invitation. Those children deserve joy and laughter as much as any other child. You should have seen them! While I was there, it didn't even seem as if any of them were sick! With all due respect, Your Majesty, I stand by my decision."

Mother bristled. "You may stand by it, but that does not make it right. There are reasons we make plans. There are expectations to be met. I will not have you derailing things with your sentimentality."

"Sentimentality?" Grace repeated incredulously, boldly stepping closer. "Is caring about sick children mere senti-ment to you? I cannot believe bringing a small measure of happiness to those kids can be seen as problematic."

Mother frowned. "Happiness is not the issue. Security and logistics are. Those children require medical care we cannot provide on-site. It is simply not feasible."

Grace folded her arms across her chest. "The hospital administrator assured me it could be done since the hotel for the gala was located right next-door. I trust his expertise in this area. Are you telling me you don't?"

Mother narrowed her eyes, unused to being contradicted so openly. "I really do not have time for this right now." For a moment, it seemed she might continue the argument, but then she spun on her heel and strode toward the palace doors, leaving me speechless.

Mother called out over her shoulder. "Oliver, in my office! Now!"

I sighed, feeling bad for not helping Grace. "I'm sorry about that. She is quite set in her ways."

"No need to apologize," she said. "I can handle a stern talking-to. I just hope she doesn't rescind the invitation from those children. They would be heartbroken."

"Not to worry," I said firmly, impressed by Grace's courage and conviction. "The children will be there. I'll make sure of it myself."

Grace smiled. "Thank you, Oliver. I appreciate your support on this."

I found her boldness captivating.

And though it angered my traditionalist mother, a part of me hoped Grace would continue disrupting the status quo. I only wished she would wait until we got to the wedding planning for her to turn things upside down.

Chapter Seven

GRACE

I sat at the largest solid-wood executive desk I had ever seen in my entire life, carefully going through the royal wedding files left behind by Miss DuPont. Her meticulously printed pages of notes, plans, and charts that seemed to cover every imaginable detail for Oliver and Veronica's wedding. There was no doubt in my mind that she was a true professional.

I got up to take a break and stretch, staring out the window of my room. The view was simply stunning, with the lush gardens spreading out as far as the eye could see, and the sparkling sea in the distance.

My thoughts drifted back to my confrontation with Queen Annabelle about the fundraiser. I had been incredibly nervous, but I had stood up for my idea about including the children. Yet, despite my fear, I had held my ground against the formidable queen, and I felt a swell of pride within me.

"I won't be a pushover anymore," I vowed to myself.

In all my years as a wedding planner, I had learned that

when clients didn't listen to me, problems were usually just around the corner. If I wanted to avoid another colossal failure, I needed to make sure Oliver and Veronica understood my expertise and followed my advice. And if I were even luckier, the queen would completely stay out of my way.

I sat back down and continued to sift through Miss DuPont's files, realizing that there was a difference between our approaches. She clearly had a wealth of knowledge and experience for planning weddings, but she always leaned more toward the conservative side. I'm guessing this had something to do with tradition, more than a reflection of her personality, but I saw it as an opportunity to add my personal touch and create a wedding day that would be more unique, more magical, and unforgettable.

I sighed, taking a deep breath as I felt my determination solidify within me like a suit of armor. No more fear, no more second-guessing myself. It was time to show the world what Grace, the determined and passionate wedding planner, could do.

"Please pardon my interruption, Miss Grace," Henri, the head steward, called from the doorway, his voice smooth and professional, "I trust your accommodations are satisfactory."

"More than satisfactory—this place makes a five-star resort look like a pup tent in the outback," I said, smiling. "It's amazing. Thank you for asking."

"It is our pleasure to make your stay as comfortable as possible," he replied with a smile. "Please, follow me to the terrace. Prince Oliver, Princess Veronica, and Mrs.

Masterson are waiting for you there to discuss the wedding."

"Mrs. Masterson?" I said, not understanding who she was.

"Yes," Henri answered, not giving me any more information.

I guess I'll find out soon enough.

I gathered my notes and my laptop, trying to suppress the sudden flutter of nerves in my stomach since this would be our first official wedding planning meeting. As I followed Henri through the opulent halls of the palace, I mentally prepared myself for the upcoming discussion. I knew I had to present my ideas with confidence to gain their trust, and I couldn't allow my past to hold me back.

As we stepped out onto the sun-drenched terrace, I took a moment to catch my breath.

"Ah, here she is!" Oliver's voice boomed from his seat under the umbrella, dark hair tousled, and a mischievous glint in his eyes. Veronica looked poised and elegant in the chair next to him.

"Your Highnesses," I said, curtsying awkwardly. I could feel my cheeks heating at the clumsy maneuver, but I pushed through my embarrassment and held up the files. "I've got lots of updates on the wedding."

"I look forward to hearing about them," Veronica said kindly.

"Grace—please allow me to introduce Georgina Master-son," Oliver said, gesturing to the *very* pregnant woman with short brown hair in the dark green maternity dress.

"Georgina will document our journey to the altar. She's a journalist with the *Royal Gazette* who works with us often."

I hesitated for a moment, then shook her hand.

Suddenly, flashes of past headlines swirled through my mind. I felt dizzy. "World's Worst Wedding Planner" and "Grace the Disgrace" taunted me like ghosts from my past. My heart raced, and my palms grew clammy.

"A pleasure to meet you, Georgina," I stuttered out, releasing her hand quickly and taking a step back.

"And you as well . . ." Her eyes narrowed slightly at my reaction, but she nodded and turned her attention back to her notebook.

"Excuse me, Prince Oliver," I said, my voice barely above a whisper, "may I have a word with you in private?"

He studied me for a moment, then said, "Of course." He gestured for me to follow him to a more secluded corner of the terrace.

As we walked, I clasped my hands together to hide their trembling, and I tried to steady my breath. Once we were out of earshot, I blurted out in a low voice, "You told me no more surprises. I didn't know there would be a journalist documenting the wedding planning process. It makes me feel . . . exposed."

Oliver regarded me thoughtfully before responding. "I see. You're worried that Georgina might write something unfavorable about you, and you have already been through enough in the recent past."

I hesitated, surprised he knew what I was thinking. "Yes . . ."

He nodded. "I understand your concerns, Grace. I really do. But having a journalist present is a long-standing tradition in Verdana. The people of our kingdom cherish our royal weddings and expect to have every moment documented for posterity and transparency. Georgina has proven herself as an objective and truthful journalist. I assure you that her job is to focus on the beauty and grandeur of the wedding. The *Royal Gazette* is not a tabloid."

His words were comforting, and I felt some of my earlier tension melt away. Oliver truly had a way with words and an innate ability to put others at ease. I let out a sigh, feeling somewhat foolish for letting my fears get the best of me in public.

"Thank you, Your Highness," I said, offering him a tiny smile. "I apologize for my reaction earlier. I just want everything to be perfect for you and Princess Veronica. I hope you know that."

"I do, and your apology is accepted," he replied graciously. "Now, shall we rejoin Veronica and Georgina to discuss the wedding?"

"Sure," I said.

We returned to the table, where Veronica was telling Georgina about the time she accidentally stepped on the queen's foot. Their laughter filled the air, and I couldn't help but smile as the prince and I took our seats.

"Grace has informed me of her concerns regarding the presence of a journalist during the wedding planning process," Oliver surprisingly announced, effectively drawing Veronica and Georgina's attention to me. "However, I have assured her that the reporting will be fair and discreet, and will focus on the royal couple."

I looked at Georgina, feeling a mixture of embarrassment and trepidation. "I apologize for my reaction earlier when we were introduced, Georgina. It was a surprise that a journalist was here."

"Think nothing of it," she said as she rubbed her belly.

I was honest with Georgina. "My experience with the media has been less than positive. I confess I'm quite nervous about having my every move scrutinized again. I didn't mean any offense."

"None taken," Georgina said with a reassuring smile. "I understand the pressures you're under, and I assure you, I'm here to capture the magic of this beautiful event, not to cause any trouble."

"I appreciate that," I said.

"I've seen the videos, and have read a few of the articles," Princess Veronica said, her eyes filled with sincerity. "I want to say how sorry I am that you had to go through all that bad publicity. It must have been so difficult for you, all the lies and cruel remarks."

I blew out a breath. "You have no idea, but I've learned from my mistakes, even though none of the things that happened in those viral videos were my fault. But people believe what they want to believe. It's as if they're entertained by other people's failures."

"Wasn't there one bride in particular who blamed you for her wedding being called off?" Veronica asked, looking genuinely interested. "Do you mind sharing what happened?"

Georgina nodded. "Off the record—of course."

I hesitated, unsure if I wanted to delve into that story, but I took a deep breath and was honest, since the three of them were looking at me with interest.

"I guess I can share, since you can find most of it online anyway," I said. "The groom, Bradley, was a prominent entertainment lawyer. Very Type A personality, he had to control every detail. As the planning went on, I noticed some odd behavior from him. He was increasingly secretive, spent a lot of time on his phone, and seemed disinterested in the actual wedding plans, much more than the average groom. Anyway, we were just a week out from the wedding when I saw him through the window, at a small cafe across the street. He was with another woman, holding hands, laughing. It was clearly a date."

"How awful!" Veronica gasped, her eyes widening in shock.

"Sounds like a real charmer," Oliver muttered sarcastically, shaking his head.

I sighed. "You have no idea. I confronted him about it the next day. He said he just needed to get it out of his system, that it was a onetime thing. Then he threatened to fire me if I said a word to the bride."

"But you could not help yourself, I suspect?" Georgina asked.

I shook my head. "The guilt of not saying anything to her

was getting to me. So, when I was alone with the bride during the final dress fitting, when she mentioned the groom had been acting weird lately and she was worried, I spilled the beans. I told her everything, what I saw and what he said."

"What did she do?" Veronica asked.

"She confronted him," I said. "She told him exactly what I had said. Then he gave an Oscar-winning performance, telling her she was crazy for believing the *stupid* wedding planner over him, and that I was a liar. He said he could not marry a person who didn't trust him over a gossiping nobody. Then he broke it off with her on the spot and demanded the ring back. The bride sued me for ruining her life, for emotional damage, and for the lost deposits from the venue and wedding vendors."

"Preposterous!" Oliver declared, shaking his head in disbelief. "How could you possibly be responsible for his actions?"

"Exactly," I agreed, feeling a mix of relief and vulnerability at having shared such a painful story. "In hindsight, maybe I should have just kept my mouth shut and let her suffer in that horrible relationship. Let her learn a hard lesson. But I did what I thought was right, and what I would hope someone would do for me if I had been in the bride's shoes."

"I probably would have said something as well," Veronica whispered, her sympathetic gaze meeting mine. "It is absolutely dreadful that you paid the price for his indiscretions, and your honesty."

"Dreadful" didn't even cover it.

The humiliation, the anger, the endless sleepless nights spent wondering how everything had gone so wrong—those memories still haunted me. But I couldn't afford to dwell on the past. Not when I had a royal wedding to execute.

"It was," I confessed, offering her a small, rueful smile. "But like I said earlier, I'm doing my best to move forward and learn from my mistakes. And on that note, maybe we should talk about something a little more upbeat. I've been given the incredible opportunity to help you achieve your wedding, which I'm determined to make a success."

"And speaking of that," Veronica said, her eyes sparkling with curiosity, "how are things going, Grace?"

"Actually, I've already made progress in the last few hours," I said, eager to show my competence and commitment. "I've reserved an additional room block at the Four Seasons Verdana since it appears we are going to run out of rooms for guests. I also arranged shuttle bus transportation to and from the hotel, scheduled final fittings for the bridesmaids with the designers, updated the wedding website with details on royal wedding traditions and etiquette, plus I added an interactive map of the carriage procession route. And I checked in with the five people on the wedding planning team to make sure we were all on the same page."

Oliver startled, and he exchanged a strange glance with Veronica. It seemed as if they weren't expecting me to have accomplished so much in such a short period, which was a boost to my confidence.

Georgina had pulled out a tablet and was furiously

typing notes. I tried not to let it affect me, but it was hard not to feel self-conscious under such scrutiny.

"Wow, that's . . . impressive," Oliver admitted, and a curious expression flickered across his face as he exchanged another glance with Veronica.

She shot a raised-brow look at Oliver, then turned back to me. "Well done."

Neither of them looked as pleased as I had hoped, though.

I set my ego aside and brushed it off, reminding myself this was an arranged marriage. The two of them might not be so overjoyed about their impending nuptials and the little details that went along with it. In fact, I would not have been surprised to learn that they just wanted to get the whole endeavor over with.

"However," Oliver said, leaning back in his chair and adopting a more serious expression, "we do have an idea for the wedding that we'd like to discuss with you. It's rather unorthodox, but we think it could make the wedding even more memorable."

"Of course," I responded, my curiosity piqued. "I'm open to any ideas you may have, and I'll do my best to make your vision come to life."

"Good," Oliver said. "Because we've grown tired of the same old royal traditions and protocols. It's time for something fresh and exciting."

"What did you have in mind?" I asked.

He leaned closer. "We'd like to have a pirate-themed wedding, complete with treasure chests and eye patches.

The guests would have to walk a plank to enter the reception, and I could even have a parrot on my shoulder during the ceremony."

I could not help myself and immediately erupted with laughter, and was quickly joined by Veronica and Georgina. Then the prince himself.

"Good one," I said, impressed again that he had a sense of humor.

"A pirate wedding would be so unique!" Veronica said, clearly wanting to keep the joke going. "You'd look so dashing dressed like Jack Sparrow. Don't you think he resembles Johnny Depp?"

"Oh, please—the prince is much more handsome than Johnny Depp!" I blurted out without thinking.

Oliver's head drew back in surprise.

Veronica stifled a giggle behind her hand.

I froze, feeling my cheeks flush hot with embarrassment.

"Your Highness," I stammered. "Forgive me—that was unprofessional."

Oliver waved it off with an amused chuckle. "No need to apologize, Grace. I'll gladly take the compliment." He gave me a roguish wink.

Wait—should the prince be winking at me?

I shot a quick glance at Veronica. Luckily, she hadn't seemed to notice, although Georgina had a hint of a smile tugging at the corner of her mouth as she typed feverishly.

"I'm trying to imagine you with a parrot on your shoulder under the altar," Veronica said, continuing to laugh. "Imagine what the queen would think if she were here."

"Imagine what the queen would think about what?" Queen Annabelle asked, approaching and stopping in front of the table.

The laughter stopped.

Georgina jumped to her feet and curtsied. "Your Majesty . . ."

"I was just having a little fun, joking about dressing up as a pirate for the wedding," Oliver said.

Queen Annabelle stood there, tight-lipped, the veins in her temples appearing to throb, like she was going to burst a blood vessel.

How could she not think that was funny?

"The royal wedding is not a joke, Oliver," she finally said. "The entire world will be watching us." She glanced over at me. "We have traditions to uphold, many dating back centuries. I expect them all to remain intact. Please do not stray from the course with any wild notions of trying to be unique. Unique is for the weak. I hope I am making myself crystal clear."

Unique is for the weak?

What does that even mean?

"Verdana is all about tradition," Queen Annabelle added. "Understood?"

I held her gaze and tried to stay relaxed, having dealt with many overbearing parents and parents-in-law of brides and grooms in the past.

But before I could respond, Oliver cleared his throat.

"Mother—I'd like to talk to you privately." He stood and walked away, not waiting for her to respond.

She glared at me, then spun around and marched away to follow Oliver.

Veronica forced a smile in my direction, then kept her voice low. "The queen has not been the same since the king passed away last year. They loved each other dearly. Then her trusted companion, Ruby, the royal dog, died a few months after that. A beautiful Pembroke Welsh Corgi. That's why you don't see any dogs around here. An order from the queen."

I nodded, glancing toward the queen, imagining the loss and heartbreak she must be feeling. "That's horrible."

Veronica nodded. "Oliver says we need to be patient with her, but sometimes it's easier said than done."

Oliver returned by himself and took a seat again. "I apologize for that."

"Not a problem," I said, watching the queen return inside the palace, but not before giving me one last nasty look.

"Where were we?" the prince asked, preferring not to mention anymore of his mother's interruption. "That's right. Me and Johnny Depp. Shall we explore that further?"

Veronica gave me a knowing smile. "Men and their egos."

I laughed and pointed to the ground in front of Oliver. "Careful when you get up. You might trip over it."

"Fine," he said with an amused smile. "We can talk about the wedding, if you prefer."

Over the next two hours, we drank more than a few cups of tea and finished every single pastry on the platter. Our conversation had shifted to other important planning topics, including the potential entertainment for the wedding reception and whether we should include a fireworks display. I chimed in with suggestions and ideas for everything, on top of my game, feeling more confident with every minute that passed.

Which was why Oliver's creased forehead worried me. What was on his mind as he suddenly ignored me and scrolled his phone like he was looking for something more important and interesting than my ideas?

"Is everything okay, Your Highness?" I asked.

"Yes . . ." He nodded and finally looked up from his phone. "I just had an idea I would like to incorporate into the wedding."

"Don't tell me—you would like to turn the wedding reception into a pajama party?" Veronica joked.

Oliver chuckled. "Not a bad idea. Let's table that discussion for another day." He tapped a couple more times on his phone. "Ah, here we go." The prince handed me his phone.

I glanced at a picture of a beautiful six-lobed flower with purple and silver petals, then read the caption out loud. "The Adana Orchid." I glanced up at Oliver. "It's gorgeous. Is this something you're growing in your royal garden?"

"If only we were so lucky," he said. "This orchid only grows wild in northern Europe in the old-growth beech forests of the Carpathian Mountains in Romania. It prefers damp, shady areas and is very difficult to cultivate."

I nodded, a little confused. "I'm sorry, but I don't understand. Are you saying you want this flower for the wedding?"

Oliver nodded. "For the centerpieces. We'll need one hundred and twenty-five of them, one for each table."

"What happened to the magenta peonies?" Veronica asked.

"I've changed my mind," he firmly said.

"As you wish," the princess said, studying Oliver but not saying any more on the subject.

I was surprised the two of them hadn't discussed this change ahead of my arrival to avoid any awkward conversations. I had seen my fair share of disagreements between couples on certain aspects of wedding planning, especially when one of them changed their mind at the last minute.

"No problem," I said. "I can cancel the order for the peonies and search for ethically cultivated Adana Orchids from reputable growers."

"You won't find them," Oliver said. "The Adana Orchid is one of the rarest flowers in the world. The only way to get them is to go directly to the source."

I blinked twice. "You want me to go to Romania?"

"In my private jet, of course," he said. "With as many people as you need to complete the task. Bring the flowers back and get them situated in our garden shade house, so they can slowly adapt to our climate in time for the wedding."

Speechless, I glanced down at his phone, scrolling for more information on the Carpathian Mountains in Romania.

What I found did not look encouraging. Steep mountain slopes and valleys. Rocky outcrops, cliffs, and elevation changes. Trails requiring climbing over boulders and up inclines. Mossy rocks, muddy trails, wet leaves, and even occasional snow patches that would make footing slippery and unstable.

I glanced back over at Oliver. "It says here that accessing remote, rugged Romanian locations to collect these flowers in large numbers would be extremely difficult logistically. It would take careful planning, several permits for access, collection, and importation, and experienced local guides for the rustic conditions."

Oliver nodded. "I have every faith in you, Grace. Whatever you need to make it happen. Georgina can accompany you on the trip and document everything."

"It would be a pleasure, Your Highness," she said.

If I did not put my foot down, this would turn into another wedding disaster. I was sure of it.

"No," I said, handing his phone back to him as my heart rate picked up speed from my defiance.

Oliver cocked his head to the side. "Pardon me?"

I turned to him and squared my shoulders. "This is not realistic. There are a million flowers under the sun. You heard the queen, *unique is for the weak*. Please choose something that is more easily accessible. Your guests won't know the difference between the Adana orchid and a hundred other beautiful orchids that are available for your wedding."

"*I* will know the difference," Oliver said, standing up.

"And *the queen* will know as well, since the Adana orchid was my father's favorite flower. This will be our way of honoring him at our wedding. And just so we're clear, this is non-negotiable. Now, if you'll excuse me, I need to meet with Dante."

Just like that, the meeting was over, and I was sitting there on the terrace alone. As much as I wanted to prove to myself and everyone else that I could pull off the most spectacular royal wedding Verdana had ever seen, I couldn't help but worry about the possibility of making one tiny mistake that would bring it all crashing down around me. The last thing I needed was another viral video, or to be splattered across the front page of the *Royal Gazette* because I could not fulfill the prince's wishes to honor his father.

I had no other choice in the matter.

"Looks like I'm going to Romania," I mumbled to myself.

Chapter Eight

PRINCE OLIVER

Two Days Later . . .

The large white tent in the parking lot at the Royal Children's Hospital had been transformed into a magical wonderland, with twinkling lights, colorful murals, and balloons arching high above the dance floor.

My gaze swept over the space, taking in the sights.

A juggler was surrounded by a circle of delighted kids, his clubs twirling hypnotically through the air. At a face painting station, a volunteer carefully traced a butterfly across a little girl's cheek. By the photo booth, children waited their turn to strike silly poses while pop music played from the speakers near the makeshift dance floor, where kids were showing off their best moves.

How Grace could make this happen with fewer than three days of preparation was beyond me. Especially since I had sent her on that impossible task of finding the rare orchids in Romania.

"Can you believe how quickly this all came together?" Veronica said. "Grace has turned a simple tent into a vibrant, joy-filled space where these children appear to have forgotten about their troubles and are simply having fun. It's just what she said she wanted to do. Her vision came to life."

"I was just thinking the same thing," I said sincerely, even though my eyes scanned the room for something amiss.

Everything looked perfect.

"Grace said she would return in time to see the children," Veronica said. "It doesn't worry you that you haven't heard a single word from her in the last forty-eight hours?"

"Not at all," I said. "She was adamant about doing things her way and not being managed. I respect that."

Veronica thought about it. "What if she were to actually get those orchids?"

I shook my head. "Impossible. I chose one of the rarest flowers in the world, in a location that few have traversed. The only thing I expect is for her to return to tell me she could not accomplish the task, and for Georgina Masterson to write about it."

"I must say—this is so out of character for you," Veronica said. "You don't feel the slightest bit of guilt for this plan of yours?"

I sighed. "I would be lying if I said I didn't, but there

really is no other way. The alternative is you and me being married forever."

Veronica nodded. "Good point."

"Prince Oliver!" called out a little girl, running toward me with arms wide open, effectively pulling me from my thoughts. I bent down to catch her in a big embrace, feeling her infectious giggle vibrate against my chest.

"Hello there, Carmen," I said warmly after reading her name tag. "Are you enjoying yourself?"

"Uh-huh!" she exclaimed, her eyes shining with excitement. "I got my face painted like a butterfly, see?" She pointed to the colorful design adorning her cheeks, and I couldn't help but smile at her enthusiasm.

"Absolutely beautiful," I said, causing her to blush and giggle once more.

"I agree!" Veronica added as the girl ran off.

"Well done, Your Highness," said Mr. Thomas, a major donor, dressed in a perfectly cut tuxedo. "Including the children was a brilliant idea. Several parents have already told me their kids seem happier and more optimistic. It's not surprising that their involvement has inspired many guests to increase their donations."

The fundraiser had been the same monotonous affair year after year, full of stuffed shirts donating for the prestige, so his words were music to my ears.

"Thank you, but I can't take the credit," I replied. "Our wedding planner, Miss Fullerton, was the one who proposed it."

"Then I would like to personally thank her myself," he said.

"We're hoping for her arrival at any minute," I said.

"I look forward to making her acquaintance," Mr. Thomas said before being called away by another guest.

I plastered on my best princely smile as the cameras flashed, trying not to blink against the blinding lights. I exchanged pleasantries on autopilot, nodding and making small talk, all while scanning the room for any sign of Grace.

"Oliver, she's here," Veronica said, gesturing to the entrance.

As we walked in her direction, a group of children immediately flocked to Grace, nearly knocking her over with their enthusiastic and affectionate hugs.

"Miss Grace! You look like a princess!" one exclaimed.

"Please take a photo with me!" another said.

Grace's smile lit up the tent as she exchanged more hugs and high-fives than I'd seen in my entire life. I couldn't help but marvel at the impact Grace had on these children.

"Your Highnesses." Grace curtseyed as we approached her, then admiring Veronica's elegant black sequined dress, said enthusiastically, "You look stunning."

"Thank you—you are far too kind," Veronica said, offering her a warm smile as she admired Grace's red, floor-length gown. "I was just about to say the same thing about you."

"Thank you," Grace said, glancing at me and nodding. "Nice tux, Prince Oliver."

"Oh, uh, thank you," I said, adjusting my bow tie. "It's obvious this event means a lot to the children. Just look at them." I gestured to the impromptu dance party that had broken out behind her. "This was an inspired idea, I must say. You should be proud."

"Thank you, Your Highness. That means a lot to me," Grace said, her cheeks flushing pink.

A server stopped by and offered champagne to the three of us.

"Perfect timing," I said, holding up my glass. "To the children!"

"Cheers!" we all said, clinking our glasses.

"And to the Adana orchid!" Grace added, beaming. "Mission completed. I've got all one hundred and twenty-five of them."

I nearly choked on my champagne.

Veronica's eyes went wide. "I must say, I am quite surprised."

"Unbelievable . . ." I finished my champagne in one gulp, then stopped a server, swapping my empty glass for a full one. "How on earth were you able to accomplish that?"

"It was much easier than I thought," Grace said. "After I mentioned the orchids were for your wedding, I had more volunteers than I could handle! You have many fans in Romania."

This was a nightmare.

A young boy of about ten came running up to me, holding a colorful painting close to his chest. "Prince Oliver! Look what I painted! Do you like it?"

"Let's see what you've got there." I took the painting and saw a detailed landscape of the palace rendered beautifully for someone that age. "My, oh, my, you've captured the north tower splendidly. And the use of one-point perspective draws the eye right to the main entrance."

The boy looked at me, perplexed.

"And blending the shadows on the west wing to show depth—very skilled," I continued, impressed by his artistic abilities. "But my favorite part by far is the brush technique on the gardens. Marvelous!"

"Um, okay," the boy finally replied with a shrug before scampering back into the crowd.

Grace looked at me in surprise. "You seem to know a lot about painting."

"I dabble a bit in my spare time," I said casually, not wanting to make a big deal of my hobby, since few people knew about it. Before Grace could ask more, a booming voice interrupted us over the speakers.

"Attention, esteemed guests!" the man said. "Please welcome Prince Oliver to the stage!"

"Please excuse me," I told Grace, spinning on my heels toward the stage, wondering what in the world I was going to do with one hundred and twenty-five Adana orchids since there would not be a wedding.

"Good evening, ladies and gentlemen," I began, my voice echoing throughout the tent. "I would like to extend my deepest gratitude to every one of you for attending this year's gala. Your generous donations will make an incredible difference in the lives of these extraordinary children."

I paused my speech briefly for the applause, glancing at Grace, who still seemed on cloud nine from her accomplishment in Romania. It would only be fair to give credit where credit was due, in regards to the fundraiser.

"Before we transition to the hotel for dinner, I would like to acknowledge someone who was adamant about including the children this year," I said. "Grace, could you come to the stage and say a few words?"

She hesitated, clearly not expecting me to acknowledge her, but then graciously smiled, handed her glass to a server, and walked to the stage as the children chanted her name. But just as Grace reached the top step of the stage, her heel caught on the hem of her dress, and she stumbled forward.

"Whoa!" she cried out, arms flailing as she came careening into my chest.

Luckily, I caught her, my arms instinctively wrapping around her waist to help her regain her balance.

Cameras flashed wildly around us.

Grace gazed up at me, flustered, inches from my face.

"Are you all right?" I asked, holding on to her tightly as the flashes continued.

"Yes—thank you," Grace said, her face reddening with embarrassment. "I'm not drunk."

That made me laugh.

She smoothed down her gown, regained her composure, then stepped up to the microphone. "I really know how to make an entrance."

I laughed, along with the attendees. Then she launched into a heartfelt speech about the children that had half the room dabbing their eyes. I had to admit, she had a way with words.

"Whether it's through art, music, or just spending time with one another, we have the power to make a difference in their lives," Grace continued. "Let's remember to celebrate not only tonight, but every day we have the privilege of being part of this wonderful world."

The crowd erupted into applause, with my sister Adriana leading the charge. She beamed at Grace, clearly impressed by her heartfelt speech.

My brother Theodore stood off to the side, grumpy as ever.

"Now, please join me in transitioning to the ballroom next door for dinner and dancing," I said. "The night is still young!"

"Grace, your speech was truly touching," Adriana gushed, once the applause had died down and the guests began to exit the tent. "You're an inspiration to us all."

"Thank you, Your Highness," Grace replied, looking touched by her kind words. "And I'm sorry I haven't had a chance to talk with you much since I arrived."

"Well, we need to do something about that, don't we?" Adriana said. "I would love to get to know you better."

"I'd like that very much," Grace said.

My mother pulled me aside while Grace and Adriana continued to chat, irritation flashing in her eyes. "That woman is a menace, Oliver."

I sighed. "What are you talking about, Mother? We

doubled the donations this year because of Grace. You should be happy."

"While I appreciate that, such uncouth behavior toward a prince simply won't do!" she said. "She does not know how to be proper and act accordingly."

"Uncouth?" I said, trying to keep my voice down. "She tripped!"

Before I could inform my mother that she was dead wrong about Grace, she turned to talk with someone else.

"What was that all about?" Veronica asked.

"Mother just being Mother," I said, tugging on her arm to step away from Grace and Adriana to talk in private. "It appears that we have underestimated Grace."

"That is a gross understatement," Veronica replied with a tiny laugh. "But I really don't know what we can do at this point."

"Neither do I." I sighed. "She has miraculously gotten her act together, and if she continues on this trajectory, you and I are going to be royally screwed."

Chapter Nine

GRACE

I went viral again.

Why do these things always happen to me? Do I attract them or do they attract me? Was this payback for something horrible I had done in the past? I considered myself a decent human being.

Tired of staring at the online photo of myself in the arms of Prince Oliver, I closed my laptop screen.

My phone rang with a video call from Cristina, her eyes bulging in a dramatic fashion. "Grace! You're all over the internet again. And why are you *all over* the prince? Details! Now!"

I cringed, recalling the moment I face-planted into Oliver's muscular chest. "It was an accident, I swear. My stupid heels failed me at the worst possible moment, as I was going up the stairs to the stage."

Cristina clicked her tongue doubtfully. "Mm-hmm, sure.

And what about that picture of you ogling his behind as he walked away? Don't even try to deny it, Grace Marie!"

"I have no idea how they could have even seen that, let alone gotten a picture of it because it was a split-second!" I said, trying to brush it off. "And come on, every woman in that tent was ogling the prince. Like my mom always says, great butts need to be appreciated."

Cristina cackled approvingly. "Preach, girl! Your momma raised you right."

"I'm only human, after all," I said with a shrug and a smile. "But seriously, I wonder what's going to happen when the queen sees those photos. She already hates me."

"Oh, stop—I'm sure she doesn't hate you," Cristina soothed.

"You haven't seen the death glares and bulging forehead veins," I said. "A royal banishment is coming. I can feel it."

Cristina scoffed. "Please . . . that's hardly a scandal. You're lucky it happened at a public event and you two were not alone. Now, if you got the prince naked in a jacuzzi, that's a different story."

I did *not* need that image in my head.

She smirked knowingly. "You're picturing it right now, aren't you?"

"No comment," I muttered. "And I'm being serious. This trip is crucial to me, you know that."

"Of course I do," she said. "This too shall pass."

"I hope you're right," I said.

"Just relax and try to enjoy it, okay?" Cristina said. "You deserve to be happy, Grace. And if that includes ogling some royal booty now and then, well, I say go for it. As long as you remember he's betrothed and not to touch."

"Seriously?!" I burst into laughter, shaking my head at her ridiculousness. "Okay, I need to run. I just got a text from Oliver to meet him and Veronica downstairs."

We said our goodbyes, and I descended the spiral staircase to pick up the wedding files from the top of the desk, but they weren't there.

"That's so bizarre," I muttered, scanning the room. "Where the heck did I put them?"

My eyes landed on the sitting area with its embroidered settee and velvet armchairs. I lifted the cushions and peeked behind the curtains. I rifled through the things on top of the desk and inside the drawers. I peered out toward the table on the terrace, even though I was certain I hadn't taken them out there.

Nothing.

How could the files have just disappeared? My memory doesn't fail me like that. It was the strangest thing, because I wasn't drunk either.

Smoothing my dress, I hurried from the room, knowing I would figure out where I had left the files later.

As I approached the grand foyer, I spotted Veronica with her hand on the handle of a suitcase, engaged in conversation with Dante. Oliver stood nearby, looking concerned. I hesitated for a moment, wondering if I should come back later, but they noticed my presence.

"Ah, Miss Fullerton," Oliver said. "Please join us."

"Hi, everyone," I said, offering a small smile. "Am I

interrupting something? I can come back." My eyes lingered on the suitcase in Veronica's hand, my curiosity piqued.

Veronica sighed, her elegant posture wilting. "I'm afraid I have some unfortunate news. My mother is unwell back in Kastonia, and I must return home to be with her."

"I'm sorry to hear that," I replied. "I hope she gets better soon."

"Thank you, Grace," she said appreciatively. "A couple of things before I go. We've received a delivery of lavender candles for the ceremony that are in the storage in the hallway near your room, with some of the other wedding things. Also, I had my tiara professionally cleaned and polished for the wedding. I hate to ask this of you, but would you mind going into town and picking it up? They said they would drop it off later this week, but I'd feel safer if I had it here at the palace. It is very special to me."

"I'm happy to help in any way I can," I responded.

"Grace, you really are a lifesaver," Veronica said. "And while you're in town, you must stop by the sweets shop and try the Verdana Banana."

I smiled. "Cute name. What is it, exactly?"

"Frozen banana bites covered in dark chocolate and sea salt," she said. "They are absolutely divine."

"It's our most popular treat on the island," Oliver chimed in, giving me a grateful smile. "Dante will provide you with the details, and Marco will take you once he's back from dropping off Veronica at the airport. I'll be available to meet up with you when you return to go over any other details that need attention."

"Sounds perfect," I said, grateful for his help.

After Veronica left, I couldn't help but bring up the elephant in the room. "Oliver, did you see those photos? I'm so sorry."

He chuckled, a mischievous glint in his eyes. "Yes, Grace, I saw them, but please don't worry about it. The press is always desperate for something, anything to garner people's attention. They blow things out of proportion because it means more clicks and likes. It's not the first time, and it won't be the last."

"Great," I sighed, rolling my eyes. "Just what I needed."

"Hey now," Oliver said, his tone light and teasing. "At least it proves you're human, right?"

My mouth dropped open. "That's what I was telling my friend Cristina!"

"We've all had our moments," he said.

"You?" I asked, surprised.

"Trust me—you don't want to know," he said with a chuckle.

"I kind of think I do," I teased, then glanced over at Prince Theodore, who was sitting nearby with his nose buried in a newspaper.

I swore I heard him grunt at Oliver's comment.

"Is he always so quiet?" I asked.

"Moody is the term I prefer," Oliver replied with a low voice, amusement dancing in his eyes. "That conversation would also be for another time."

Prince Theodore looked up and observed us from the corner of his eye.

"All right," I said as I wondered how two brothers could be so different. It was almost as if they were from entirely different parents.

Suddenly, a loud screeching sound came from outside the palace.

We rushed to see what it was. The sound only grew louder.

"Good heavens!" Queen Annabelle said on the front veranda, hand on her chest. "This is unacceptable! Someone please stop this madness!"

It was the most bizarre scene—a hundred vibrant peacocks, maybe more, roaming across the palace lawns. I stood there in shock as the colorful creatures strutted around the grounds, letting out ear-piercing screeches.

The queen's face was scrunched up in horrified dismay. "Why are there peacocks roaming my gardens?" She turned to me, her face flushed with irritation. "Do you have an explanation?"

"Me?" I asked, placing a hand over my heart. "I had nothing to do with this."

We watched as the bold birds started pecking away at her prized royal roses and tulips, eliciting more ear-piercing screeches that sounded more like the shrilly meows from angry feral cats.

"My word—make them stop this instant!" the queen commanded. "How could this have happened?"

Thankfully, Dante spoke up then. "Pardon me, Your Majesty, but I seem to recall from Miss DuPont that the original order was for one hundred white doves for the ceremony. It appears there was a mix-up and they sent peacocks instead."

"A mix-up that I'm sure Grace was in charge of," the queen huffed. "Am I correct in that assumption? How could you not catch that error?"

I blinked. "This order was placed before I—"

"Fix it!" Queen Annabelle thundered. "And what is this one doing here? Why is he looking at me in such a manner? Get away from me, you wretched beast!"

The bold peacock strutted right up to the queen and fanned out his feathers, as if attempting to woo her.

"I think he likes you, Mother," Oliver said, unable to contain an amused smirk at the entire fiasco unfolding before us.

I shot him a subtle but pleading look.

Now was not the time for humor!

Okay, sure, it was sort of funny that a peacock was hitting on the queen, but I didn't like the fact that she was blaming me for this.

"Shoo! Go away!" Queen Annabelle said to the peacock, then turned to me. "I refuse to have my garden turned into a zoo! Grace, I demand you fix this."

With that, she hurried back inside the palace, muttering something about incompetent help, which I assumed meant me.

I turned desperately to Oliver. "I have no idea how this happened."

He gave me an encouraging smile and said, "You can handle it."

That was all he had to say about this fiasco?

Why was he so relaxed?

I immediately went back to my room, then froze when I entered and saw the wedding files on the desk.

I shook my head in disbelief. "I must be losing my mind."

There was no other explanation.

I immediately called the company in charge of the dove release and told them about the mix-up, then requested they get to the palace as soon as possible to corral the peacocks and remove them from the property. I also informed the royal gardeners about the half-eaten flowers and droppings, which they got to work on immediately.

After getting the mess cleaned up, I met Marco out front to go into town.

I marveled at the quaint beauty of Verdana City, the capital. The cobblestone streets wound through the heart of the village, lined with charming old buildings with terracotta rooftops, adorned with ornate iron balconies. The impressive cathedral towered over everything, its steeple reaching for the sky like a divine beacon. It reminded me so much of some of the small towns I'd visited in the north of Spain a decade earlier.

"Wow, there are so many people out walking," I commented to Marco as we passed by throngs of pedestrians on both sides of the street.

"It's common here, even in winter," he explained. "In Amsterdam, everyone rides bicycles. Here, we walk."

We pulled up to Verdana Jewelry, nestled between a cafe and bakery.

"We have arrived," Marco announced as he parked the car in front of the shop. "I'll get the door for you."

"Thank you," I said.

Marco opened the door, and I stepped out of the vehicle and took a deep breath. The air was crisp with the faint smell of freshly baked bread wafting from the bakery.

I entered the jewelry shop and was greeted by a friendly, middle-aged woman with warm brown eyes and hair pulled back into a bun. She wore a simple yet elegant dress with a diamond necklace.

"Hello! You must be Grace," she smiled. "I've been expecting you. I'm Isabella, the owner."

"Nice to meet you, Isabella," I replied, shaking her hand. "How did you know it was me?"

She gestured to the black SUV that was visible through the front window. "I know Marco, and he doesn't drive around just anyone."

"Ahh . . ." I nodded. "Of course."

"I have Princess Veronica's tiara for you," she said excitedly, leading me to the back of the shop.

As she retrieved the tiara, she proudly told me about the history of her shop, showing me photos on the walls of royalty and socialites wearing her family's designs dating back generations. "Our shop has been hand-crafting jewelry for royalty and the people of Verdana and other countries for generations. Notice the intricate filigree metalwork and gem settings on each piece." Her fingers traced the delicate patterns. "Few jewelers do this type of detailed work by hand anymore. It's a form of art."

"It's truly stunning," I said, feeling honored to be tasked with transporting such a precious heirloom.

"Thank you," she said, her eyes glimmering with pride. "I'll pack it up for you, so you can be on your way back to the palace."

I smiled. "I was told to try the banana bites at Verdana Sweets."

Isabella placed her hand on her chest. "Heaven. That's all I will tell you. And do not get a large bowl unless you want to explode. It is enough for three to four people."

I nodded. "Thanks for the tip. Can't wait to try it."

As Isabella carefully placed the tiara in a velvet case, I chatted with her about the royal wedding and my role as the substitute wedding planner in charge of a small team following my orders. She wished me luck and assured me that everything would be perfect. I liked her even more after her kind words of encouragement.

"Next stop, Verdana Sweets!" Marco announced as I set the velvet box on the seat next to me. We drove through the picturesque streets, my head practically hanging out the window like a dog, admiring the beauty and grandeur.

We arrived at the sweets shop, and Marco pulled up across the street, then opened the door for me to get out. "Please take your time to enjoy your Verdana Banana. I will be here after you have finished."

"Thank you," I said, then crossed the street, walking by the pet shop and the bank, and finally parking myself in the long line outside of Verdana Sweets. I inhaled the overpowering scent of tempering chocolate from within.

Once inside, I was greeted by another smiling face, an older gentleman with a neatly trimmed white beard and round spectacles perched on his nose. I tried not to stare at the chocolate stains on his green apron, but for some reason, they made me smile.

"Welcome to Verdana Sweets—what are you in the mood for today?" the man asked.

"Someone told me you have the best frozen banana bites on the island, so I'm here to try them." I said.

"I must humbly tell you that whoever told you that was a wise person," he said, chuckling. "Regular or large?"

I glanced over at the display, then remembered what Isabella said about the large being too much. I also contemplated getting a bowl for the queen, to smooth things out between us, but opted against it.

With my luck, she'd be allergic and would suggest I was trying to poison her.

"Regular, please, with a bottle of water," I said. "Is this a secret family recipe?"

He nodded as he piled the chocolate-covered banana bites into the bowl, then heaped two giant spoons of fresh whipped cream on top. "My great-great-grandfather opened this shop before cars were even allowed on this street. We take great pride in creating the most delectable treats. Can I interest you in some almond toffee, hazelnut chocolate, or our exotic truffles?"

"Not this time, thank you, but I have a feeling I will be

back, just based on the smell alone," I said, taking the bowl of banana bites and bottle of water from him and paying for the goodies.

"Of course you will!" he said, then gestured to the bowl. "Please try."

I forked one of the banana bites into my mouth.

He pointed to me. "Tell me it is not the best."

"Mmm." A moan escaped from my mouth. "The best for sure!"

"This pleases me more than you know," he said. "We make everything here with love. And plenty of chocolate, of course."

I adored how the people of Verdana were so proud and passionate about their work. After thanking him, I sat at an open table and enjoyed every bite as I watched the man work, dishing out sweets and smiles to every single person who came through the door. When I finally finished, I stood with a happy stomach, gave the man a thumbs-up, tossed the bowl in the garbage, then walked outside.

I was about to cross the street back to Marco's SUV when I heard a dog yelp happily. I turned and saw a woman with her young son, both smiling brightly as they came out of the pet shop with the most adorable floppy-eared puppy.

"Oh my goodness, what an absolutely precious dog!" I gushed to them.

"I named him Oliver—after the prince!" the boy replied.

Now, that was funny.

"We just adopted him," the woman said, pointing back to the pet store.

My curiosity piqued, I said goodbye to them and walked over, peering through the window of the pet store.

A sign read "Pet Adoption Fair Today!"

I obviously was not in any position to adopt an animal, but I could never resist a chance to cuddle an adorable dog. I went inside and glanced around eagerly. My eyes were immediately drawn to the dog frolicking in a playpen near the window. It had a fox-like face, big dark eyes, stubby legs, and soft red and white fur, with tan accents around its brows and muzzle. He was having a jolly good time all by himself, shaking a toy in his mouth, his little tail wagging excitedly.

"Would you like to hold him?" asked the woman, noticing my interest. "He's the last one."

"I would love to," I replied, my heart swelling with affection for that adorable pup.

As she lifted the fluffy puppy into my arms and my eyes caught his, I felt an overwhelming sense of love and connection wash over me. Its soft fur tickled my cheek as I nuzzled it close, and I could feel its heartbeat against my chest.

Then he nibbled on my finger.

"Ouch!" I said, laughing.

The woman nodded. "Watch out—he's got sharp tiny teeth. He's quite rambunctious and is in the biting stages, wanting to put everything in his mouth. But this stage is only temporary. He'll be changing teeth soon. Your furry friend here was the most lively of the bunch. Now, he's all alone."

"Aww, poor thing," I said. "People don't want you just because you're in your chewing stage. Every puppy goes through that, but some people don't know and didn't pick you for that."

"We're hopeful someone else will adopt him soon," the woman said.

"What kind of dog is he?" I asked.

"A Pembroke Welsh Corgi."

I blinked, then glanced down at the dog again, thinking. *Pembroke Welsh Corgi.*

The same breed as the queen's dog that passed away.

At that moment, a brilliant idea struck me . . .

I needed to adopt this dog for Queen Annabelle.

She was obviously grieving from the loss of her husband, then from her beloved pet. This would surely make her feel better, and it might even get me on her good side, melting her icy heart or at least warming it up a little. She at least would appreciate the peace gesture, I would think.

"I would like to adopt this little guy," I said to the woman as I cradled the puppy protectively.

She beamed, her eyes shining with happiness. "That's wonderful! I'll just need you to fill out some paperwork, and then he's all yours."

With a newfound sense of purpose, I signed the adoption papers, imagining the look on Queen Annabelle's face when I presented her with this precious gift. Surely, she couldn't resist such a heartwarming gesture, even if it came from the person she seemed to hate the most in the world.

The woman double-checked the paperwork, then glanced up at me, looking quite confused. "Your address is at the royal palace?"

I nodded. "Yes, I'm the royal wedding planner, and this dog is for Queen Annabelle. Is that a problem?"

Her eyes lit up. "Not at all! It is a great honor, indeed."

I paid the adoption fee and also bought a crate carrier, food, and bowls for food and water. I had also planned on paying for treats, pee pads, toys, and a leash and collar, but the kind woman insisted on throwing them in for free, since it was for the queen. I could always come back if I forgot something or wanted to get a name tag after the queen chose a name for her dog.

"Best of luck," she called out as I stepped into the sunlight with the carrier and the big bag of dog supplies, already picturing the joy and laughter that this dog would surely bring to the palace. Some members of the royal family could benefit from smiling more.

As I crossed the street with a bounce in my step, Marco jumped out of the SUV when he spotted me, his gaze dropping to the carrier with raised eyebrows. Then his jaw dropped.

"Is that . . . a dog?" he asked.

"Yep! I'm going to give it to the queen as a gift," I replied confidently, then held the carrier closer. "Isn't he just the cutest thing you've ever seen?"

Marco's face went pale.

"Why do you look like you're going to pass out, Marco?" I asked. "She's going to love it."

"I don't think that's a good idea," he warned, his eyes wide with concern. "The queen has not permitted dogs on the property since she lost her beloved Ruby. She was very adamant about it. Disobeying direct orders from the queen is never advised, and could have dire consequences."

"Trust me," I insisted. "Once she lays eyes on this little guy, she'll be smitten. Plus, I didn't get those direct orders, so this is on me."

Marco hesitated for a moment before sighing and opening the door for me. "I had nothing to do with this."

"You did not." I laughed. "I will make sure the queen knows. Don't worry."

Back in the palace, every single employee greeted me with wide eyes and they whispered as I passed them in the halls, their gazes on the dog carrier.

I snuck quietly, not wanting the Queen to see the dog before the big reveal during her teatime. I entered my room, quickly setting the carrier down and opening it up so the dog could stretch. He immediately ran to me, as if he were asking for some love.

Scratching him on the head, I said, "You are so darn cute. You're going to love your new home. I hope she'll give you a name that matches your cuteness."

I pulled the paw print-covered ceramic bowl from the bag, then poured some water from the bottle I had gotten at the sweets shop. Just in case, I laid out a couple of pee pads on the floor, so there were no accidents.

"Be right back—you be a good boy," I told him, then closed the door behind me.

The plan was to find Oliver to share my surprise.

Instead, I ran into Henri, the head steward.

"Good day, Miss Grace," he said.

"Hi, Henri," I replied. "Have you seen Prince Oliver?"

He nodded. "I believe he is in his art studio at the moment."

That caught me by surprise. He said he dabbled in art, but he had an entire studio? Of course, a prince could have anything he wants.

"Follow me." Henri led me down the hallway, knocked on the studio door, then opened it. "Your Highness, Miss Fullerton is here to see you."

I stepped inside the art studio and froze.

Easels, paints, frames, and other supplies were scattered throughout, and the beautiful natural light from the windows illuminated Oliver's latest work-in-progress.

"This is amazing," I said. "I thought you said this was just a hobby. It looks like a real art studio."

"It *is* just a hobby," he said.

I pointed to one of the finished paintings. "That looks like a Van Gogh!"

"Thank you," was all Oliver said. "Is there something about the wedding you wanted to discuss?"

I shook my head. "Not at all. I just wanted to share a surprise with you. Can you come with me? It will just take a moment."

"Of course. Show me what you've got." He jumped up from his stool, quickly pulling off his smock, then followed me to my room.

"Uh-oh," I said, noticing the door to my bedroom was open.

I peeked inside and glanced around.

The dog was gone.

Not good at all.

"What is it?" Oliver asked.

A blood-curdling scream echoed through the palace.

We sprinted down the hallways, our footsteps echoing off the polished marble floors. My heart pounded in my chest as I tried to keep up with Oliver's long strides. As we rounded the corner, we skidded to a halt in front of the open doorway of the biggest bedroom I had ever seen, which I assumed was the queen's.

One servant gestured inside the room, her hand over her mouth.

There, amidst a sea of ivory silk and tulle, was the adorable puppy I'd adopted for Queen Annabelle. Unfortunately, he was currently gnawing on an exquisite wedding gown train.

"No!" I shrieked, running inside the room to salvage what was left of the dress. "Drop it. Drop it."

"Grace, what have you done?" Oliver whispered as he pulled up next to me. "And where did that dog come from?"

"What is all this ruckus?" came a furious voice from behind us. "And what are you doing in my room?!"

I flipped around, just as Queen Annabelle appeared in the doorway, her silver hair perfectly coiffed and her blue eyes blazing with anger.

I tried to unclench the dog's jaws that were attached to

the wedding dress. His vice-like grip and growl were impressive, but not helping in the least.

"What in heaven's name?!" the Queen cried. "My wedding dress!"

Things were getting worse by the minute.

I blinked twice. "Your wedding dress?"

"Why did you take it out of the display, Mother?" Oliver asked.

"I was going to surprise Princess Veronica and offer her the privilege of wearing my dress for your wedding," Queen Annabelle said. "I just had it cleaned, and it was lying on my bed." She glared at me. "You ruined it! And what is a dog doing in my palace?!"

I swallowed hard, not liking the feeling in my gut.

This would not end well.

Chapter Ten

PRINCE OLIVER

I had to admit I didn't see that coming.

Grace was on her hands and knees, wrestling with a very cute, but stubborn dog. Its jaws were clenched tightly around the bottom of my mother's precious wedding dress, refusing to let go despite Grace's best efforts, along with the efforts of two of our employees. The poor girl looked both embarrassed and frantic, her hair sticking to her forehead with perspiration, while the dog was having the time of his life.

Mother stood in the doorway, her eyes close to bulging from their sockets, lips pressed so tight they disappeared completely.

Henri hovered behind her.

"Miss Fullerton!" Mother said, her usually regal voice raised several octaves higher. "This is unacceptable!"

"I apologize, Your Majesty." Grace held up the end of

the dress, finally free from the dog's teeth. "But I have great news!"

Mother's jaws were now clicking back and forth, to the left and to the right. "There is no such thing as good news in this situation. You've ruined my wedding dress."

"I understand why you would be upset, and once again, I apologize, but the dress is fine! It just needs a little repair, and a good cleaning from the dog saliva, and it will be as good as new. I promise. Do you want to see?"

"No!" Mother said. "That dog is a savage!"

Grace stood and set the dress down on the bed. "This is completely normal behavior. Puppies are born with an instinct to suckle at their mother's teats, and when the mother is no longer around, they look for blankets or something else as a substitution."

Mother tapped her foot on the floor. "Do I look like I'm in the mood to learn the intricacies of canine rearing? I asked you why there is a dog in the royal palace. Are you planning on answering the question?"

I was curious as well.

"Actually, Your Majesty," Grace replied, "he was meant to be a gift. For you."

"For me?" Mother's eyebrows shot up in disbelief.

Grace nodded. "Yes—I adopted him for you."

"Whatever possessed you to think I would want a dog?" Mother asked.

"I heard about Ruby," Grace said. "And I thought you might like, well, this little guy." She gestured to the now-released dog, who wagged his little tail happily, oblivious to the tension in the room. "I had the best of intentions. I apologize if I've overstepped."

"Overstepped?" Mother said. "I'd say you vaulted over the line."

The dog turned toward us—we could finally see his face.

"He is quite adorable." I crouched down to get a better look at the dog. "And the spitting image of Ruby, don't you think? Is he a Pembroke Welsh Corgi?"

Grace nodded. "He is. That's why I knew it was meant to be. He was the last dog available for adoption at the pet store. I had nothing but positive motives, I swear."

I could detect a softening in Mother's demeanor. Especially when the puppy wriggled free of Grace's arms and trotted over to sit happily at Mother's feet. His tail swept back and forth across the floor.

It was hard not to smile at the sight, despite the dress fiasco.

Even Mother seemed taken aback by the dog's boldness, but it would take a lot more than that to get her to come around.

"I think he likes you," I pointed out.

"Have you become a comedian, Oliver?" Mother asked dryly, her gaze locked on the dog. She seemed to be fighting a losing battle against her curiosity. "As I have said before, dogs are not allowed in the royal palace. I never asked for another dog, nor do I want one."

Grace called her bluff. "Fine—I'll keep him for myself then." She scooped the corgi back into her arms. As she walked past my mother, she paused, meeting her gaze steadily. "He needs a loving home. And I understand if you can't provide that for him. Or if you just don't care about dogs anymore."

"Do not put words in my mouth," Mother said.

Grace did not give up. "Well, my point is, since you don't *appear* to want this precious little creature, Your Majesty, I will take him back to the US with me when I leave. I'll give him the most loving home possible."

Mother stiffened a little, but did not respond.

I glanced at Grace, impressed by her confidence, but held up a hand to defuse the situation. Obviously, she had let go of the idea of decapitation and didn't fear my mother anymore.

"We don't need to make any rash decisions," I said. "Why don't we give it a few days? The dog can stay with Grace until we figure things out. Mother, you won't even see him."

"I'm fine with that," Grace said. She turned to walk out, then stopped to glance back at Mother. "Your Majesty, again, I truly am sorry about the dress. I accept complete responsibility, even though I have no idea how he could have left my room. I will have it repaired immediately."

"That is unnecessary. I believe you've done quite enough already," my mother replied, glancing at the dog one more time. "You may go now."

Grace nodded, not saying other word.

I walked out of the room behind her, the door closing behind us.

After Henri walked away, I couldn't help but shake my head at the absurdity of what had just transpired. Grace looked up at me. Her expression was one of pure mortification.

"Did that really just happen?" she asked.

"Indeed, it did," I confirmed. "And I must say, Grace, only you could manage to introduce such chaos into the palace with something as innocent as a living surprise gift."

"I hope she believed me," Grace said, as we made our way down the hallway back toward her room. "I had only positive intentions."

"I don't doubt that for even a second," I said. "It may have been one of the kindest things anyone has ever attempted to do for my mother. Just give her some time. She'll come around to the idea of having a dog again. It's uncanny how he looks like Ruby when she was a puppy. He's going to melt my mother's heart, you'll see."

"That would be nice . . ." Grace sighed, her shoulders slumped. "Honestly, I just feel like nothing is going right in my life. Something is off. I really don't get it."

I'd brought her to Verdana for the sole purpose of failing and getting me out of my arranged marriage, but I was feeling a little more guilty about it now. Especially with that vulnerability clearly etched on her face and in her voice. I suddenly felt the urge to make her feel better.

"You're being much too hard on yourself," I reassured her. "The gala was a raging success. You pulled it off with panache, despite the tight timeline."

"Except when I climbed up your chest like it was Mount Everest," she said.

"It was barely enough to land you in jail," I said, grinning. "I think what you deserve is a break from all this wedding planning pressure. How about joining me in the billiard room? Do you play pool or darts?"

She hesitated for a moment, then nodded. "Yes, but not very well."

"Perfect," I said. "Because I love winning."

That finally got a smile out of her. "Men and their egos."

"Look out, this one is huge," I said, tapping the side of my head.

"Somehow, I doubt that," she surprisingly said, as we stopped in front of her bedroom door. "I'm still wondering how he got out of my room." She ran her fingers through the pup's fur. "I just need to make sure he doesn't destroy anything else in the palace."

"We'll have to keep a close eye on this cute little troublemaker." I scratched him on the head. "How about I hold him while you grab his food and water and things? It's time you had some fun. How does a bottle of beer sound?"

"Just one? Sounds like you'd better stock up." Grace smiled, then grabbed the pet shop bag and followed me.

I was determined to help her relax and forget about the wedding planning debacle and my mother's harsh words. We took the puppy outside for a pee on the royal lawn, then made our way back inside.

"Welcome to my sanctuary," I announced as we entered the billiard room and I set the dog down.

Grace's eyes widened in awe, taking in the grandeur of the room. "This. Is. Incredible."

"Probably my favorite place in the palace, after the art studio," I said. "Here, let me help you with this stuff." I reached for the dog's belongings Grace had been carrying, setting them down in a spot in front of one of the leather chairs.

She immediately set about arranging a comfortable spot for the dog, complete with food and water bowl. She even laid down pads and explained that they were there in case he had to "do his business" as she called it, even though he had just gone. It was obvious she had a genuine care for the little guy.

She pulled one of the chew toys from the bag and tossed it. "Get the toy!"

The dog scurried across the room, his nails clicking against the tile floor. He grabbed the toy, then plopped down to play with it.

I pulled two bottles from the refrigerator behind the bar and held one up. "Straight from the bottle or frosty mug?"

"Straight from the bottle," Grace said.

I popped the tops off, handed her a cold one, then clinked it. "To forgetting about our troubles for a while."

"I'll drink to that," she said, taking a pull of her beer, still glancing around. "How many rooms does the palace have?"

"I can't remember," I said.

That made Grace laugh. "Seriously? You've lived here

all your life and you don't know how many rooms there are?"

"It's not as simple as ABC," I said. "For instance, you are standing in what many would consider a room, but some might call it the billiard *hall*."

Grace nodded. "Okay, for simplicity's sake, let's convert the halls to rooms. How many are there in total?"

"What about the ballroom?" I asked.

She took another drink of her beer. "Ball*room*. This ain't rocket science. Start converting."

I nodded, then took a sip of my drink, thinking. "Seventy-seven."

Grace almost spit out her beer. "For a family of four?!"

"You're right—it feels cramped sometimes." I chuckled, then said, "And please don't ask me how many staff members there are."

"I don't think I want to know," Grace joked, then began inspecting the paintings on the walls, her eyes flickering from one piece to another. "Did you paint any of these?"

"A few of them," I admitted, feeling oddly bashful about my talent, but still gesturing to them. "Those two of the palace over there, the portrait of my brother Theodore, and the one of Dante in front of the fountain."

Grace pointed to the wall behind me. "This painting is such a contrast because you don't expect to see a prince sitting on a BMW motorcycle. Is he a member of your family?"

"My brother, Prince Augustus," I said.

"He lives here at the palace as well?" Grace asked.

I chuckled. "No, no. August is what you might call the free spirit of the family, always opting to do his own thing. He is presently riding his motorcycle across South America."

"Why is he able to do what he wants, but not you?" she asked.

"Because he is not next in line to be king," I answered. "Do yourself a favor and do not mention his name around Mother." I pointed to the large painting behind the bar. "Oh, and that one over there is my father, King Henrik, right before his passing."

Grace turned to me. "I'm sorry, but I don't know the story of your father."

"He was a great man, a great king, but even more, he was the best father a child could ask for," I said, reminiscing. "Although he would occasionally get irritated with me because I would follow him around like a puppy dog." I wrinkled my nose after admitting that. "I guess you could say I was clingy when I was younger."

Grace smirked. "I don't know—you were kind of clingy at the gala."

"And here I thought I had broken the habit." I chuckled and took another pull of my beer, then glanced back over at my painting of Father. "He was always busy, but I couldn't understand that at my young age. I just loved him and wanted to be with him. Nothing wrong with that, right?" I turned to Grace when she did not answer immediately.

She was studying me. "No . . . nothing wrong with that

at all." She turned to admire the pieces with genuine appreciation. "These are wonderful."

"Thank you," I replied, touched by her words. "My mother doesn't quite share your sentiments. She finds my painting a waste of time and often reminds me I should focus more on my royal duties, that I need to prepare myself for being the king of Verdana."

Grace frowned, concern etching her brow. "You should be able to do what you love."

"Unfortunately, life as a royal isn't always about what we want," I sighed, feeling the weight of my future responsibilities.

Grace nodded. "Like your arranged marriage . . ."

"Exactly . . ." I nodded. "It's about tradition and duty. The union is meant to strengthen ties between our kingdoms. Love, in this case, is secondary, or maybe even third. It is what is expected of me. It's in my veins. That's who I am and who I am meant to be."

"Sounds kind of . . . sad," she mused, her expression softening with sympathy.

"Yes . . . well . . ." I cleared my throat, eager to change the subject and lighten the mood. "Let's not dwell on that. How about we have some fun? No more talk of weddings and royal duties today."

"Deal," she agreed with a smile, then clinked my bottle.

"Perfect." I gestured to the billiard table, then the dartboard. "Are you in the mood for pool or darts?"

"Let's go for darts—I'm kind of in a stabby mood," she said.

"Remind me to not turn my back on you," I joked, taking six darts from the top of the bar and handing three of them to Grace.

We took turns throwing them, each shot getting worse and worse.

"Who knew the prince of Verdana was so unskilled at darts? " she asked playfully, a smirk tugging at the corner of her mouth. "You're just as bad as I am."

"It's all part of my master plan to lull my opponents into a false sense of security before I move in for the kill," I shot back, winking at her.

"Sure. Whatever you say." She laughed, then tossed her dart right into the painting of the dashing knight professing his undying love to a swooning maiden. "Whoops."

"I'll pretend I didn't see that," I said.

Grace was about to pull the dart from the painting, then ran her fingers across it. "It looks like I am not the only one who has been so far off target."

"I've never seen those three holes in my life," I said.

"Four holes," she said, laughing, then turning back to me with a mischievous look on her face. "How about we make this interesting?"

"Are you suggesting a wager?" I asked.

"I am," she said, moving closer. "Why? You're not scared, are you?"

I chuckled. "Hardly. What did you have in mind?"

Grace thought about it for a moment. "If I win, you have to wear your royal robe inside-out for an entire day!" She laughed.

"I already do that," I joked.

"I should have known," Grace said, then her eyes lit up. "If I win, you have to send your 'Macarena' video to the press, so the entire world can see you dance."

"I see you like high-stakes bets," I said. "And what makes you think I haven't already deleted that video?"

Grace shrugged. "Call it a gut feeling. Maybe deep down inside, doing something so fun, or silly, depending on who you asked, makes you feel normal. Like a regular guy. I'm willing to bet you still have that video. Let me see your phone."

"Sorry—one bet at a time." I gestured to the chair. "And should I be sitting down for this therapy session?"

"Ha! I was right!" she said, moving closer and patting me on the side of the arm. "Don't worry, your secret is safe with me. And what do you have to lose, anyway? You're going to beat me at darts anyway, aren't you, Mr. Confident?"

It was good to see she had completely forgotten about the episode with my mother. Grace looked a lot more relaxed.

"Very well—I accept your terms," I said. "And if I win?"

She shrugged. "You tell me."

I nodded, thinking about it, my gaze popping over to the portrait of my sister. "If I win, I will paint you."

Grace blinked, then glanced down at her body. "You mean like body paint?"

I chuckled. "Your portrait. You'll have to pose without moving for hours."

She hesitated. "Why would you want to paint me?"

I shrugged. "Why not? You're not scared, are you?"

Grace scoffed. "Dream on."

I pointed to the dartboard. "Okay then . . . ladies first. We can keep it simple and play Around the World. Start by throwing at the number one, then move on to two after a successful hit, then three, and so on until you reach twenty, then the bull's eye."

"Very well," she said, stepping up to the line and taking aim as she squinted.

To my surprise, her first dart landed squarely on number one.

She glanced at me with a triumphant smile.

"Beginner's luck," I said.

At least that was what I thought.

Then her second dart hit number two.

"Why do I get the feeling I've been set up?" I asked.

"I don't know what you're talking about," she said, throwing her third dart, which hit number three. "Can you believe that? Must be my lucky day." She stepped aside to give me room.

"All right, here goes nothing," I said, faking nervousness as I took my position. I threw my first dart, hitting the number one perfectly.

My second dart hit the number two right in the middle.

"You played me!" Grace exclaimed with mock indignation, her eyes dancing with delight. "You played me, pretending to be horrible!"

"Ha! Says the woman who nailed her first three shots!" I retorted. "Seems like I've underestimated you."

"You got that right," she said, laughing along with me.

We continued our game, growing more competitive and playful as we drank our beers. At one point, the dog fell asleep, sprawled out on the hard floor.

"That can't be comfortable," I said, picking him up and setting him on the leather chair. "Much better."

"You like dogs a lot," Grace said, smiling.

I nodded. "Very much. And so does my mother, you'll see. Now, where were we?"

Grace stepped up to the line and hit her next three shots.

"I see how this is going to be," I said.

As the evening wore on, we both continued to play very well as we engaged in lively conversation. Grace's playful nudges and lingering looks seemed to increase as well. At one point, she purposefully brushed against me just as I was about to throw the dart.

"Foul!" I protested through my laughter.

"All's fair in darts and war!" Grace crowed victoriously, her eyes dancing with joy.

We were tied, with only the bull's eye left to win for either of us.

"All right—this is it," I announced, feeling the enjoyable tension and fun between us. "Winner takes it all. Whomever hits the bull's eye wins."

"Let's see what you've got, Your Highness," Grace

taunted. "The entire world is hanging in the balance. No pressure."

"I'm not listening," I said.

As I lined up my next shot, I felt her gaze trailing over me in appraisal. "Gotta say, I'm surprised some princess didn't snatch Your Highness up ages ago. With a face like yours? The royal matchmakers must be slipping."

I blinked, momentarily surprised. Was she flirting with me? Letting out an awkward chuckle, I launched my dart, missing the board entirely.

I turned to her and crossed my arms, finally figuring out what was going on. "Quit trying to distract me. You need to play fair."

"What?" Grace said. "Can't a girl give a guy a compliment? It was completely innocent."

"Uh-huh . . ." I tried to shake off her words, but it wasn't easy.

Obviously, it was the alcohol and nothing more. The interesting thing is, if I weren't a prince in another country and we were just two average people, I could picture us as friends, the two of us hanging out, enjoying each other's company. Grace was a good person, had a wonderful sense of humor, and was down to earth. Most people I encountered lately wanted something from me. Grace was not impressed with my royal status, and for some reason, that appealed to me. She was authentic.

I lined up the final winning shot, ready to triumphantly end our silly game.

"You know, you have remarkably muscular arms for a

prince," Grace mused, not-so-subtly touching my bicep. "Been lifting more than just royal decrees, eh?"

My next shot missed the board completely. Again.

"I've had enough of this." I huffed. "Do you really think you can distract me again?"

Grace smiled. "As a matter of fact—"

I let my next shot fly before she could finish her sentence. My dart flew swift and true, piercing the bull's eye dead center with a thwack.

I pumped my fist and crowed, "Huzzah!" I turned to Grace with a swaggering grin. "It appears the crown prince remains unmatched in all pursuits, darts and otherwise. In other words, I win."

"What?!" Grace said. "I get a chance to tie the game."

"Making up rules now, are we?" I asked.

"No," Grace said, playfully pushing me out of the way. "That's the way the game is played and you know it."

I knew that.

Obviously, this was my chance to exact my revenge on the sneaky American who thought she could fluster me with her faux flirts.

Two could play her flirtation game, after all.

As Grace lined up her first dart and furrowed her brow in concentration, I cleared my throat conspicuously. "You know, you have the most captivating eyes, Grace. I could get lost in them forever."

Her dart sailed past the board entirely, bounced off the wall, and fell to the floor. Grace turned to gawk at me, momentarily paralyzed. A vibrant blush bloomed across her cheeks.

I felt an odd surge of masculine satisfaction at rendering her uncharacteristically speechless.

"Okay, I see how this is going to be," she said. "You're afraid I'm going to win, and you're trying to distract me."

"Can't a guy give a girl a compliment?" I mimicked her. "It was completely innocent."

That elicited a snort out of her, which was cute, but then she pointed at me and said, "Behave, Your Highness."

"I will try my best, but it won't be easy," I said, as she lined up the next shot. "Especially since I am in the presence of the most breathtaking woman I have ever met in my entire life. I simply can't take my eyes off you."

Her second dart flew high and right, striking the painting again, this time hitting the dashing knight in his royal jewels.

I winced. "There goes his hope of having children."

Grace sighed and turned to me. "This is not princely behavior. What if the queen found out you were being mischievous?"

"And you're the one who is going to tell her?" I said. "Oh, yes, please. I would pay to see that."

Grace thought about it. "Fair point, but I could send an anonymous letter."

"One. Dart. Left," I said. "Bull's eye or you lose. Good luck."

I didn't think I'd ever had this much fun playing darts.

Grace lined up her last shot.

I moved closer, close enough that my breath was sure to touch her hair when I spoke, but then I caught the scent of her lovely floral perfume.

"Your fragrance is completely intoxicating," I murmured, then inhaled loud enough to make sure she heard it.

Grace blinked twice, then turned toward me.

My eyes trailed from her graceful neck down along her shoulders, hoping to make her uncomfortable enough to miss her last shot. "I simply cannot place the flowers. It must be an exotic strain known only in heaven, since you are absolutely angelic." I punctuated the fawning compliment with a roguish wink.

Grace stood there, stunned into silence.

I smiled in satisfaction at having flustered her so, but then her eyes flew wide, gaze fixed over my shoulder. I pivoted to see Dante standing frozen in the doorway, eyes as big as saucers.

"Oh! Uh, Your Highness, I apologize for the intrusion," he stammered. "I simply came to confirm our meeting tomorrow, but I see you are otherwise engaged. Another time, perhaps." With that, he spun on his heel and positively ran from the billiard room.

As soon as the door clicked shut, Grace and I turned to each other and both dissolved into raucous laughter.

"Oh my word, did you see his face?" Grace said, fanning her still-flushed cheeks. "That was hilarious."

I nodded. "I only wish we had it on video."

"Imagine if it had been your mother—I wouldn't be

laughing at all," she said. "Okay, back to business. Let's get this over with."

Grace stepped to the line, but this time I let her throw without a distraction. After lining up the shot, she let the dart fly and hit the double seven.

She snapped her fingers in disappointment. "Foiled again. Well, a bet's a bet. I graciously accept my portrait fate." She gave a dramatic sigh, eyes glinting playfully.

"Excellent," I said. "Be prepared to don your finest dress and strike a pose tomorrow after lunch."

Grace looked surprised. "Tomorrow? Already? Don't you have princely matters to attend to? Dante mentioned a meeting."

I waved dismissively. "Nothing that can't wait. And do wear something purple, by the way. I find the color truly captivating on women. The color inspires me."

"Oh . . ." Grace was deep in thought. "I don't think I brought anything purple with me."

"Well then," I said with a grin. "It looks like you'll need to go shopping tomorrow."

Chapter Eleven

GRACE

"Good morning," Marco greeted me with a warm smile outside of the palace, his eyes crinkling at the corners as he opened the back door of the sleek black SUV.

"Good morning, Marco," I said, looking up to admire the beautiful blue sky, then inhaling the wonderful scent wafting over from the Mediterranean Sea. "How are you on this lovely day?"

"I'm excellent—thank you for asking," he said. "Are you ready for your Verdana shopping adventure?"

I nodded, feeling a little weird having Prince Oliver's credit card in my purse. "I'm ready. And I promise not to bring back any animals this time."

"I'm sure I'm not the only one who appreciates that," he said with a wink.

I climbed into the vehicle, sinking into the plush leather seat.

"Grace!" Princess Adriana approached before Marco

could shut my door. She had an infectious energy about her that made me smile. "Where are you off to?" She peered into the SUV with curiosity, even though I'm sure she had been in it a thousand times.

"Dress shopping, Your Highness," I answered.

"Oh, do you mind if I join you? I love shopping, and it's been ages since I've had a day out! And, please, call me Adriana!" Princess Adriana's eyes sparkled with anticipation, clearly excited at the prospect of an impromptu adventure.

"Of course!" I exclaimed, delighted by her eagerness. "I would love for you to come with me, Adriana."

It would be nice to have some company, especially someone who knew the ins and outs of royal fashion. It might also give me some insight into her family's tastes and preferences. Plus, it's not every day a regular girl has the chance to hang out with a real princess.

"Great! Let me just run to get my purse," Adriana said, disappearing back into the palace for a moment before reappearing, a small designer bag slung over her shoulder.

Right behind her was a tall man wearing all black with dark sunglasses, one of the same guys who was with Oliver when he had come to see me in Los Angeles. Her bodyguard, obviously, with some type of communication device in his ear. He hopped in the passenger seat up front, as Adriana got into the back with me.

"I'm surprised you can just go out into public any time you want," I said as Marco drove to the center of town.

"Most outings are planned far in advance—true,"

Adriana said. "But I refuse to be cooped up in the palace all day and all night like a chicken. I just want to feel like a normal person sometimes, even though I happened to be born into a royal family with too many rules."

I nodded. "Prince Oliver mentioned something similar to me."

Adriana smiled. "We're very much alike, Oliver and I. We both have yearnings to spread our wings. My mother dislikes this side of us with a passion."

"Prince Oliver told me something like that as well," I said.

Despite our vastly different backgrounds, we both seemed to share a desire for genuine connections and a love for life's simple pleasures. Although having carte blanche to go on a shopping spree and spend as much as I want is not something the average person would ever get to experience.

"What about you?" Adriana asked. "Living in Los Angeles must be exciting with Hollywood and Beverly Hills just outside your door."

"I don't know . . ." I shrugged. "I really could do without the traffic and smog. Sometimes I think I should live somewhere else. Like I don't fully belong there."

"Well, you're in for a treat today—fresh air, no traffic, and plenty of shopping," she promised with a conspiratorial grin as Marco pulled up in front of a charming boutique called Demetrio Couture. "And here we are!"

After we got out of the SUV, I pointed to the sign on the door that read, "Closed for Private Appointment."

"Uh-oh," I said.

"Closed for us—Oliver said he would call to let them know we were on our way," Adriana said with a smile, then gestured to the front door when a few people spotted her. "We should probably head inside."

A slender man with long dark hair emerged from the back room sporting an open-collared grey silk shirt layered over a slim-fitted white tee, as well as black ankle-cropped wool trousers. Silver rings and leather bracelets adorned his hands and wrists.

Demetrio, I assumed. He looked Greek, but his accent was confusing me.

"Ah, Princess Adriana, welcome!" he said, locking the door behind us. "It is such a pleasure to see you again. And you must be Grace. Prince Oliver called to alert me of your arrival."

I smiled. "A pleasure to meet you."

"The pleasure is mine. I am Demetrio, and these are my creations." He gestured to his newest designs he thought would suit us, pulling out various dresses while commenting on their colors, cuts, and styles. Then he pointed to the wine, cheese, and snacks on the counter. "And please, enjoy some refreshments while you peruse. Take your time. The store is all yours for as long as you need."

"Thank you, Demetrio," Adriana replied graciously. "Hmmm, let's see what catches our eyes, shall we?" She linked her arm through mine like we were besties, then guided me deeper into the boutique as we browsed the racks, admiring the luxurious fabrics and designs.

"Mother would just die if she caught me wearing this,

but I just have to try it on for giggles," Adriana said, pulling a frilly pink cocktail dress from the rack and ducking behind the curtain to try it on.

She doesn't waste any time.

A minute later, she stepped out, spun around like a model, then grimaced. "Okay, maybe not." She headed right back to change.

That made us both laugh.

As soon as Adriana stepped out again, she said, "So, tell me about yourself, Grace. Any romance in your life? I'm curious about you, and this is our opportunity to get to know each other better."

I shook my head. "I haven't been on a date in over a year. The last guy I went out with was a model. Worst decision ever."

"Let me guess, he spent more time in front of the mirror than you did?" Adriana said.

"Actually—it was much, much worse than that," I said. "He was always posing in front of it, flexing, checking out his abs, then his chest, then his arms, then right back to his abs. I don't think I have ever met a man quite so in love with himself."

We both got a good laugh out of that.

"To be fair—he was a nice guy," I said. "But it's not like I need a man to have six-pack abs and walk around shirtless all day. There are other things far more important to me in a relationship than good looks."

"Such as?" Adriana pulled a black, floor-length gown from the rack and held it against her body, looking at herself in the mirror. "What qualities do you look for in a man?"

I considered the question while idly flipping through a rack of dresses, waiting for one of them to catch my eye. "Well, I've always been drawn to men who are kind-hearted, genuine, fun, and laid-back. A guy who can make me laugh is gold. And generosity is also a trait I admire."

Adriana tilted her head to the side. "Someone who showers you with lavish gifts?"

I blinked. "No—sorry. I don't mean generous with me. True generosity in my eyes is doing something kind for someone you don't even know." I sighed and placed my hand on my heart. "That kind of man will win my heart every single time."

Adriana nodded. "If my brother weren't getting married, he'd be perfect for you." Her tone was teasing, but there was a hint of wistfulness in her eyes. "He's the most generous man I know. It's one of the things I love most about him. But alas, fate has other plans for the two of you."

"Such is life," I joked with the back of my hand to my forehead, but then curiosity got the best of me. "What has Prince Oliver done, if you don't mind me asking?"

Adriana pulled another dress from the rack, then shook her head and put it back. "Well, we do have many charitable organizations that rely on us for fundraising, but this is something Oliver does completely on his own, with no prompting, fanfare, or recognition. He has auctioned off almost a hundred of his paintings and donates all the money to charities that benefit children or the elderly."

"Wow—that really is a very kind gesture," I said. "Does that mean he's going to donate my portrait when he's done painting it?"

I assumed he would give it to me to take back to L.A.

Adriana turned, her brows furrowed. "He's painting you? I did not know."

I nodded. "Today. After lunch. That's the reason I'm shopping today. He wanted me to wear something purple."

"Interesting," was all she said, then she nodded, looking deep in thought.

"Why do you say that?" I asked.

"It's just . . . Oliver has never painted a woman before," Adriana said. "I'm quite surprised, that's all."

"Never?" I asked. "Not even you or your mother or Princess Veronica?"

She shook her head. "No. None of us. He has always stuck to landscapes, inanimate objects, animals, or men."

"Why is that?" I asked.

"He says it's just a coincidence, but I think there's more to the story," Adriana said. "Do let me know if you find out."

I didn't know how I felt about being the first woman he had ever painted. Honored? Terrified? The more I learned about Oliver, the more fascinated and intrigued I became with the man. Not only was he handsome but also generous, funny, and now mysterious.

Adriana was right.

He was just my type.

Oliver would be perfect for me, if it weren't for the tiny

fact that he was getting married to Veronica and would eventually become the future king of Verdana. I couldn't help thinking about our dart game and what he'd said to me.

You have the most captivating eyes, Grace.

I could get lost in them forever.

I knew his little flirts were just a ploy to distract me, but why had my body had such a visceral reaction when he gave me a compliment or whispered in my ear? And why did I want him to do it again?

Wait . . .

Did I have a crush on the prince?

It certainly felt as if I did.

Oh, no . . .

How could this have happened?

The man was getting married! Having a crush would mean pain and torture for me because there would be nothing I could do about it. I had to get distracted and erase that thought from my head immediately.

"Grace?" Adriana said, snapping me out of my thoughts.

I cranked my neck in her direction. "Huh? Yeah?"

"I said I think you should try this on," she said, holding up an elegant strapless purple dress with intricate stitching and a silk band around the waist. "I think you would look fabulous in it. Try it on!"

"Okay . . ." I nodded and took it from her. "Be right back."

I slipped into the dressing room, took a deep breath, cleared my head of those ridiculous thoughts of Oliver, then tried on the lovely garment.

Emerging moments later, I had to admit I felt like a princess in the elegant dress. As I twirled around in front of the mirror, the bottom flared out gracefully, making me feel like I was floating on air.

"Grace, you look absolutely gorgeous!" Adriana gushed, clapping her hands with delight. "And that color is perfect on you."

"Thank you," I said, then glanced down. "You don't think it's too low-cut for the portrait?"

"Heavens no," Adriana said. "It's the perfect combination of sexy and elegant. You have to get it."

I nodded and smiled. "Okay then." I changed out of the dress, then we took a break with a glass of wine as we chatted more about men on the couch in front of the dressing rooms.

"What about you?" I asked. "Do you have a type?"

Adriana grinned. "This may sound a little odd, but I've always had a thing for American firefighters. Who knows? Maybe one day I will marry one."

"Seriously?" I asked.

"Must be from watching all those episodes of *Chicago Fire*," she said. "I love the courage, strength, and selflessness that firefighters embody, knowing that they dedicate their lives to protecting others and the community. And the uniform certainly doesn't hurt." She laughed and clinked my glass.

That was when I noticed Demetrio casting furtive glances at Adriana from across the room. It wasn't the first time either.

I leaned in closer to Adriana and whispered, "I'm sure Demetrio will be sad to know you want to marry an American firefighter. He seems to be enamored with you, unless he is one of your mother's secret spies."

Adriana's eyes widened in surprise, but then she let out a soft laugh. "Oh, I don't know about that. He's always been very attentive when I visit. He treats all his customers like royalty."

"I beg to differ." I gave her a little nudge with my elbow. "He's been watching you like a hawk since we got here. And that gleam in his eye has nothing to do with providing excellent customer service."

Adriana glanced in his direction just as Demetrio looked over.

He smiled and rushed our way. "Is there anything I can help you with, Your Highness?"

"No, thank you," Adriana said. "We're just taking a break." She held up the glass. "And the wine is divine."

He gave a slight bow, not even glancing my way once. "Always a pleasure, Your Highness."

Demetrio walked away, and I leaned closer. "See? I'm pretty sure he likes you."

Adriana smiled, glancing back in his direction again. "Well, I will most definitely take it under advisement. He certainly is a kind and good-looking man." Her eyes sparkled with interest.

"Where is his accent from?" I asked. "He doesn't have the same as yours."

"Demetrio is from Greece but has lived in Verdana for

the last ten years," Adriana said. "Speaking of Greeks and big fat weddings, Mother has suggested more than a few times that I should marry the royal prince of Greece." She grimaced. "He's a good-looking man, and kind, as far as I can tell, but he's much too young for me. That won't happen."

I shook my head. "I just don't understand why you get a choice, but Prince Oliver doesn't."

"As next in line to the throne, there's intense pressure on him to marry strategically and produce heirs," Adriana explained. "Tradition is what it comes down to, although I think it's time for a few changes. I'm sure the people of Verdana would be open to it, as long as we put their best interests first. They've done it in other countries. We wouldn't even be the first."

My heart ached for Oliver's predicament. Every person deserved their chance at true love. I truly believed that.

As Adriana and I continued our shopping, we laughed and chatted as if we'd known each other for years. Both of us found dresses that we absolutely adored, along with a few accessories. We eventually paid for our selections, gathered our many bags, said goodbye to Demetrio, then were escorted by the bodyguard across the street to the SUV. As we settled into the back seats of the SUV, I had a sudden feeling of guilt as Marco loaded the bags in the back.

"Adriana," I said hesitantly, "I hope it doesn't seem like I'm taking advantage of Prince Oliver. I mean, I know he offered, but this is just so extravagant."

"Grace, trust me—you are not even close to taking

advantage of him," Adriana assured me, her voice as earnest as her expression. "And that you're worried about it speaks volumes. Most people wouldn't give it a second thought."

I nodded, thinking about it. "That's good to know. The last thing I want to do is ruffle feathers after the fiasco with the dog and the wedding dress. I'm sure you heard about it."

"Oh, yes," she said, a smile on her face. "There are no secrets at the palace. And you're not the first person to ruffle the queen's feathers. You certainly won't be the last."

My amusement faded as a sudden thought struck me. "Oh no, what am I going to do with the dog during the portrait session? Dante is watching him now, but I can't ask him to continue for the rest of the day. I totally forgot, and I don't think having him in the art studio with us is a smart idea either."

"Leave it to me," Adriana volunteered enthusiastically. "I've always had a way with animals, and I'd be more than happy to help. I miss Ruby."

"Are you sure? He's sweet, but he can be a handful . . ." I trailed off, unsure if I should impose on her any further. "He's definitely not like Ruby."

Adriana placed her hand on top of mine. "Nothing would bring me more joy. Consider it done. Does the dog have a name yet?"

I shook my head. "I was going to let your mother name him, but now I don't know if she even wants to see him anymore."

"She wants that dog more than she is leading you to

believe. Just give her a little time," Adriana said. "And if you want her to come around faster, name the dog Freddie."

"Why, Freddie?" I asked.

Adriana smiled. "Father's middle name was Alfred, but Mother used to call him Freddie occasionally. It would be a way to honor him, and nothing would bring my mother more joy. Trust me."

I nodded. "Okay, Freddie it is then."

Between the excitement of shopping and my constant gazing out the window to admire the coast, we were back at the castle in no time. The plan was to head to my room to drop off my bags, then get Freddie from Dante to pass him along to Adriana before changing for my session with Oliver.

Seeing Dante in the hall without the dog was not a good sign.

"Welcome back, Grace," he said with a smile, eyeing my bags in both hands. "I trust you had a pleasant shopping experience?"

"I did, thank you," I said. "Sorry, but where is the dog?"

"Oh, that," Dante said. "Queen Annabelle asked me for a few favors. She said she would take care of the dog."

Take care of the dog?

I certainly did not like the sound of that.

What if she sent him back to the pet store? That would be a nightmare because I was serious when I told her I would be happy to take Freddie back to the US with me. I needed to find her before it was too late.

"Have you seen Queen Annabelle?" I asked him.

Dante nodded. "She's presently on the terrace."

"Could you do me a huge favor and have someone take these bags to my room?" I asked.

"It would be a pleasure," he said.

"Thank you," I said, dropping the bags and running as fast as I could out onto the palace terrace, my chest heaving, hoping the dog would still be on the premises. My eyes darted around, desperately searching for Freddie.

Suddenly, I froze, not believing the sight before me.

There, under an umbrella, sat Queen Annabelle, gently stroking a wriggling Freddie on her lap. She was murmuring softly to him, a hint of a smile on her usually stern face. I did a double take, wondering if the summer heat was causing a mirage. The formidable Queen Annabelle was being affectionate to Freddie? To a dog she did not want or like? I couldn't wrap my mind around it.

As the queen laughed lightly at Freddie licking her face, she said, "You're such a mischievous little boy. All you need is some training and you'll be fine. Lucky for you, you have an adorable, forgivable face."

It was like she was a completely different person.

The queen's gaze hardened when she saw me.

I approached and gestured to the dog. "I can take him off your hands."

With pursed lips, she handed him over without a word.

I let out a sigh of relief, clutching the squirming dog to my chest. "Come on, Freddie. Let's go get you some food."

"What did you call him?" Queen Annabelle asked.

"Freddie," I said. "Why? Do you not like the name?"

"I did not say that," she said. "Why on earth would you name him Freddie?"

I shrugged. "I like the name."

Queen Annabelle glanced at the dog, then back at me, speechless.

"Well, then . . . we'll be going now," I muttered, still reeling from the discovery that even the coldest of queens could not resist a cute puppy.

I quickly dropped off Freddie and his things to Adriana, then went back to my room to change into the purple dress, and touch-up my makeup and hair.

Fifteen minutes later, I paused outside the art studio door, my heart pounding. Why was I so nervous?

I took a deep breath and knocked.

When the door opened, Oliver froze, his eyes trailing over my dress.

"Wow," he breathed.

My cheeks burned under his admiring gaze.

Last night came flooding back, the flirty glances, his smooth voice whispering playful compliments in my ear.

I am in the presence of the most breathtaking woman I have ever met in my entire life. I simply can't take my eyes off you.

"Grace?" Oliver asked, his brows furrowing. "Are you all right?"

I jumped. "Yes! Sorry, just nervous, I guess. I don't know if I'll be able to stay still for such a long time."

"Not to worry," Oliver said with an affable grin. "You'll

have breaks and you'll be able to move. I promise to be gentle with you. Trust me." He winked.

My mouth went dry, then my pulse quickened.

I avoided eye contact as I stepped inside the studio.

"Shall we get started?" I chirped too brightly.

What had I gotten myself into? I had a crush I did not want or need. And now I was going to let him intensely stare at me for hours as he painted every inch of my body. Let the torture begin.

Chapter Twelve

PRINCE OLIVER

The moment Grace entered the art studio, I could feel the nervous energy surrounding her like a dark cloud. It was a stark contrast to her fun and flirty demeanor from the night before, but I would do my best to get her to relax. It was just a portrait, after all. Nothing more.

"You look absolutely beautiful in that dress," I said.

"Thank you," she replied shyly as she nervously fidgeted with the hem of her dress, then glanced around the room, avoiding eye contact with me.

"There's no need to be nervous," I said.

"I can't help it—I am," Grace replied.

"Fair enough," I said. "Let's see if we can do something about that."

An idea struck me that would surely cut through this awkward tension. There was no way we could work under these conditions.

"Grace, let's try something," I said, motioning her to the

center of the room. "This is an icebreaker to get us out of our heads. Humor me and strike an exaggerated pose. The more theatrical, the better."

"Seriously?" she asked.

"This will relax us both—trust me," I said. "Give me your most dramatic gesture possible. Channel your inner Broadway diva, if you'd like."

She grinned, appearing more open to the idea. "I think I can do that."

Grace cleared her throat and struck a pose worthy of the Bolshoi Ballet, leg kicked in the air, one arm curved gracefully over her head, the other resting on her hip. She batted her eyelashes at me as she wobbled in place, struggling not to burst into giggles or fall over.

"Yes—I think you've got something there." I pretended to scrutinize her posture studiously. "Now, can you hold that position for three to four hours?"

That did it—Grace finally laughed, but then her arms flailed in the air as she teetered sideways.

Stepping to her, I scooped her into my arms.

Now we were both cackling uncontrollably.

"Looks like my trick worked," I said, still holding her. "You look much more relaxed now."

She nodded. "I guess I am."

I was about to release her from my arms when there was a knock, then the studio door opened.

Dante stepped inside and froze, mouth agape. "Oh, dear . . ." His gaze shot upward to the ceiling. "Sorry for the intrusion, Your Highness. I was looking to reschedule your appointment, but it can wait until, well, whenever." He backed out, colliding with the door frame before making his flustered escape.

I finally released Grace and shook my head in amusement at Dante's reaction. "That's the second time he's walked in on us like that."

She straightened her dress. "Careful, or he's going to think there's something going on between us."

"Imagine that," I said, trying *not* to imagine that. "Anyway, we should get started." I asked Grace to sit in the chaise lounge near the window where the light was best. "Now, I just need a little something to set the mood. I like to listen to music while I paint. I hope you don't mind."

"Not at all," Grace said, taking a seat on the chaise lounge. "How about the 'Macarena'?"

"Not on your life," I said, then grabbed my phone and selected the playlist with my favorite painting music: Opera Classics.

I queued up "Nessun Dorma" by Luciano Pavarotti.

Soon, the emotional crescendos of that iconic love song filled the studio. I closed my eyes for a few moments and swayed back and forth, taking in the heartfelt emotion of Pavarotti's voice. There was nothing like it in the world, and, as always, it instantly put me in the mood to paint.

Opening my eyes, I noticed Grace studying me intently.

"What's on your mind over there?" I asked lightly.

"Nothing," she said, fidgeting with her hands.

"You don't like the song?" I asked.

"Actually, I do—it's beautiful," Grace said. "I guess I'm just surprised that you like opera, that's all."

"I'm full of surprises," I said.

She nodded. "That's an understatement."

I was tempted to ask what she meant by that, but let it go. As Pavarotti's soaring vocals continued, I prepared my easel, eager to capture Grace's beauty on canvas.

Fidgeting on the chaise lounge, she kept brushing her hair back repetitively and crossing her arms in jerky motions. Her eyes darted around the room, looking at everything except me.

Why was she acting so strange?

And here I thought my trick had worked to relax her.

It hadn't worked even a little bit, apparently.

"I've never been a subject for a painting before," Grace said out of nowhere.

"Nor have I," I confessed, hoping to lighten the mood.

A genuine smile finally graced Grace's face.

"Now, a serious question, Mister Prince," she said. "How should I sit?"

I shrugged, attempting to put her at ease. "I want you to be comfortable, in a natural state. How would you sit in that chair if you were at home?"

After a moment of contemplation, Grace leaned back and casually crossed her legs. The hem of her dress hitched up slightly, revealing more skin.

That definitely got my attention.

An audible gulp escaped me.

I found it difficult to look away.

"Okay, then, that should work," I said.

"What?" Grace inquired, glancing down at her lower extremities. "Is there something wrong with my legs?"

I quickly redirected my gaze to meet hers. "No—they're perfect."

Grace blinked twice.

"I mean, your positioning is perfect," I said.

She gave me a dubious look. "Uh-huh—if you say so."

What did she mean by that?

Grace tilted her head to the side, listening to the song from Pavarotti. "So, you speak Italian then?"

"Yes," I said. "Also French and Spanish."

She nodded, but didn't say more.

I tried making more conversation to put her at ease.

"Puccini's *Turandot* is one of my favorite operas," I remarked over the soaring Italian vocals. "It's about a defiant princess who challenges her suitors to answer three riddles, with death awaiting those who fail. I like to joke with Adriana that the opera is based on the true story of her life."

Grace simply blinked at me.

No response, not even a hint of a grin.

"Adriana is kind of the rebel in the family," I explained.

Still nothing from her.

At least I thought it was funny.

I focused on my work rather than on her puzzling behavior.

"All right, let's get down to business," I said. "I'll start with a preliminary charcoal sketch and then move on to watercolors. If time becomes an issue, I can always snap a picture and finish the rest on my own."

"Sounds good," Grace replied, her shoulders tense, her jaw clenched, and her breathing shallow. She went right back to fidgeting.

It was utterly baffling.

I reached for my charcoal pencil and became absorbed in capturing Grace's likeness on canvas. The sweep of her jawline, the waves of her hair, the sparkle in her eyes. I wanted to portray the spirit within as much as the external beauty. As I sketched, I glanced at her rose-colored cheeks, the curve of her body, her sexy lips, her graceful neck, and even lower to her . . .

Realizing my thoughts were drifting into dangerous territory, I gave myself a mental shake.

Focus, Oliver.

This is about art.

Not . . . whatever else you're thinking.

This was going to be more difficult than I thought.

"I appreciate your modeling for me," I said, hoping some conversation would clear the naughty thoughts that were floating around in my head. "I know you lost a bet, but this is one of my genuine passions."

Grace nodded. "How old were you when you first started painting?"

"Five," I answered. "I started with my fingers, then worked my way up to brushes." I grinned proudly. "We used to have a Royal Academy of Arts, much like the one in

London. It was my favorite place to visit on the island by far."

"What happened to it?" Grace asked.

I frowned. "It was destroyed when Mount Verdana erupted. It's my dream to build another one, but focused more on classes for children. I think the arts are an important part of a child's life. It helps them express themselves when they don't have the language level to do so yet."

She nodded. "I agree. Well, hopefully your dream comes true."

I nodded. "Thank you. Mother has made it perfectly clear she prefers to use the money for what she considers being more important things, which does not make it easy."

"O Mio Babbino Caro" by Maria Callas began to play.

"What is she singing about?" Grace asked as she listened intently. "She sounds tortured and heartbroken."

I paused my sketch and gestured to the speakers. "Actually, she's not. She's conveying her profound love and compassion for the man she's in love with, and begging her father to approve of him. If he doesn't, she will throw herself in the river."

Grace nodded. "Parental approval is important for some people, I guess. Good thing you don't have to worry about that since your mother arranged a marriage for you."

I blinked, not sure how to respond to that.

Grace winced. "I'm sorry—I probably shouldn't have said that. I apologize if that was rude or insensitive."

"No—it's okay," I said. "You merely spoke the truth."

After I finished the rough sketch, I moved on to the watercolor paint, starting with her hair.

A few songs later, Grace broke the amiable silence. "I'm curious . . ."

I stopped painting and glanced in her direction. "About what?"

She shrugged. "What fate awaits your masterpiece? Are you going to sell it and donate the money to charity?"

"Ah, you've been chatting with Adriana, the gossip queen," I teased.

Grace smirked. "Hey—she's not a gossip queen. Girls talk. It's called communication. And I think your whole 'paint and donate' thing is noble. No pun intended."

"Well, thanks for keeping my secret, Grace. And as for your painting, I was thinking of giving it to you as a souvenir. A little piece of me to take back to America."

"I would love that," she said. "I have another question for you. How come you've never painted a woman before?"

That question caught me off guard.

I thought about it, deciding to tell the truth. "Well, my mother and Adriana turned me down, and besides them, I guess I never found a woman who intrigued me enough to want to paint her." I shrugged.

Grace blinked twice. "Wait—I intrigue you?" She looked down bashfully, and her cheeks evidenced her embarrassment. "Why is that?"

Not wanting to get in too deep, I answered by saying, "Beat me at darts and I will confess all."

"Are you serious?" Grace asked.

"I am," I said, then frowned. "And you really need to stop moving around so much. You're in a completely different position than when we started, and your hair is not the same. I should have taken a photo earlier."

She glanced down at her body on the chaise lounge. "Sorry. Do you remember my position?"

"Luckily, I do," I said, standing and walking over to her. "I can adjust you and get you back to where you were, if you don't mind."

Grace nodded. "Okay . . ."

I hesitated for a moment, then sat beside her on the chaise lounge.

Tentatively, I reached for one of her legs, the warmth of her soft skin beneath my fingertips sending a jolt through me. My touch lingered longer than necessary, but she didn't seem to mind one bit. In fact, it was almost as if she were welcoming it.

"It's okay, I don't bite," Grace said, and then ironically bit her bottom lip. "And you're not going to hurt me. I'm limber."

Why did she have to tell me that?

An unexpected intimacy unfolded between us as I repositioned her legs. There was also a language spoken that went beyond words, and a tension that hinted at something unexplored and completely unexpected.

"There," I murmured, meeting her gaze.

Grace held still, not a muscle twitching.

Yet our connection was undeniable.

"Anything else?" she whispered, her gaze now on my lips.

"Yes . . ." My heart pounded in my chest as I swallowed hard, nodding. "Just your hair." Leaning in, I gently tucked a few strands behind her ear, my thumb grazing her cheek.

There was something crackling in the air between us, and it wasn't a campfire. Our eyes locked, as the feeling intensified. In that charged moment, my gaze drifted to her lips, and an unexpected desire surged within me. I couldn't shake the thought of kissing her.

Was I out of my mind?

What was going on with me?

"Just beautiful." The words escaped from my mouth before I could stop them, and I could not take my eyes off her.

The urge to kiss her only intensified.

This was madness, but she wasn't moving away.

Not being able to control my body, I leaned closer and—

"Ahem," came a sudden cough from the doorway.

Grace and I both jumped apart.

Mother stood there, her eyes wide as she took in the scene before her.

"Oliver—what in the world is going on in here?" she asked, her tone carrying a hint of disapproval.

"I'm painting a portrait of Grace," I explained, jumping to my feet.

Mother raised an eyebrow. "From over there?" She glanced back over at the easel. "Exactly how are you able to accomplish that without a paintbrush?"

I sighed. "I came over here to adjust her positioning. Is there something I can help you with?"

"I don't understand why you waste so much time in here," Mother said. "I'm sure Grace has plenty of work to do with the wedding. And where is Freddie?"

"Who's Freddie?" I asked.

"The dog," Mother said. "Miss Fullerton, you were in such a rush to take him off my hands, and you don't even have him with you?"

"He's with Princess Adriana, Your Majesty," Grace said, pulling the bottom of her dress down to cover more skin. "She really wanted to spend some time with him, and how could I say no?"

"Who named the dog Freddie?" I asked.

"I did," Grace said.

I nodded my approval. "Great name. What a wonderful way to honor Father." I turned to my mother. "Don't you think so?"

Her gaze popped back and forth between me and Grace, before finally answering, "I suppose so." Then she huffed. "On to more important topics, where did you put the tiara, Miss Fullerton? I would like to put it in the royal vault until Princess Veronica's return."

"Oh . . ." Grace fidgeted nervously again, clearly at a loss for words. "Well then, I will get it for you as soon as we've finished here."

Mother's lips thinned into a line. "See that you do. You can bring it to dinner with you." She turned to me. "Honestly, Oliver, between this and the wedding tasks, you both seem utterly distracted."

I cringed internally but maintained a diplomatic front. "We appreciate your letting us know, Mother. We will try to do better. Is there anything else?"

"I'm sure there is, but I do not have time at the moment." Mother eyed us both severely before turning on her heel and walking out the door.

Once alone, I shot Grace a grin. "I can't believe you named the dog Freddie! Thank you for doing that. It means so much."

Grace was deep in thought, biting her lip, still staring at the door.

"Hey—don't worry about Mother," I said. "She'll come around, eventually."

"I'm not so sure about that," she said.

"Why is that?" I asked.

"Because," Grace said, wringing her hands and wincing. "I have no idea where the tiara is."

Chapter Thirteen

GRACE

The missing tiara was almost enough to send me into a panic attack of epic proportions, but I mustered every ounce of strength to keep a clear head as I changed out of my purple dress and into a black skirt and white blouse for dinner. I might've looked like one of the palace staff, but my conservative wardrobe was the least of my worries. Oliver assured me that the tiara had to be somewhere in the palace, and that we would find it, but I continued to wrack my brain for clues.

Where could it be?

The tiara had been in the SUV with me after I had adopted Freddie. I was sure of it, and so was Marco, the driver. But had I brought it inside the palace? That was the part that was fuzzy to me.

The impending dinner with the queen loomed, just minutes away, and I envisioned the awkward moment of presenting myself without the cherished tiara. These mishaps seemed to befall me with alarming frequency, but this one was bigger than ever. Barring a last-minute miracle, the queen would surely send me packing now.

As I left my room, intent on retrieving Freddie from Adriana and passing him off to one of the palace staff who had agreed to watch him during dinner, I couldn't help but find a small silver lining. The tiara debacle had provided a temporary distraction from the lingering thoughts of that dangerously intimate portrait session with Oliver, where the threat of a kiss had hung tantalizingly in the air between our lips.

Just as I rounded the corner, Adriana emerged from her room. A sinking feeling hit me in the gut when she didn't have the dog with her.

"Hey, Grace!" she said. "I'm heading to dinner. Shall we walk together?"

"That sounds good, but where's Freddie?" I asked.

"He's with Mother," Adriana said.

"Excuse me?" I gasped. "Again?"

"Don't worry—he's fine," she said. "While I was playing with him on the lawn, Mother showed up and said she'd heard that Theodore was looking for me, then she offered to watch Freddie for me. And you know what? Theodore hadn't been looking for me! Can you believe her?" Adriana shook her head in amusement. "Don't think for a second she does not want Freddie, because she does. Anyway, one of the footmen is watching him at the moment, so we can have dinner in peace."

That was where Adriana was wrong.

Showing up to the dinner without the tiara was going to be the start of World War III, and I would be the blame for it.

"Adriana, there's something else I should tell you," I said hesitantly, my heart racing as I decided she'd be the perfect person to have on my side if things went south. "I can't find Princess Veronica's tiara." I shared the saga with her, wondering how she would respond.

"That is the strangest thing," Adriana said. "Did you check with Marco?"

"Yes, and he has no clue what happened," I said.

Much to my surprise, Adriana didn't seem to be worried about it. She was convinced, like Oliver, that the tiara had to be somewhere on the property.

"I can help you find it. Please don't worry," Adriana said with a reassuring smile. "We'll figure this out together. Let's just focus on getting through dinner first, then we can search for the tiara afterwards."

"But Queen Annabelle is expecting me to bring it to dinner," I said. "What am I going to say? I can't lie to her."

"You don't have to," Adriana said. "Just let me handle it if she brings up the subject. I'll buy you some time. Promise."

"Okay . . ." I felt a little relieved, but wondered what she was going to say.

I steadied my nerves before we entered the dining hall, but much to my pleasant surprise, Queen Annabelle was not seated at the head of the long table.

Had I gotten lucky?

Was it possible she was going to skip dinner?

Only time would tell if I got *that* lucky.

I let out a sigh of relief and quietly slid into the seat next to Oliver.

He leaned in close and whispered, "Still no sign of it?"

I bit my lip and leaned in to whisper back, "No—I can't find it anywhere. I even asked Marco. Adriana said she'd help me look again after dinner."

Oliver's eyebrows shot up in surprise. "You told my sister?"

I gave a small nod and smiled at her as she placed a napkin on her lap.

"I'm impressed," Oliver said. "Looks like you're getting the hang of this royal inner circle business." He wiggled his nose. "Gardenia, right? Your perfume?"

"No," I said. "Not even close."

My muscles tensed as Queen Annabelle entered the dining room and took a seat at the head of the table.

A few seconds later, she glanced in my direction.

"Miss Fullerton," the queen said. "Before I forget, did you remember to bring the tiara with you?"

I picked up my napkin and slowly wiped my mouth, even though I had eaten nothing yet, delaying a few precious seconds as I waited for Adriana to jump in and hopefully take over like she had mentioned.

"I have the tiara, Mother," she lied.

"Why do you have it?" Prince Theodore asked suspiciously.

I bristled at his tone, wondering why he even cared, then

took a slow look at everyone at the table. The queen was obviously irritated. Add to that Adriana had just lied through her teeth, and even Theodore's behavior was out of character. Then there was Oliver, who acted like he didn't give a fig if the darn tiara was ever found. What the heck was going on with this family?

"Why does it matter if I have it?" Adriana deflected Prince Theodore's questions. "I also have one of Veronica's scarves, as well as a sterling silver bracelet. Would you like to know why I have those as well?" She was practically picking a fight with her brother, it seemed.

Luckily, Theodore did not press any further on the subject.

"We don't need to take an inventory of your belongings." Queen Annabelle's expression softened. "After dinner, please ensure the tiara is placed in the royal vault."

"Of course, Mother," Adriana agreed easily.

I could hardly believe that she had lied like that for me.

The panic in my chest loosened slightly.

Adriana had saved me, and the tiara debacle seemed temporarily forgotten as servants began placing plates of food on the table. The aroma of the sumptuous feast filled the air, a culinary masterpiece that would've been the high-light of any event: lobster bisque, filet mignon, turnip greens, and truffle-infused risotto.

I shot Adriana a grateful look, then we ate. I could totally see us as good friends, if she weren't a princess.

As for the food at the palace, it was amazing. Every

meal, every time. It surprised me I had yet to meet any of the kitchen staff, including the chef.

"Please give my compliments to the chef," I said to one of the dining room staff. "This food is heavenly."

The employee bowed politely and said, "Of course, Miss Fullerton."

Henri entered, exclaiming, "May I present Miss Honey Buttermaker, Your Majesty!"

The room fell into a sudden silence.

The queen's complexion turned several shades paler.

Oliver leaned in, a mischievous glint in his eye, and whispered, "Honey is my step-aunt from Oklahoma, my uncle's second wife. He passed away a few years back. Brace yourself. Things are about to take a very interesting turn."

Puzzled, I asked, "Why's that?"

"She's Mother's worst nightmare," he replied.

"Then why was she invited to the wedding?" I questioned.

Oliver shook his head. "Believe me—she wasn't."

"Oh, she definitely was," I retorted confidently. "Honey was on the backup list. I sent out the invitation."

Oliver blinked. "We don't have a backup list."

"Uh-oh," I mumbled under my breath, realizing there was the possibility an enormous error had been made, even though all I did was follow instructions.

In the wedding files, there had been a note emphasizing the invitation of backup guests to maintain the guest count around one thousand. I had sent out email invites to twenty people the day after I arrived, as it was too late for traditional mail for invitees in other countries.

I wondered how many other invitations were not supposed to go out. One thing was certain—the impending firework show was going to start any minute if the queen was not a fan of Aunt Honey.

I turned toward the dining-room door, just as Honey strolled in with an ear-to-ear grin. She appeared to be in her early sixties, wearing a vintage, pink velour Juicy Couture tracksuit that clung snugly to her curves. Her big hair, enormous chest, even her stacked white sneakers were impossible to ignore.

"Y'all don't get up now," Honey said, her eyes wide with amazement as she surveyed the opulent dining room, then pointed to the vacant chair next to Adriana. "That must be my spot to get my grub on."

Honey sashayed over to the empty chair, treating us to a view of the word JUICY emblazoned across her posterior. A member of the waitstaff rushed to set her place, while another poured a generous glass of wine.

Honey took a long sip of wine. "Oh, that really hits the spot. What a long-ass flight! I still can't believe I'm really here in Verdana." She lifted her glass toward Oliver. "So great to see you again, sweetie pie. I'm just tickled pink for your wedding!"

"A pleasure to have you here, Aunt Honey," Oliver replied politely, then gestured to me. "This is Grace, our wedding planner."

"Hey, Grace!" Honey practically screamed. "Bless your

heart for sending me that invitation. I'm just thrilled to pieces to be here. For some silly reason, I didn't think I was invited!"

You have no idea.

Queen Annabelle stiffened, then shot an icy glare in my direction. "So, we have *Miss Fullerton* to thank for your visit."

"Sure do," Honey said.

"Henri," the queen called out.

"Yes, Your Majesty," he said, moving to her side.

Queen Annabelle motioned him closer, then whispered something in his ear. His eyes went wide, then he glanced at me before leaving the dining room.

"But the wedding isn't for another three weeks," Queen Annabelle said.

"I know, ain't it grand?" Honey said cheerfully, oblivious to the queen's foul mood. "Gives me a chance to enjoy a nice long vacation here at the palace. I just couldn't wait to celebrate! When I got the invite, I booked the very next flight and high-tailed it over here."

The waiter topped off Honey's wine.

"Thank you!" She took another sip, then starting eating her meal, her long, jewel-encrusted nails clicking against the fine china with every single bite. "Mmm, this food is dee-licious, although the greens could use a little kick, if you ask me. It kind of reminds me of a hound without its howl." She picked at the turnip greens with her fork, then waved the dining room employee back over. "Y'all got some pickled pepper juice back in the kitchen?"

The man looked baffled. "I'm uncertain, madam, but I would be happy to check for you."

"That'd be amazing, sugar." Honey batted her fake lashes. "If not, check to see if the chef has got any of my favorite hot sauces, like Tapatio, Devil's Revenge, Slap Ya Mama, Tony Chacheres, Nuclear Meltdown, or Rectal Roustabout."

Queen Annabelle choked on her wine.

"Of course," the employee said politely, quickly turning and heading out of the dining room.

"Where are you from, Grace?" Honey asked as she chewed on a piece of her filet.

"I live in Los Angeles," I said.

Honey placed her hand on her heart. "Oh, I just love L.A. I had a layover there once on the way to Portland and ate at the Panda Express at the airport. I'm from Hooker, Oklahoma, about four hours west of Oklahoma City. And just so we're clear, Hooker is a destination, not a vocation." She winked, then chuckled. "Hooker is in my DNA. In fact, they crowned me the Hooker Queen three years in a row back in the eighties. There was that unfortunate incident during the Hooker parade when I fell off the float in my Sunday dress and landed on my back with my legs high in the air. Thank The Lord I was wearing undies that day! And the crown stayed on my head!"

"You must be so proud," the queen deadpanned.

"Darn tootin'!" she said. "I come from a long line of Hookers, going back four generations. Some people like to make fun of our little town, but you know what I say? Screw them all!"

Adriana cracked a smile as the servant returned with a bottle of Tabasco sauce. "Miss Buttermaker, your sauce."

"Bingo! That'll work. Thanks so much," Honey exclaimed, grabbing the bottle from the man and dousing her turnip greens liberally with the sauce. "These are some good groceries, my friends."

For the entire dinner, Honey continued chatting away like a twister that had just touched down in the palace. I thought she was a breath of fresh air, positive and bubbly and sweet. Queen Annabelle obviously thought otherwise. She kept shooting me looks that could've frozen a sunflower in full bloom.

When we had finished our desserts, Henri returned and leaned in to tell the queen something, her eyes glaring at me the entire time as she nodded.

What was that all about?

Finally, the time came to retire for the evening.

I snuck by the queen, avoiding eye contact.

Oliver was right behind me.

The only thing I wanted to do was find the tiara, then double-check the wedding file to see if I had misunderstood the instructions. I was certain I hadn't.

"Miss Fullerton, a word please!" Queen Annabelle's voice cut through the air just as I reached the door.

Turning back around, I forced a polite smile. "Yes, Your Majesty?"

The dining room was now a tense triangle, with only

Oliver standing alongside me, about to be caught in the crossfire.

Queen Annabelle fixed me with a penetrating gaze. "It has come to my attention that there is more to your story than meets the eye."

Her words reverberated in my ears.

My stomach sank.

She knew.

"Your Majesty, I can assure you—" I began, but she cut me off with a dismissive wave.

"I had my people dig into your background after that atrocious dinner display with Aunt Honey," Queen Annabelle said. "Something just did not add up. Well, it all makes complete sense after having learned of your sordid past. The viral videos, the lawsuits—you're completely unqualified for this position."

The words struck like a verbal slap, and I struggled to compose myself.

"Yes, Your Majesty," I stammered. "I've had some setbacks, but I've learned from those experiences. I can make Prince Oliver's wedding an event to remember."

"Miss Fullerton," Queen Annabelle said, her voice turning colder. "Do you think I can afford to take risks with something as vital as our family's legacy?"

I shook my head. "No, it's just—"

"It was a rhetorical question!" she snapped. "You have to be the most incompetent person I have ever met."

I blinked twice, stung by the harshness of her words.

Why did she have to be so mean?

As frustration bubbled within me, I mustered the courage to defend myself. "I would be happy to go through the wedding files with you, to make sure there are no other misunderstandings."

"It's too late, Miss Fullerton," she asserted. "You must understand that the future of our kingdom and my son's happiness are at stake here."

I couldn't hold back any longer.

"That's a laugh!" I said. "You don't care about your son's happiness!"

Queen Annabelle jerked her head back. "I beg your pardon?"

"You want him to marry someone he doesn't even love! Do you really think he is going to be happy with that? Well, I've got news for you—you're dreaming! And it will be a nightmare for both of them if you think they'll ever have a happily-ever-after."

Whoops. I had not envisioned those words coming out of my mouth. Maybe it wasn't the brightest idea to verbally spar with the queen at that moment, since I was sure she was about to fire me.

"How dare you!" Queen Annabelle said, her eyes bulging. "I will not be addressed in that insolent tone." Then she turned to Oliver. "And what do you have to say about all of this? You're the one who hired Miss Fullerton. I have no doubt that you did a background check on her as well. How could you hire such a person for the wedding? What were you thinking?"

"Mother, please be reasonable," Oliver said. "Grace is highly qualified. She's just had a string of bad luck."

"A string?" Queen Annabelle barked out an unhinged laugh. "More like a frayed rope that stretches from Verdana to Los Angeles."

"Grace does everything with good intentions and is a talented woman. She deserves a second chance," Oliver pleaded.

The queen placed her hands on her hips. "If Grace is looking for chances, perhaps she could have a go at the roulette table, but the royal wedding is not a game to be played."

"Mother, please," Oliver said.

"Enough!" Queen Annabelle said. "This has gotten completely out of hand, and I will deal with you tomorrow, Oliver." She turned back to me, completely livid, with fire in her eyes. "As for you, Miss Fullerton, you are dismissed. And just so there are no misunderstandings, that means your services are no longer required. Go back to L.A. You're fired."

Chapter Fourteen

PRINCE OLIVER

The Next Morning . . .

The steady hum of the two side-by-side treadmills filled the air in the royal gym. I reached for my towel and wiped my forehead, then glanced over at Dante, who seemed to be effortlessly keeping pace beside me.

"Last night was a disaster," he said, his eyes never leaving the digital display in front of him. "The *Royal Gazette* would have had a field day with the latest news, but Mrs. Masterson went into premature labor and won't be writing about it."

"I hadn't heard," I said. "Who will be taking over the reporting for her?"

"I haven't been informed yet, but I do know they are short-staffed," Dante said. "Still, with recent developments, how come you don't look worried?"

I hung the towel back on my treadmill, then increased the speed. My legs burned, but I welcomed the sensation, focusing on something other than the circus my life had become.

"Because I have no intention of giving up easily," I said. "It was merely a minor setback."

Dante glanced at the display on my treadmill, then increased the speed on his to match mine. "Minor? The queen fired Grace."

"*Attempted* to fire Grace," I said. "Luckily, I had my bases covered."

Once I had shown Mother the contract that stipulated Grace was under my employment, she knew she was power-less, which made her even angrier with me. She knew she did not have the legal right to terminate Grace's employment. She was furious with me for taking such a bold stand against her, but I held my ground firmly, knowing I did not have any other options.

"Besides, I'm starting to like having Grace around," I added.

Dante smirked. "That's obvious."

"What do you mean by that?" I asked.

"With all due respect, Your Highness—I'm not blind," he chuckled. "The way you look at her, the way you defend her. It's clear you're smitten."

Smitten was a strong word.

I couldn't deny that Grace intrigued me—her quirky sense of humor, her endearing vulnerability, and her unwavering passion for her work, even when things were not going her way. There was something refreshing about her presence. I wanted to protect her, to save her from my mother's wrath, even though I was the reason she was in this predicament.

"All right, fine—maybe I'm a tad smitten," I admitted, thinking of that delightful moment when we almost kissed. "But that doesn't mean anything is going to happen between us, nor will it change the fact that we need a new plan to make sure this wedding does not happen. Now, more than ever, Mother will be watching us intently, but I'm not giving up without a fight."

Both of our phones pinged at the same time.

"Sounds like someone might be looking for us," I said. "Would you mind checking to see if it's important?"

"Not at all . . ." He glanced at his phone, his eyebrows furrowing in concern. "It's an urgent message from Henri. Our presence is required in the private sitting room for an emergency meeting with the queen in thirty minutes."

"An emergency meeting?" I frowned, my mind still occupied with thoughts of Grace and our yet-to-be-devised new plan. "Did he say what for?"

"No," Dante replied, stopping his treadmill and hopping off. "I guess we will find out soon enough."

"Right," I sighed. "Guess we'd better get ready, then."

Ready for what, I did not know.

After a quick shower and change of clothes, I made my way to the private sitting room, trying to suppress the uneasy feeling churning in my gut. What could be so important for Mother to call an emergency meeting? The last one had been years ago, after Father had died.

As I entered the room, I was shocked to see Adriana, Theo, and Grace already seated, their faces a mosaic of concern and confusion. Grace's eyes met mine, and a subtle pang of guilt hit me for my part of thrusting her into this mysterious scenario.

Theo cut through the uneasy silence, breaking the tension with a puzzled inquiry, "Does anyone have a clue as to why we've been summoned to this so-called emergency meeting?"

"I'm putting my money on Oliver," Adriana said, her tone a blend of teasing and genuine concern, interjected with a mischievous smile. "What did you do this time?"

Feigning innocence, I raised an eyebrow. "Why is it always me?"

"Because it usually is," Theo quipped.

"If Grace is here, it must be wedding-related, but what could be so urgent?" Adriana pondered aloud.

Seating myself next to Grace, I leaned in and whispered, "How are you holding up? Did you get any sleep?"

"Yes, it was possibly the best night of sleep I've had in years," she said.

Surprised, I chuckled. "I wasn't expecting you to say that, especially after enduring Mother's wrath. How is that even possible?"

Grace shrugged. "Last night, I realized it was time for a significant change in my life. Wedding planning isn't working for me, no matter how hard I try. I thought coming here, to a different country, to a different culture, would change things and get me moving in the right direction, but I was wrong. I'm not the klutz and disaster that you see, though. Anyway, I've been trying to figure out for the longest time why these things keep happening to me. It felt like I was trying to fit a square peg into a round hole repeatedly, forcing it, instead of looking for a square hole. And that square hole is something that truly fills me and brings me joy, something I am passionate about."

"And tell me, have you figured out what that is?" I asked.

Grace shook her head. "Not exactly. I think I have some good options to consider."

"I would love to hear about them, if you don't mind sharing," I said.

Grace smiled. "I'd love to share them with you. It was like I finally had a wake-up call and realized I needed to make some changes. And because of that, I felt peace for the first time in a very long time. Then I slept like a baby."

Nodding, I said, "That's a wonderful perspective, something I could learn from. It's good to go after our dreams and do something we are passionate about."

"Like painting?" Grace said.

I thought about it. "Maybe . . . Although in my case, it may not be as realistic. I have duties."

"You never know . . ."

"True," I said. "Well, hopefully, we will both emerge with the same healthy mindset after this mysterious meeting."

"Trust me," Grace said. "There's nothing the queen can say or do to change my mind or alter my state at this point. I'm in a pretty good place right now. Who knows how long it would have taken me to figure that out if I hadn't come here. I want to thank you for that."

I smiled. "Glad to help."

A newfound confidence resonated in her words, and I couldn't help but admire the clarity she had found during so much uncertainty.

The royal sitting room, usually infused with warmth and familial joy, echoed with tension as Mother entered and paced restlessly in front of the stone fireplace. Henri stepped inside the room and stood off to the side against the wall. Abruptly turning to us, Mother's gaze practically pierced through each of our souls, a mix of disappointment and fury evident in her eyes.

"Tell me," she demanded. "Do you all take me for a fool?"

I blinked in astonishment, the weight of her words settling in. We exchanged confused glances as we waited for further explanation.

"Did you seriously think I wouldn't find out?" Mother continued, her tone accusing. "Every one of you is a liar. It's bad enough dealing with the wedding mishaps, but my own children lying to me is the last thing I would have expected."

"What are you talking about?" Adriana asked.

Queen Annabelle scoffed. "Fine—let's start with you, young lady. You told me you had Veronica's tiara. That was a lie."

Adriana nodded hesitantly. "Well, yes, technically a lie, but I didn't hurt anyone. I was just trying to protect Grace until we found it. It was a little white lie, to buy some time."

"How kind of you," Mother retorted, her words laden with sarcasm. She then turned her attention to Theo. "As for you, Theodore, you are a liar *and* a thief!"

The room buzzed with shock at the strong accusation.

Theo, caught off guard, nervously avoided eye contact. "I don't know what this is about, but you're obviously mistaken."

"Am I?" Mother motioned to Henri, who ushered in a footman carrying a large velvet box. It was placed on the table, capturing everyone's attention.

Henri and the footman left the room, closing the door behind them.

"Wait a minute," Grace exclaimed, sitting up in her chair and pointing to the box. "Is that Princess Veronica's tiara? You found it!"

Mother opened the box with a deliberate, dramatic pause. "Yes. The very tiara stolen by Theodore."

"What?" Grace said as she spun to face Theo.

All eyes turned accusingly to Theo, who sat there open-mouthed, yet speechless.

"I have just been shown security footage of Theodore removing it from the SUV and taking it to his room," Mother said. "We found it on the floor of his closet."

Grace was the first to speak up, the hurt and confusion clearly showing in her eyes. "Why would you take the tiara and then allow me to take the blame? What have I done to you?"

"Nothing, and I really didn't steal it from anybody. I was just hiding it." Theo let out a weak chuckle. "Life can be dull here sometimes, and I thought it would add some mystery to our lives. It was just some innocent fun."

I didn't believe him. This was completely out of character for Theo, not to mention the fact that he never looked for fun.

"Innocent fun?" Grace shot back, the betrayal evident in her voice. "I don't buy it. Do you hate me that much?"

Theo opened his mouth and closed it.

"I felt absolutely horrible that I couldn't find it, especially knowing what it means to Princess Veronica," Grace added. "You should be ashamed of yourself."

After everything that had previously happened to Grace, I'd never seen her with such a pained expression. She was truly hurt. And it was all my fault for bringing her here.

Before Theo could respond, Mother shifted her focus to Grace. "You've caused quite enough wedding chaos yourself, Miss Fullerton. My damaged dress, the unwanted guest in the palace, and the alarming quantity of peacock droppings that are still being found in the royal garden as I speak. And, I was just alerted to the fact that the lavender wedding candles that arrived for the wedding ceremony are black-licorice scented."

"I just ordered what was listed in the wedding files," Grace defended.

"And you think black licorice is a popular wedding

scent?" Mother asked. "You should have spotted the discrepancy and at least inquired about it."

"Maybe you're right, Your Majesty," Grace admitted. "Maybe I would have noticed or questioned it if I had been here when they had arrived or had actually seen the boxes to begin with. But that doesn't give you the right to treat me this way, queen or not."

"I beg your pardon!" Mother said.

Grace stood and boldly took a step toward Mother, her gaze unwavering. "You've got anger issues. You need to work on that."

I didn't know whether I should cheer for Grace's gumption or step in front of her to protect her.

"How dare you talk to me in that tone!" Mother said.

"My tone?" Grace said, not backing down. "Just because you have the title of queen does not give you the right to be mean. I admit I've made mistakes, but the peacocks were not my fault. The candles were not my fault. Aunt Honey was not my fault. And the tiara was obviously not my fault. It feels impossible to please you when I am mis-characterized and blamed for things I can't control."

Grace's stance was impressive. It made me like her even more, but it was difficult to intimidate the Queen of Verdana. In fact, it was almost an impossibility.

Mother held her ground as well. "None of those issues would have occurred under the supervision of Miss DuPont. And as for respect, it is not given freely, like candy to a child. Respect must be earned."

Grace nodded. "You're right. So, I will let you know

when you have earned mine. Because right now, I have no respect for you at all." She glared at Mother for a long moment, then walked toward the door.

"Where do you think you're going?" Mother asked. "This meeting is not over!"

Grace stopped and turned around to answer, but I interjected, growing weary of the negativity in the room. "Mother, you've made your point. This kind of talk is not healthy. Let's just end this now." I stood and walked over to Grace, stopping next to her.

"On the contrary, Oliver," she declared, her stern gaze fixed on me. "We haven't even touched on your unimaginable deceit."

This meeting took another unexpected turn. I could feel the weight of her words pressing down on me. I swallowed hard, wondering how much she knew.

"You had knowledge of the missing tiara, but said absolutely nothing," Mother said. "Did you not?"

There was no use lying now. "I did."

"And when you had told me that Grace was the new wedding planner, I said I would expect nothing less than perfection and stellar reviews. I specifically asked you if she had achieved that level of client satisfaction, and you replied people couldn't stop talking about Grace."

I nodded, wondering when she had suddenly acquired the memory skills of an elephant. "That was the truth."

"But also misleading, since they could not stop talking about her negatively," Mother said. "You also left out the part where her clients were suing her."

"I object!" Grace said. "Suing me doesn't mean I'm guilty. They're opportunists, nothing more, looking to make a buck."

Fortunately, a disturbance in the halls of the palace distracted Mother, at least for the moment.

"What is going on out there?" she asked.

The noise was getting closer, and much to my surprise, the lively conversation was in Italian.

"The Tuscany Twins," I mumbled in disbelief.

Lorenzo and Vincenzo Vitale, otherwise known as Renzo and Enzo. They were distant relatives on my family tree, third cousins connected to my great-grandparents on my father's side.

And one more nightmare for my mother.

I had a feeling I knew the answer, but I still had to ask Grace. "Did you invite Lorenzo and Vincenzo Vitale to the wedding?"

She nodded. "Yes. They were on the backup list, just like Aunt Honey." She studied me and grimaced. "They were not supposed to come, were they?"

"No," I said. "Brace yourself for a category five testosterone tornado inside the palace."

The door banged open, and the Tuscany Twins entered with the energy of a thousand espressos, clad in vibrant azure and marigold plaid suits that seemed to defy the laws of color coordination. Fashionably tieless, the top buttons of their shirts hung open, highlighting their olive skin and sculpted collarbones underneath. Their hair, an explosion of dark waves, had grown out since the last time I had seen them, framing their expressive faces with mahogany locks. Despite the assault on the senses of their attire, they somehow pulled it off with confidence and panache. Especially for a couple of men in their late twenties.

Henri came running in behind them, out of breath, looking frantic. "I apologize for the intrusion, Your Majesty!"

"Queen Annabelle!" Enzo said, always the charmer, swooping in and addressing Mother with enthusiasm. "You look more radiant than ever! *Bellisima!*" He planted a kiss on her hand, while Renzo mirrored the gesture.

Mother's discomfort was palpable, her face growing paler as she endured the unexpected and unwanted attention from the two people she considered loose ornery cannons. In fact, she had never wanted to see them again, let alone invite them to my wedding. But here they were, embracing her, then moving on to greet Adriana and Theo with kisses and hugs.

I was next.

"Prince Oliver!" Enzo exclaimed, enveloping me in a bear hug that left me gasping for air, following it up with a kiss on both my cheeks. "You look fantastic. You have been working out in the gym, no?" He reached for one of my biceps and gave it a squeeze. "*Grande!*"

Renzo echoed his brother's sentiment with a squeeze of my bicep. "Enzo is right! Big muscles! Good to see you, my cousin!" He laughed and kissed me on both cheeks.

They saved Grace for last and stopped in their tracks, both of their mouths dropping open.

"And who is this stunning vision?" Enzo marveled, his eyes widening as he admired her from head to toe.

"This is Grace, our wedding planner," I answered.

"Yes! The wedding planner!" he gushed, grabbing her hands, then kissing her on both cheeks. "Thank you for the invitation." He shook his head in amazement, then patted his chest with his hand. "I do not know if my heart can withstand your beauty for a long period."

"Then please take a break, my brother!" Renzo said, moving Enzo out of the way with his arm and stepping closer to kiss Grace on both cheeks. "I want to freeze this moment and enjoy it longer." His eyes were filled with admiration as he gave her the once-over.

Or maybe that was lust.

"It's a pleasure to meet you both," Grace said, appearing to enjoy the attention, and the break from Mother's grilling.

"Believe me—the pleasure is all mine," Renzo said, winking at her playfully, then giving her an extra set of kisses on her cheeks that were completely unnecessary.

I cast a quick glance at Mother, who could not hide her ire at two more unwelcome guests. I got the last laugh, though. I thought they were both absolutely delightful and upbeat.

"I hope you do not mind that we arrived early." Enzo flashed a grin at Mother. "We couldn't resist the allure of a family reunion."

Renzo chimed in with his infectious enthusiasm. "We were craving some quality time with you, that is all. We have not seen you since the funeral last year. Family is important, you know. Now, more than ever."

"We also saw a video on TikTok of your *grande* amusement park here in Verdana that just opened," Enzo interjected.

"Bigger than Disneyland!" Renzo chimed in.

"What is the name?" Enzo snapped his fingers, struggling to think of it.

"Atomic Adventures," I replied with a proud grin. "Yes, we're very proud of it. We have twenty-two rollercoasters, the most in the entire world."

"Yes!" Enzo said. "We must enjoy Atomic Adventures in all its glory for ourselves and ride all twenty-two roller coasters."

I chuckled. "That is a very ambitious goal. It will take more than one day to accomplish, I think."

Just then, Aunt Honey sauntered into the room. "There y'all are! I wondered where everyone was hiding!"

Mother's blood pressure was surely about to be tested.

Right on cue, she massaged her forehead. "I feel a migraine coming on."

Aunt Honey's eyes sparkled with delight as she eyed Enzo and Renzo like they were candy. "My goodness, who do we have here?"

Aunt Honey was at least thirty years older than the Tuscany Twins, maybe more, but neither of the three seemed to mind the age difference.

Especially Enzo, who took a step toward her and turned his charm up to eleven. "My name is Enzo, and please allow me to say that I'm enamored by your beauty. You, my dear, are the crowning jewel of this palace." He grabbed her hands, then kissed her on both cheeks. "Please tell me your name so I can write it on my heart."

Aunt Honey blushed as she soaked up the attention. "Well, aren't you just as sweet as molasses!" She gave him a playful smile. "I'm Honey Buttermaker from Oklahoma. Hooker, to be exact."

"Hooker?" Enzo tilted his head to the side, blinking rapidly. "I do not understand."

Aunt Honey smiled. "It's a destination, not a vocation."

Enzo's eyes went wide. "Ah! Yes!" He nodded enthusiastically. "Much better."

"Did I hear y'all talking about Atomic Adventures when I came in?" Aunt Honey asked.

"Yes!" Renzo said. "We want to visit this magical kingdom."

"Me, too!" Aunt Honey said. "We should all go together."

"A wonderful idea!" Mother said, suddenly perking up. "In fact, I'll have someone fly you there in the royal helicopter. You can leave immediately. Grace, you should join them. I'll have someone watch Freddie for you."

Grace and I both stared at Mother.

The suggestion completely caught us off guard, but her motive was crystal clear. She wanted a temporary reprieve from the charismatic Italian duo, as well as Grace and the Hooker. It would also give her an opportunity to spend more time with the dog she claimed she did not want. Mother's plan, however, wasn't about to unfold quite as smoothly as she contrived.

Enzo frowned. "We just arrived, Queen Annabelle. It would not feel right leaving without spending time with family."

"It is true!" Renzo said. "It would be rude of us to leave you and our cousins."

Mother's smile, though insincere, held its charm. "There will be plenty of time for that when you return. Please, go enjoy yourself. And take your time. There is no hurry. In fact, I insist you spend the night in the royal suite at the Atomic Adventures Hotel as our guests. One day is simply not enough time to enjoy everything. Make it two."

Welcome to the lying club, Mother.

The Tuscany Twins celebrated the impending amusement park adventure, hugging and kissing everyone again, including Mother.

"Fantastico!" Renzo exclaimed. "We will enjoy Atomic Adventures with two of the most beautiful women in the world. This will be a day to remember!" He winked at Grace.

Something about that didn't sit well with me. Grace was going to spend the night with the testosterone twins? Not on my watch.

"I think I'll go with you!" I blurted out. "That way, you will at least be with one member of the family while you enjoy the amusement park."

"Don't be ridiculous, Oliver," Mother said. "You can't just go out in public like that. You'll create a scene."

"Then I will go incognito," I defended. "I did it in Los Angeles when I met Grace and not a single person recognized me."

Mother hesitated, still looking like she did not like the idea. "I thought you had a videoconference with the Prince of Liechtenstein."

"That was rescheduled," I lied, making a mental note to tell Dante to reschedule the meeting for later in the week.

Mother eyed me suspiciously. "Very well . . . enjoy yourselves then, but please try to avoid going viral. The last thing we need is a royal scandal." She turned to leave, then walked out.

Theo followed her, but I reached for his arm and said, "We need to talk. You owe me an explanation. The truth."

He just nodded, avoiding eye contact as he walked out.

The thought of spending more time with Grace ignited a warmth within me. Yet, beneath the surface, conflicting emotions brewed. Guilt crept in, like a shadow casting doubt on the choices I was making. My feelings were getting stronger for a woman who would most likely hate me for the rest of my life if she found out why I brought her to Verdana.

I don't want to live a lie, but I also don't want to hurt her.

"Are you okay?" Grace asked. "You look deep in thought."

I nodded. "I'm fine. Just thinking of the amusement park."

However, the truth lingered in my gut, a silent whisper

reminding me I was digging myself deeper into a hole that I might not climb out of.

Chapter Fifteen

GRACE

After checking in to the Atomic Adventures Hotel and leaving our overnight bags in our rooms, the private shuttle took us to the amusement park located on the same property. During the short drive, I contemplated the bewildering unpredictability that had woven itself into the fabric of my existence.

Arriving in Verdana with aspirations to rejuvenate my career, I now found myself marked as public enemy number one by none other than the queen. Adding to the intricacies of my situation was the uncharted territory of harboring romantic feelings for her son, emotions that surpassed the bounds of possibility.

There was no doubt the queen wanted me out of her perfectly coiffed royal hair, and frankly, I could use a break from her as well. I gave myself permission to enjoy some time away from all things wedding-related, although a dark, not-so-proud part of me just wanted to sabotage the darn thing and ask Oliver to run away with me. A ridiculous fantasy, I know, but it was hard to not wonder what might have been if he weren't in an arranged marriage, or didn't belong to royalty.

As the driver passed through a private entrance into the back of the amusement park, my attention shifted to the imposing bodyguard with the serious face seated at the front of the shuttle. He was dressed in black from head to toe, with matching sunglasses to boot.

"Has that guy ever cracked a smile?" I whispered to Oliver, who was sitting next to me in the same incognito outfit he wore in Los Angeles, a blue Santa Monica T-shirt, an "I Love LA" baseball cap, and dark sunglasses.

Oliver smirked. "Mr. Stoic? He only smiles after he's taken down a man."

"Excuse me?" I exclaimed, turning my head toward the mysterious security guard. "Are you serious?"

Oliver burst into laughter, and I realized he was merely joking.

"No," he reassured me, flashing a playful grin. "Or at least, as far as I know."

Disembarking the private shuttle, we were promptly welcomed by an Atomic Adventures employee dressed in a light-blue polo shirt, khaki pants, and brown shoes, proudly sporting the amusement park logo on her chest. Standing alongside her were two men in dark suits, their expressions mirroring that of Mr. Stoic, who was now standing off to the side monitoring the area.

"Welcome to Atomic Adventures, Your Highness," the

employee said with a respectful nod. "It's a genuine honor to have you and your guests here with us today."

"Thank you," responded Oliver. "We've been looking forward to it."

"That is wonderful," she said. "My name is Janice, and I'll be your contact at the park throughout your visit. Should you require anything, and I mean anything, call my direct and personal number, conveniently provided on my card. In addition, you can use these VIP cards, granting you and your guests unlimited complimentary meals and drinks at any park location. These cards also entitle you to skip the lines at all our attractions."

"Thank you," we chorused appreciatively as we accepted the VIP cards from her.

Janice unlocked the side gate with a metallic click, swinging it open to welcome us with a broad smile. "Enjoy your day at Atomic Adventures!"

We thanked her and strolled through the gate into the amusement park. Colors popped everywhere, from the rides to the food stands. The air was thick with the wonderful scents of buttered popcorn, funnel cakes, grilled hamburgers, and cheesy pizza. Laughter, screams, and upbeat music filled the air. The weather was perfect, warm, but not sweltering.

"Ready for some fun?" Oliver asked.

"Ready as I'll ever be," Aunt Honey drawled, her eyes scanning the map she held in her hands. "What's first?"

Enzo didn't hesitate with an answer. "A rollercoaster!

That one." He pointed to the towering, twisting metal behemoth in front of us that seemed to reach the sky.

"Sounds like a plan," I agreed.

Oliver glanced up and grimaced. "Have fun—I'll wait right here for you."

"Nice try," I said, laughing and tugging his arm toward the entrance.

Oliver and I sat next to each other at the very back of the rollercoaster, while Mr. Stoic sat in the seat in front of us, monitoring the surroundings. Luckily, the vast majority of park attendees were tourists from other countries, so there was less likelihood of him being spotted.

"I guess this would be a good time to say I've never been on a roller coaster before," Oliver admitted, surprising me.

"Never?" I asked incredulously as the security bar lowered across both our laps. "In your entire life?"

"Never," he confirmed.

"This should be fun to watch," I teased, earning a playful glare from him.

As the rollercoaster began its ascent to the top, I felt a thrill of excitement well up inside me. From high above, I could see the Mediterranean Sea shimmering in the sunlight as Oliver gripped the safety bar tightly, his knuckles turning white.

"Here we go!" I cried out, raising my hands in the air as the rollercoaster crested the top of its first hill. Oliver, gripping the bar like it was a lifeline, glanced over at me with wide eyes and a pale face.

"Are you sure about this?" he asked, sounding more than a little nervous. "Maybe it's not too late to make it stop."

"No way!" I replied. "Trust me, you're going to love it."

"I don't believe you," he said.

The roller coaster plummeted down, and I laughed with joy, a stark contrast to the screams of terror coming from His Highness. We bounced off each other as the ride twisted and turned, our bodies pressed close together by the forces of gravity. When the coaster finally came to a stop after what must have been twenty loops, I stumbled out of the car, breathless, exhilarated, laughing like a teenager.

"Best roller coaster ever!" Renzo cheered from the first car, his enthusiasm contagious. "And there are still twenty-one more!"

"Let's do it!" Enzo said, walking with Renzo and Aunt Honey toward the exit of the ride.

I turned back to find Oliver still frozen in his seat, his face a hilarious mix of abject fear and relief.

"Hey!" I called out, extending my hand. "Come on!"

Oliver nodded, accepting my hand. "People call that fun, do they?"

I laughed. "We do."

After exiting, Renzo, Enzo, and Aunt Honey studied the park map, trying to decide which ride to conquer next. I spotted the photo booth selling snapshots of rollercoaster riders and knew what I had to do next. Mr. Stoic stood off to the side, monitoring our surroundings, as usual.

"Hang on," I said to Oliver, walking over to the booth and browsing the display board for our picture.

Oliver protested, "That's unnecessary."

Ignoring him, I said, "For me, it is. Come on, you appreciate art. I'm sure our photo is a masterpiece."

"I seriously doubt that," Oliver said.

There it was—a close-up shot of us mid-plunge, Oliver's eyes wide, hair askew, and an expression of sheer unadulterated horror on his face.

I burst into laughter. "Where's your hat?"

Oliver reached up to his head and felt around. "Oh . . . I hadn't even noticed it came off." He gestured to the employee's head. "I'll give you forty euros for your hat."

The employee pulled the hat off his head so quickly, I almost missed it. "Sold."

Oliver paid the guy and slipped the hat on. "Much better."

"This is gold!" I said, gesturing to the photo. "I'm buying it."

Oliver tried one last time, "You don't have to—"

"Sorry—it's a must," I insisted, grinning and paying. "This will immortalize my trip."

We regrouped with the gang, and Renzo exclaimed, "We've discovered the next thrill: Death Drop, the roller coaster to end all roller coasters. Let's do this!"

Oliver groaned, and his face was still flushed from the wild ride. "Can we ease into it and pace ourselves? How about something less heart-stopping?" He pointed to the log ride. "That looks like a good time."

Renzo eyed the ride suspiciously. "Isn't that for kids?"

Deciding to cut Oliver some slack, I chimed in, "Not at all. Plenty of adults love it. Just be ready to get wet."

Enzo shot a mischievous glance at Aunt Honey. "Well, what are we waiting for? We can do the next rollercoaster after this ride."

To my amazement, not a single soul in the amusement park suspected we had Verdana's prince in our midst as we hopped into the log boat. An even bigger surprise awaited us after we splashed through the water and got off at the end.

We were all soaked.

I snuck a peak of Oliver's wet T-shirt that was glued to his body, hugging every glorious muscle.

Luckily, my blouse was spared, but Aunt Honey's shirt turned transparent from the soaking, revealing a stylish leopard-print bra underneath.

Enzo couldn't take his eyes off her and blurted out, "Will you marry me?"

"I appreciate your enthusiasm, sugar," she replied with a laugh. "But I'm probably fifteen years older than you."

Thirty, I thought.

"Age is just a number!" Enzo insisted, undeterred. "You're a mature woman who knows what she wants. And luckily, I want to give it to you."

"Is that so?" Aunt Honey asked, raising an eyebrow as she fanned her face.

If I'd have been wearing glasses, they would've been steamed up from those two. They seemed to be the most unlikely of couples. Almost as unlikely as the prince and me, although Oliver was grinning at me at that very moment.

"What's that mischievous look for?" I asked, raising an eyebrow.

He pointed to the carnival games area, his eyes sparkling with excitement. "They have darts."

I followed his gaze just in time to witness a teenager triumphantly popping a balloon with a dart, earning herself a giant pelican as a prize.

"Seriously? You've got a thing for stuffed birds?" I quipped.

"Not at all," he replied smoothly. "I'm just in the mood for another bet."

I chuckled, curious about his next move.

"Fine," I said. "If I win, you have to—"

"Post my video of the 'Macarena' on social media," he interjected. "So predictable."

"And if you win?" I challenged him.

I was confident I would be victorious this time, but I at least had to ask, so he thought he had a chance of winning.

Oliver gestured to the "Face Painting" sign with a twinkle in his eye. "You get your face painted."

I considered the wager. "That's it? You're on!"

He smirked, his gaze lingering mischievously. "And I am the one who gets to paint your face."

"Oh . . ." I was surprised by the unexpected twist. The prospect of Oliver painting my face added a thrilling layer to the bet. There was no doubt about that. I couldn't help but imagine what he might create, not to mention the closeness that would be involved.

I cleared my throat, attempting to conceal the sudden flutter in my stomach. "Alrighty then, you've got yourself a bet."

Enzo, Renzo, and Aunt Honey abandoned us, deeming darts too vanilla, opting for the thrills of Death Trap. We'd catch up with them later.

"Ladies first," Oliver said.

I shot him a playful look. "How gentlemanly of you. No distractions this time, though. Play nice."

Oliver smirked mischievously. "Can't make any promises on that front."

The employee handed me three darts with a wish of good luck.

"Thanks." I positioned myself in front of the wall adorned with balloons, raising the first dart, eyes fixed on the targets.

Oliver sidled up, his warm breath caressing my ear. "Had the most interesting dream about you last night, Grace. Checked into a hotel, and surprise, surprise, there was only one bed. Quite the scandal."

My initial throw missed the mark, bouncing off the wall and narrowly avoiding the employee's foot. I kept my composure, ignoring the effect of Oliver's proximity and his words.

With the second dart in hand, I aimed for the red balloon. I did my best to not think of the one bed in the hotel and focus on the target. My dumb brain took it a step further, and I imagined myself walking in on him in the shower.

My second dart veered left, impaling a stuffed pelican.

I huffed, crossing my arms in frustration, though Oliver's amused expression made it hard to be upset with him.

"Is cheating the only way you can win?" I quipped.

"I didn't even say anything that time!" Oliver raised his hands in surrender. "I'll be silent as a church mouse. Promise."

I took my time as I focused my aim on the green balloon, but it really didn't matter. The vision of Oliver in the shower still lingered in my brain.

My third and final dart sailed wide right.

The balloons remained unscathed, taunting my lack of accuracy.

Oliver flashed a confident grin, swaggering up to the line and collecting three darts from the employee. "Such a shame. I just need to hit the target once in three tries to win. It's as easy as taking candy from a baby."

I needed to take it a step further if I had any chance. It was time to get out of my comfort zone and show him he was messing with the wrong person.

Oliver took aim at the first balloon.

"Hang on—what is that?" I said, playfully closing the gap between us. I reached my hand up to his face, letting my fingers slide slowly across his cheek. "I swear, I spotted something on your face." Tilting my head, I lingered inches from his mouth. "Your skin is like velvet. I can't resist touching it." My hand casually dropped to his chest, and I drummed my fingers lightly. "But hey, don't mind me. It's your turn to dazzle with those darts. Good luck."

Oliver shot me a glare, swallowed hard, and then tossed the dart. It ended up sticking into the wall far from any balloons.

"Oh, what a pity," I said, wincing. "That wasn't even close."

"I still have two more," Oliver replied, his confidence undeterred. He raised the second dart to eye level. "Let's finish this."

Closing in with a playful smirk, I murmured, "Great plan. Hey, do you have any Chapstick? I've been licking my lips a lot lately."

His second dart flew far right and bounced off the fire extinguisher on the wall with a resounding clank, then dropped to the floor.

"Uh-oh," I teased. "One dart left. Feeling the pressure?"

"I can handle it," he declared.

"Confidence suits you," I nodded. "And I won't mention a thing about the dream I had of us in a hot tub."

This time, Oliver remained unfazed.

He released the dart into the carnival breeze, hit the orange balloon with a satisfying pop, then turned to me with a triumphant grin. "Looks like I win, Grace. Again."

I huffed, incredulous. "How did that not distract you? We were in a hot tub together, slipping and sliding!"

Oliver shook his head, chuckling. "Maybe it would've worked if I hadn't had a similar dream two nights ago."

His playful confession blindsided me.

"Come on—time to paint your face," he added, grabbing my hand and walking with me.

That's right, we were holding hands.

I was speechless.

When we arrived at the face painting, Oliver released my hand, excusing himself for a quick chat with an employee. The man's eyes widened as he nodded enthusiastically, pointing to the lone face-painting station that was open among the five.

Curiosity piqued, I settled into the chair in the corner of the tent and waited, watching as Oliver rejoined me.

"What did you tell him?" I inquired.

Oliver shrugged with a mischievous grin. "The truth. I told him I was Prince Oliver, and in exchange for keeping it a secret and letting me paint you, I promised him a tour of the royal palace."

"Huh," I said. "That was easy. Are you sure the queen won't mind?"

"No—we do tours occasionally," Oliver said. "The real challenge will be keeping my focus while painting you." He grabbed a paintbrush and dipped it into a vibrant blue.

"What are you going to draw?" I asked.

Oliver's grin widened. "You'll see."

As Oliver began to paint, the atmosphere turned suddenly more intimate than I could have ever imagined, considering we were in public. Each stroke of the brush on my skin sent shivers down my spine. His gentle touch awakened senses in me I thought were long dead. Even our conversation became more intimate when he brought up the unfinished portrait session at the palace.

"I wanted to kiss you," he admitted in a whisper as his gaze met mine. "More than you can imagine."

I felt a surge of courage, and I said, "Me, too."

The air between us crackled with unspoken tension. As he continued to paint, the brush glided across my skin, and a magnetic force seemed to pull us closer.

It was impossible to ignore our chemistry.

I finally broke the charged silence.

"What are we going to do about our . . . situation?"

Oliver paused, eyes locked onto mine, and countered with a playful smirk, "What would normal people do?"

"I may be normal, but you are far from it," I replied, meeting his gaze with a teasing glint. "You're the prince of Verdana, engaged to Princess Veronica. I don't see any logical way for us to explore our feelings."

His eyes softened, and he met my gaze with sincerity. "What if I weren't marrying her? Would you want to explore this?"

I nodded, feeling my heartbeat quicken. "Yes. Without a doubt."

"Good," Oliver said. "That's all I need to know."

The silence that followed only amplified our connection, the bond between us growing stronger with every passing second.

A minute later, Oliver finally said, "I've finished painting your face. Take a peek."

Turning to the mirror, I was greeted by a romantic

masterpiece. Delicate swirls of blue intertwined with soft pink hearts adorned my cheeks, chin, and nose. An intricate pattern mirrored the connection we were both discovering.

"I love it," I said, admiring the art. "How long can I keep this on my face?"

Oliver's smile faltered. "Didn't I tell you? It's permanent."

I snorted, then stood. "Very funny."

"One moment—we need a selfie." He pulled out his phone and held it in front of us. I smiled, and he took a couple of photos.

As we were exiting the face-painting booth, Oliver pointed to the ride across the way. "I think that right there should be our next adventure. Are you up for it?"

I glanced over at the Tunnel of Love.

"You can't be serious," I said, skepticism in my voice. "You really want to go in there?"

"Why not?" he asked. "It could be fun. It's private. We can sit in the last row of the boat, and you know, explore our feelings a little more, if you'd like." He glanced at my lips.

My heart raced at the implication.

He was talking about a kiss.

I nodded. "Oh . . . okay."

Oliver texted Aunt Honey and told her our location, so they knew where to find us, then we wove our way through the entrance of the Tunnel of Love and skipped to the front of the line with our VIP cards. The boat had ten rows of seats, two seats in each row. We were next to ride and sat in the very last row, for more privacy. Mr. Stoic sat in the row directly in front of us, glancing to his left, then his right.

My heart was beating so fast.

I was sure I was going to pass out.

Was this really going to happen?

It was almost too surreal for me to fathom.

The fear running through my bones was real, but then I realized it didn't have to do so much with the kiss, but more about me not thinking I could stop once we started.

Chapter Sixteen

GRACE

The gentle lapping of water against the sides of the boat did nothing to calm my racing heart as Oliver and I glided into the Tunnel of Love. With my hands clenched nervously at my sides, the noise of the amusement park faded away, and we were enveloped in the mysterious darkness. I could barely see Oliver beside me, but I felt his presence, his warmth, and the volts of energy dancing between our bodies.

"I can't see a thing with these sunglasses on," Oliver said. "Remind me to put them back on before the end of the ride."

"Remind me to remind you," I joked.

Oliver chuckled just as a scene illuminated before us.

It was the timeless tale of *Romeo and Juliet*. Their iconic balcony scene played out before our eyes, with the star-crossed lovers professing their undying love under the moonlit sky. The scene was adorned with cascading flowers and enhanced by soft, romantic lighting, creating an atmosphere of passion and longing. The sweet crooning of "Unchained Melody" by The Righteous Brothers echoed around us, perfectly complementing the tragic beauty of Shakespeare's most famous love story.

Oliver's hand inched closer to mine, and I felt a magnetic pull as our fingers brushed against each other. A wonderful shiver trickled down my spine, and I smiled.

More, I thought.

As if reading my mind, Oliver's fingers interlaced with mine. My breath hitched in my throat, our connection sending a delightful tingle through my entire body. I let out a deep breath and tried to relax.

As our journey through the tunnel continued, the boat carried us to the next scene, straight out of the classic film *Casablanca*. Bogie and Bergman's characters, Rick and Ilsa, stood on the tarmac of an airport, their farewell etched with bittersweet emotion. The iconic line "Here's looking at you, kid" was visually portrayed as the boat sailed past the lovers parting ways. The beautiful strains of "As Time Goes By" filled the air, casting a nostalgic spell over the timeless romance that unfolded before us.

Feeling more romantic than ever, I stole a glance at Oliver, and our eyes met in the dim light. The moment was electric, the unspoken feelings between us growing by the minute.

But I wanted more.

Needed more . . .

As the boat continued its leisurely journey through the

tunnel, I couldn't help but wonder how much longer until we reached the end of the ride. I licked my lips in anticipation of what might come. My mind ran away with the possibilities. No one would know what transpired between us. It would be our little secret. But how much longer would I have to wait? If he didn't kiss me soon, I would have to take matters into my own hands.

Come on, Oliver!

The third display in the Tunnel of Love whisked us into the enchanting world of *Breakfast at Tiffany's*, where Audrey Hepburn and George Peppard shared a rain-soaked kiss in the alley as she held her cat.

Everybody seemed to be kissing, except us.

Why hadn't Oliver made a move? I understood he was a prince with rules and duties, but he's also a man, and there is no doubt in my mind that he felt the attraction as much as I did.

My patience was growing thin.

The soft notes of "Moon River" sung by Audrey Hepburn herself, enveloped us, enhancing the dreamlike quality of this unforgettable moment from the movie, but my mind was still on the prince.

I craved his lips so badly it hurt.

It was then that Oliver's thumb traced circles on the back of my hand. His fingers gradually started moving up my arm.

My heartbeat suddenly quickened, and I felt the anticipation building within me. I was on the verge of exploding from the built-up sexual tension. I imagined my body parts flying in every direction, plopping into the water like bait for the fish. At this rate, maybe they would be the only ones who put their mouths on me, but by then I would be dead. I wanted Oliver to kiss me so badly, to feel his lips against mine. I could not stand it any longer.

Finally, as the boat approached the next display of Cupid pointing his bow and arrow right at us, Oliver turned to me, his eyes filled with an intensity that mirrored my own emotions.

This was it.

I was sure of it.

Without a word, he cupped my face and pressed his lips against mine. The kiss was soft at first, a tentative exploration that quickly deepened into something more passionate. My nerves melted away as I lost myself in the warmth of his embrace and passion. His lips moved with a gentle urgency, and my hands found their way to his chest, his shoulders, behind his neck, and then through his hair. Time seemed to stand still as we kissed, the display inside the tunnel the furthest thing from my mind. I wanted to savor this moment, this kiss, the feel of his arms around me. I also did not want it to end.

I simply could not get enough.

The thought of stopping seemed impossible.

I wanted everything Oliver had to give me.

A loud bang and a sudden jolt startled us out of our kiss as the boat slammed dramatically through the double doors to take us outside.

Just like that, we were back to reality as I felt the breeze on my face. I was in a complete daze from that magical kiss and out of breath as the sights and sounds of the amusement park engulfed us once again. But before I could bask any further in the afterglow of that kiss, our boat glided past an amusement park employee, who froze in her tracks as her eyes widened. I did a double-take, wondering what that was all about. We passed another employee, and she threw her hand over her mouth, then curtsied.

"Your Highness!" she exclaimed.

Confused, I glanced at Oliver, then jerked my head back. His disguise had completely vanished. No sunglasses. No hat. To make matters worse, blue and pink paint from my face was now smeared across his chin, nose, and mouth. I didn't know whether I wanted to laugh or die of mortification.

"Your sunglasses," I urged him. "Put them back on."

Oliver fumbled around, searching for them on his lap and on the floor of the boat. "Uh-oh," he said, panic in his eyes as he realized they were nowhere to be found. "I have no idea where they are."

"What about your hat?" I asked, even though I had a really bad feeling I'd knocked it off his head when I was running my fingers through his royal hair.

"Did I lose it again?" Oliver muttered, feeling his head. "I guess I did."

We were approaching the ramp to disembark, where there were loads of people waiting to get on the boats. Heads were turning our way.

"There's a storm brewing, Your Highness," Mr. Stoic

said from the seat in front of us. "We'll need to take swift action as soon as the boat stops. Be prepared."

"I'd like to apologize to you in advance, Grace," Oliver said.

"What for?" I asked.

"I have this feeling we're both about to go viral again," he said.

Just then, a man shouted, "It's Prince Oliver!"

The proclamation sent a ripple effect through the crowd. Camera phones were suddenly drawn, like pistols in a western shootout, all of them aimed right at us. In a swift maneuver, Mr. Stoic, the ever-watchful royal bodyguard, sprang into action, leaping out of the boat and extending his hand.

"We need to get you out of here. Now," he said, his urgency clear. "Follow me, Your Highness. Please hurry."

We ran, adrenaline pumping, through the turnstile. The pursuing crowd grew, some snapping photos and taking videos, while others screamed for selfies.

"Wait, Your Highness!" a man yelled. "Just one photo!"

"Prince Oliver!" a child screamed.

Spotting Enzo, Renzo, and Aunt Honey coming our way, I urgently called out to them, "Follow us! We need to get out of here!"

We ran past the spinning teacup ride, the chaos of the pursuing crowd amplifying with each step.

Oliver looked at me with a sheepish grin as we ran alongside each other. "That certainly escalated quickly."

I laughed. "What a royal mess you've gotten us into!"

Breathless and frantic, we followed Mr. Stoic into an eatery, through the kitchen, and out the back door, stopping next to a trash dumpster.

I bent over, hands on my knees, trying to catch my breath. "Okay, that's my exercise for the week." I stood back up and froze as Aunt Honey, Enzo, and Renzo's gazes were darting back and forth between me and Oliver.

Aunt Honey shot me a smirk. "What exactly happened to you two?" Before I could answer, she waved it off. "Never mind. I think I've got a good idea."

"It's not what you think!" I said in a pleading manner.

She crossed her arms. "When do you think I was born, sugar? It's exactly what I think."

Oliver looked genuinely confused and asked, "Why is everyone staring at me like I'm a guilty accomplice in a heist?"

"You've got Grace on your face," Renzo said.

Despite the embarrassment, I couldn't help but laugh.

Oliver blinked, then said, "You mean a little paint?" He touched his face, then glanced at his fingers that now had paint on them.

I winced. "I'd say it's more than just a little."

Oliver winked. "It was worth it."

Aunt Honey pulled out a makeup wipe from her purse and handed it to Oliver. "Here—use this, darlin'. Works like a charm. It has aloe vera."

"Thank you," Oliver said, attempting to clean up his face, but failing miserably.

I couldn't resist the opportunity to tease him. "Maybe

you should let a professional handle this." I grabbed the wipe, first focusing on the area around his lips. The very lips that had moments ago left me breathless.

"I just can't get that kiss off my mind," I said. "I want an encore."

Whoops.

I didn't realize I'd said that out loud.

Oliver's eyebrows shot up.

An awkward silence descended on us, and Enzo and Renzo stared at us like characters from a cartoon, eyes wide and mouths agape.

Aunt Honey beamed with satisfaction. "I knew it."

Heat rose to my cheeks as I quickly handed the wipe back to Oliver, trying to regain my composure. "Maybe it's best if you finish up on your own."

"You may be right," Oliver said, pulling out his phone and turning the camera to selfie mode to see himself while he cleaned up.

"I am confused, Cousin Oliver," Renzo said. "Are you still getting married to Princess Veronica?"

That question certainly got my attention.

Oliver sighed, his face reflecting the weight of the situation. "Technically, the wedding is still in the works, but do I want it? Does Veronica want it?" He shook his head, expressing doubt. "Honestly, no. Neither of us does. The issue is that both our countries would benefit significantly from our union. Veronica's country supplies over seventy percent of vital grains to Verdana. Canceling the wedding would practically shout to the citizens that we're selfish and don't care about them."

"Why should you bear the weight of your nation's future when you had no choice in the circumstances of your birth?" I chimed in, my empathy for Oliver clear. "It hardly seems fair that they just dump that on you."

Aunt Honey added her two cents. "She's got a good point."

"You should marry for love!" Renzo interjected.

Oliver appeared lost in thought, running his fingers through his hair. He looked at the restaurant's back door as an employee emerged. "You make valid points, but this isn't the place for this discussion. Who's hungry?"

"I am," everyone chimed in unison.

"Does this mean we have to leave already? After we eat?" Renzo asked.

"Don't worry—you can ride all the rollercoasters you want," Oliver chuckled. "I'll just need a change of clothes before heading back into the amusement park. And find new sunglasses and a hat."

"Let me take care of that for ya—I know just the place," Aunt Honey said. "Order me a cheeseburger and fries, if you don't mind, and I'll be back in a jiffy. Oh, and after we eat, we need to go visit that tarot card reader."

"That is not necessary," Enzo said, grabbing her hands before she could walk away. "I see my future in your eyes."

Aunt Honey batted her eyelashes. "You really are a smooth talker." She licked her lips. "I am going to eat you up."

Enzo's grin grew wider, and he pressed both his hands against his heart. "That is my greatest wish."

"Be right back, y'all," Aunt Honey said, disappearing inside the building.

Janice, the employee we had met upon our arrival, came out of the back door. "So sorry for the trouble, Your Highness."

Oliver shook his head. "Don't be—it was one-hundred percent my fault."

"Is there anything I can do for you at this point?" she asked. "Perhaps I can shut down the restaurant while you and your guests dine here."

"That won't be necessary," Oliver said. "I don't want the amusement park to lose money on my account. We can eat right over there, if that works for you." He pointed to a cluster of white picnic tables under the large canopy.

"Of course," Janice said. "I'll be right back with some menus."

We sauntered over to the tables and waited for Janice's return. After we ordered the food, Enzo and Renzo shared a little about their lives in Italy and about their olive oil business.

"Most people do not know this, but most of our olive oil comes from Spain," Renzo said.

"I've got an even better secret," Aunt Honey said, approaching with two bags. "My eyelashes are environmentally friendly, and are made from recycled plastic milk jugs." She batted them and smiled. "Anyhoo, Oliver, sugar, I got you something to help you go incognito."

"Let's see what you've got," Oliver said, starting to open the bag.

"No peeking," Aunt Honey said, pointing toward the employee bathrooms. "Go change and then come back to show us. We'll be waiting."

Oliver hesitated for a moment, eyeing the bag with suspicion, but eventually agreed and walked over to the employee restrooms to change.

"Grace, honey, you're next—here you go," Aunt Honey said, handing me the other bag.

"Me?" I asked. "I don't need to go incognito."

"Oh yes, you do," she said. "Everybody has seen you with the prince. You're easy to identify now, especially with that face paint of yours. Go wash that off, then change. And don't you peek in the bag, either."

I hesitated, then said, "Okay then . . ."

I felt a little guilty as I washed my face in the bathroom since I adored what Oliver had painted on me, but most of it was now smeared and unrecognizable, thanks to one unforgettable kiss.

I dried my face with paper towels from the dispenser, then glanced inside the bag. I smiled as I pulled out a cute pink T-shirt with the Atomic Adventures amusement park mascot on the front, an aardvark.

I slipped the T-shirt on—which fit me perfectly—then dug into the bag again, pulling out a voluminous blond wig with glamorous curls. Where on earth had she gotten it from? I had never worn a wig in my life, but reminded myself I was doing it for Oliver as I slipped it over my head and adjusted it in the mirror.

That was when I snort-laughed.

I looked like Dolly Parton, sans the big boobs.

A few minutes later, I emerged from the bathroom at the same time as Oliver. We froze when we saw each other, then both laughed hysterically.

Oliver was also wearing an aardvark T-shirt—his was blue. However, it was his wig that sent me over the edge, teased and tousled glam rock hair with cascading waves of layered locks that framed his face.

Aunt Honey grinned as we approached. "Oh. My. Word! Perfection!"

I continued to giggle at Oliver. "You look like Jon Bon Jovi from the eighties! Are you going to sing a song for us?"

"Not unless you want your ears to bleed." Oliver chuckled, looking a bit embarrassed. "Aunt Honey, I appreciate the effort, but you might've gone a bit overboard with this outfit."

"Not at all," I said, admiring him and nodding my head. "You look kind of sexy, actually."

Renzo and Enzo stared at me, both looking surprised.

Okay, I might have spoken a bit too candidly. After all, he was still the Prince of Verdana underneath that disguise.

"I'll just shut up now," I said, laughing nervously. "My mouth is going to get me into even bigger trouble."

Enzo broke the silence. "It's healthy to express your emotions, Grace." He then turned to Aunt Honey, a swoon-worthy expression on his face. "When you are near, it's like my heart is dancing to a melody only it can hear."

Aunt Honey fanned her face. "Sweetie—you keep talkin' like that and my teeth are gonna fall out from all the cavities."

We settled in, devouring burgers and fries, sipping shakes, and enjoying the casual atmosphere as Oliver and I occasionally exchanged glances. The laughter and banter continued until appetites were satisfied. Then Aunt Honey reminded us of the plan to visit the tarot card reader.

And just like that, we were back in the amusement park, off to our next adventure.

Mr. Stoic stood outside on watch as our party of five squeezed into the tarot card reader's booth. Her cozy space enveloped us in a kaleidoscope of rich, mystical colors, deep purples, velvety reds, and the shades of midnight blue. The thick tapestry behind the table depicted a star-studded night sky with a crescent moon, adding to the enchantment. The air was a mix of incense, creating a mesmerizing atmosphere, illuminated by the soft glow of candles.

Draped in flowing garments, the woman welcomed us with a mysterious smile. "My name is Celestia. Welcome to my world. I hope this will be your lucky day. Who would like to go first?"

Aunt Honey pointed at Oliver. "Why don't you go first, Mr. Bon Jovi?"

Oliver chuckled, a hint of skepticism in his eyes. "I'll pass, Aunt Honey. Let's let someone else have their fortune told."

"No, no, no." Celestia wagged her finger at him, oblivious to the royal presence in her midst. "Not fortune. I'm giving you psychic guidance."

Oliver nodded. "That's still a big no from me."

Renzo and Enzo both declined to take part as well, both preferring to continue conquering the rollercoasters in the amusement park.

That only left me and Aunt Honey.

She turned to me next with a gleam in her eye. "Grace, darlin', why don't you give it a whirl? It's all in good fun."

Celestia wagged her finger again. "Not in good fun. What I tell you is written in stone. It will happen, trust me. These cards represent significant life events, spiritual lessons, and major influences. I will reveal the powerful forces at play and the key moments on your journey. The question is, do you dare find out the truth?"

"Do you dare?" Oliver asked me, wiggling his eyebrows under his oversized wig.

I hesitated, my practical side reminding me that tarot cards couldn't predict the future. But the allure of fun and mystery, especially considering my career change contemplations, won me over. Perhaps Celestia would even drop a hint about love.

"All right," I said, finally succumbing.

Taking a seat in front of the table, I braced for Celestia's dramatic ritual. She shuffled the cards and placed them on the table in front of me. She asked me to cut the deck, then turn over the top card.

Celestia's eyes widened ever so slightly. "Ah, my dear,

the card of deceit. A shadow is lurking in the moonlit corridors of your fate." Her voice intensified. "There is a whisper of drama ahead, a dance with chaos that might test your mettle. Lies have been told. A powerful figure will try to ruin you. Be strong, child."

Aunt Honey raised an eyebrow. "Well, that got dark real quick."

I nervously chuckled. "Yeah, well, drama sounds like a normal day in my world. Let's try another card, please. Give me something good this time."

"Very well, but I do not control the cards. They control me," Celestia declared.

I turned the next one over and waited.

Celestia nodded. "Ah, my dear, the Lovers card."

"Well, butter my biscuit—Grace has hit the jackpot," Aunt Honey said.

"I'm not familiar with this expression," Enzo said as he eyed her body with a confused look. "Where is your biscuit located?"

Celestia cleared her throat, trying to regain control of the mystical moment. "May I continue?"

"Of course!" Aunt Honey said, then whispered to Enzo, "We can chat later about my biscuit." She pointed to Celestia. "You do your thing, girlfriend."

"Much appreciated," Celestia said, running her fingers along the card. "It is telling me there is a tale of profound love that is woven into the fabric of your destiny. A love that transcends boundaries and blossoms like the sweetest flower in a hidden garden. Embrace this divine connection, for it holds the promise of the greatest love your heart has yet to know."

"Okay, much better," I said with a smile. "What else can you tell me about this love story? Do you know where it takes place?"

Celestia leaned in. "My guidance does not have GPS, but this love will be a grand chapter in your life, a melody that harmonizes with the rhythm of your soul. But it does not come without drama."

I sighed. "Seriously? More drama?"

"Sounds an awful lot like the Nicholas Sparks novel I'm reading," Aunt Honey quipped. "Everything was fine and dandy until her house blew up."

"Be strong, child," Celestia added.

I pointed to the third card. "Okay, one more." I flipped it over.

Celestia's expression shifted. "Ah, the Wheel of Fortune. A turning point in your destiny. A change is coming, my dear, and it appears to be linked to your career. This is where you'll find fulfillment and do what you were meant to do. Your true destiny."

"I like the sound of that," I said, perking up.

Celestia nodded. "But the job does not come without—"

"Drama," I said with a nod and a laugh. "Well, thank you for that." I stood and gestured to the chair. "Honey, looks like it's your turn."

"I'm good," she said. "I wanted to come here for you, Grace, and we've got all the information we need. Besides, these boys are itching for more rollercoasters."

"Yes! Let's do it!" Renzo said, leading us back outside.

After exiting, the Tuscany Twins and Aunt Honey huddled around the park map, plotting their next adventure.

Oliver slid up to me with a mischievous twinkle in his eyes. "Looks like your future will shine bright as a shooting star. Positive changes are on the horizon."

I snorted. "Positive changes? More like a whirlwind of lies, deceit, and drama."

Oliver chuckled, leaning in. "But therein lies the adventure, especially since I know you can handle it. Perhaps you and I should have a little chat about . . . things."

"Things?" I teased with a playful smile. "You'll have to be more specific, Your Highness." I knew precisely what he meant.

Oliver leaned closer, his warm breath against my ear, the back of his hand brushing mine. "Let's just say, if we weren't surrounded by the prying eyes of the public right now, I'd show you exactly what I mean. Again. And this time, I wouldn't stop until you begged me."

My heartbeat quickened and heat rose to my face as I suddenly wished for a private moment. "You're giving yourself a lot of credit, Mr. Bon Jovi."

"Is it warranted, though?" he teased.

"Lucky for you, it is." I shot him a playful smile. "Must be the hair. *So* irresistible."

Oliver laughed, flipping through some strands of his wig. "Definitely the hair." He pulled out his phone and snapped a selfie of us donning our aardvark T-shirts and wigs. Then his phone dinged. "Excuse me."

He lost his smile as he read a message.

"Everything okay?" I asked.

He blinked rapidly, clearly disturbed.

Something was off.

"What's going on?" I inquired again.

Oliver pocketed his phone, grimacing. "Big trouble at home, according to Dante. Veronica is returning, and you and I are wanted back at the palace first thing in the morning. Another emergency meeting with Mother."

"I'm sure it's my fault." I sighed. "What did I do this time?"

"You only get fifty percent of the blame," Oliver clarified, then dropped a bombshell that almost stopped my heart. "Apparently, there are now millions of people who think I'm cheating on Veronica. With you."

Chapter Seventeen

PRINCE OLIVER

The Next Morning . . .

As we pulled up to the palace, a frenzy of TV trucks, cameras, and eager reporters awaited just beyond the gates, creating a chaotic spectacle.

Grace's eyes widened as she peered through the tinted windows of the SUV. "Tell me they're not because of us."

I nodded. "They are."

Grace looked at me, her expression a mix of fear and astonishment. "How can you be so calm about this, Oliver? Everybody is dragging your name through the mud. Believe me, I know what it's like. I've been there more than a few times. And it's horrible, especially when it's not true."

I smiled gently, my gaze fixed on hers. "People will talk, criticize, and speculate—it's inevitable. But if I let their words define me, I'll be living their version of my life. The only opinion that truly matters is the one I have of myself. Everything else is just noise."

Grace nodded, looking deep in thought as the SUV passed through the palace gates.

"Wow—that's pretty deep," she said.

I chuckled. "I have my moments."

"Still, you know Queen Annabelle won't be thrilled about this," Grace said.

"Yes, well, Mother hasn't been happy for quite some time," I said. "I understand she has to grieve, we all do, but I'm tired of biting my lip and tiptoeing around her. Enough is enough. It's time to speak up."

Yet, as I spoke those words, a pang of guilt settled in my chest. The weight of a promise made to my father hung over me like a heavy cloud. Before he passed away, he had extracted a vow from me, a commitment to support Mother in any way required, especially in her time of need as she mourned his passing. I had pledged not to let him down, and to do whatever she had asked, which included the arranged marriage. I also promised to take on the responsibility he carried for so long. To do what was best for our country.

But my heart yearned for something different, something that lay in the complete opposite direction. The prospect of being king and the embodiment of a monarchy I didn't entirely embrace left me uncertain. I wondered if he would understand the internal conflict tearing at me now. Would Father comprehend that my heart led me down a path divergent from his aspirations for me?

"Be careful with what you say to Queen Annabelle,"

Grace said with a mischievous smile. "You might just end up in the doghouse with me."

"Sounds like fun, if it means we're in there together," I said with a grin. "Are there darts in the doghouse? I'm in the mood for another bet."

"Next time, I'll choose the bet, and you should prepare to lose," Grace said with a chuckle. "Speaking of dogs, I have no idea how Freddie is doing. I need to check on him before the meeting."

"You won't have time, but don't worry," I assured her. "Dante says he and Mother are inseparable now."

Grace nodded, a smile playing on her lips. "Well, at least something positive came out of my chaotic visit."

"Actually, there are two positive things," I said, reaching for her hand and kissing it.

She grinned. "Right, of course. But are we being unrealistic here? You're the Prince of Verdana, and I'm not even sure what I am at the moment. Certainly not a wedding planner."

"You're not the only one trying to figure out their place in the world," I said, pondering for a moment. "Your job doesn't define you. I believe that much. Give it time. You'll figure it out."

Grace nodded. "Thanks . . ."

"I'm curious," I said. "What was life like for you before you jumped into the dazzling world of wedding planning? What did you do for a living?"

"It was the complete opposite," she said. "I was a strategic business manager and consultant."

I raised an eyebrow, genuinely intrigued. "That sounds impressive. What exactly did that entail?"

Grace shrugged. "I specialized in international business, the complexities of global markets, and implementing profitable collaborations. Strategic planning, analysis, evaluating market trends, identifying opportunities, and mitigating risks." She winced. "Sorry if I'm boring you with corporate jargon. It doesn't sound as exciting as organizing weddings, but it was my thing. I loved it."

"It's not boring at all," I said. "I find it fascinating. Why did you stop?"

Grace didn't hesitate with an answer. "Greed. Most of the companies were so driven by money, to the detriment of their employees, who were overworked and underpaid. I couldn't stomach it anymore. I was hunting for a nonprofit corporation, but then a friend roped me into planning her wedding. One thing led to another, and wedding planning became my accidental detour from the corporate jungle. It's not my passion, but it pays the bills. Well, it used to."

"And you've always been in Los Angeles?"

"Yup—born and raised there," Grace said. "By the way, you don't see that as an obstacle between us? How can we make this work?"

I shrugged, not needing much time to think. "You just need to believe, and let the Universe sort out the details. I believe in you. I believe in us. That's all that matters. We'll figure out the rest."

Marco pulled up to the front of the palace. We got out of the SUV and headed straight to the sitting room for another so-called emergency meeting. Veronica was already there by herself, looking completely relaxed as she scrolled on her phone.

"Here they come—the troublemakers," she teased as she hugged us both. "Are the rumors true?"

"Depends on which rumor you're talking about," I said, trying to keep it light. "I can't keep track of them all."

Veronica, eyeing us both, clarified, "You and Grace. Is there really something going on between you two, or was it just a ruse to get Queen Annabelle to cancel the wedding?"

I glanced at the closed door and lowered my voice. "If you're asking whether or not I like Grace, that would be a resounding yes. I do. Very much so."

It felt liberating to openly talk about it, but I was not crazy enough to say the same thing to Mother. At least, not yet.

"Aww," Grace beamed, then playfully bumped my hip with hers. "Likewise, Your Highness."

Veronica placed her hands on her heart. "This makes me so happy."

"I'm relieved." Grace held both of Veronica's hands and asked, "How is your mother? I hope she's feeling better."

Veronica nodded. "She is. Thank you for asking."

Their pleasant exchange was abruptly interrupted as Mother entered with a sour expression. "Look at the mess you have created. This has gone on long enough."

She grabbed the television remote, turned it on, and cranked up the volume of a news program, revealing the media frenzy we'd just passed outside the palace.

"We begin today's broadcast with a shocking development in the royal realm," the news anchor said. "We're live with reporter Gerald Phillips, who is outside the royal palace as we speak. Gerald? Are the rumors true?"

"That remains to be seen," the reporter said. "Indeed, Prince Oliver appears to have found himself the star of another viral video that has sent shockwaves throughout the nation. His Highness was spotted at Atomic Adventures amusement park yesterday, coming out of the Tunnel of Love with Grace Fullerton, an American wedding planner. The sighting has ignited a frenzy of rumors and speculations."

The news program showed footage of me and Grace exiting the Tunnel of Love, both of us looking flustered with paint on our faces. Then it showed us getting out of the boat and running away from the cameras.

"There are more than a few questions on everyone's mind," the reporter continued. "What was Prince Oliver doing at Atomic Adventures? How did the paint on Grace Fullerton's face get on the prince's face? Is he having an affair with the wedding planner? And what does this mean for his impending royal wedding with Princess Veronica?"

The program cut to a video of me and Grace at the gala.

"Just last week, the pair were seen together at the royal fundraising gala for the children's hospital, where Miss Fullerton took a tumble on stage, falling into the arms of none other than the Prince. Some sources suggest she may have tripped intentionally."

"What sources?" Grace said. "That is ridiculous."

"Adding to the intrigue and suspicion, Grace Fullerton is currently facing legal trouble in the United States, being sued by a former client for damages related to a canceled wedding," the news anchor said. "Speculation arises whether she may have come to Verdana on a similar mission, to disrupt the royal wedding."

"Where do they get their information from?" I said. "What a load of garbage."

Mother huffed and changed the television station to another news program, which was also talking about us.

"The public is demanding answers," the anchor said in an even more serious tone than the anchor on the other station. "Her Majesty, Queen Annabelle, appears to be caught in the middle of this scandal. Speculation is rampant, with the biggest question being—has the royal wedding been called off?"

The station played the same video of us coming out of the Tunnel of Love.

"What is truly happening between Prince Oliver and Grace Fullerton?" the reporter asked. "That is what everyone wants to know. As the nation eagerly awaits official statements and clarifications from the royal family, we will continue to follow this developing story closely."

Mother clicked off the television and set the remote on the table. "This is a disaster. Do you not remember what I said to you before you left?"

"You told us to enjoy ourselves," I answered.

Mother took a step closer to me. "Do not be coy with me, Oliver. I specifically told you to avoid going viral, because the last thing we needed was a royal scandal. It has been just one thing after another since Miss Fullerton's arrival. What do you have to say for yourself?"

"What do you want me to say, Mother?" I asked, quite tired of her behavior.

I sympathized with her grief, the void left by Father's absence, and her longing for peace and stability in the kingdom. I comprehended the reasons behind her actions, but the person standing before me was unrecognizable. The bitterness had reached a point where it was affecting everyone in the palace, and I was past growing weary.

She huffed again. "For one, explain to me how you got paint on your face?"

"Does it really matter?" I stated indignantly. "People believe what they want to believe."

"What they believe now is unacceptable," Mother said. "We need damage control. I want you to release an official statement to the press. Tell them this was all a huge misunderstanding, that you were at Atomic Adventures with relatives and a couple of *employees*." She glared at Grace when she emphasized employees, which did not sit well with me. "And most importantly, make it clear that the wedding is still on. Then I want you and Veronica to make public appearances together, let yourselves be seen holding hands and looking closer than ever. Moving forward, I forbid you and Grace to be in the same room together."

This had to end now. If it weren't for Father and the promises I'd made to him, I would have said something about her behavior months ago. No more.

"I'm sorry, but when did the queen of Verdana become a dictator?" I said. "This is ridiculous."

Mother's eyes went wide. "I have an obligation and a reputation to uphold. This is not a game. What I say goes. Do not question my authority any further!"

Before I could give Mother another piece of my mind, Grace said, "Oliver's life isn't a game! Have you ever asked him what he wants? What are his gifts? Do you know? Do you even care? You have the most amazing, wonderful son, but you are too caught up in your own world to even appreciate them."

Mother glanced at me, blinking, at a loss for words.

This was an extraordinary event.

It was the first time I had ever seen her speechless.

I absolutely loved that Grace had stood up for me.

Luckily, a jolt of brilliance hit me that could finally liberate me from the clutches of this nightmarish, arranged marriage. However, the plan would require the expertise and clever minds of both Veronica and Grace. The problem at the moment was extricating ourselves from this ridiculous meeting. The only conceivable solution was to pretend to endorse Mother's idea wholeheartedly.

"What you suggested is a great idea, Mother!" I said, with possibly too much enthusiasm. "Grace and Veronica will collaborate on the remaining details of the wedding moving forward. I won't be a part of it. And I will issue that press release ASAP. Anything else?"

Mother eyed me suspiciously.

So did Grace and Veronica.

"Is there anything else that you need?" I asked in my kindest voice.

All three of them were still staring at me.

Mother hesitated. "No—nothing else." She was still eying me like I was up to something. "And there had better not be any more surprises. Not one more. This meeting is over. You may go."

Exiting the sitting room with Veronica and Grace, we strolled toward our respective rooms. As we approached the front entrance, Henri stepped inside with an older man, then took a few steps in our direction.

"Miss Grace, you have a visitor," Henri said. "Sebastian Agosto."

His announcement stopped me in my tracks.

Despite Mother's aversion to more surprises, this revelation was monumental, and possibly would be the biggest shock of her life.

Sebastian Agosto.

A humble woodworker.

And my mother's first love.

I recalled the story of Sebastian, the one who got away, vividly told by my drunk Uncle Chester, Mother's brother, during a late-night pool game years ago. Chester spoke of Mother's passionate love for Sebastian, a man her parents wholeheartedly disapproved of. That led to an arranged marriage she was forced to accept with Father. The heart-breaking farewell to Sebastian had devastated Mother, even though she went on to love Father unequivocally.

Sebastian remained an enigma, wrapped in mystery.

Why was he in the palace now? And how would Mother react when she saw him?

Grace greeted Sebastian warmly, inviting him outside to have a look at the wedding altar, an action that left me utterly perplexed. The genuine shock, however, occurred when Mother's clicking heels abruptly stopped beside me. Her mouth fell open as she laid eyes on the infamous man from her past.

"Sebastian," she breathed, placing her hand on her chest. And then, as if succumbing to the unexpected surge of emotions, she passed out.

Chapter Eighteen

GRACE

I gasped as Queen Annabelle wobbled and began to fall over. Luckily, Oliver acted swiftly and could reach out and catch her in his arms before she hit the floor. Relief washed over me, even though I wondered if she wasn't feeling well or if it was because I had brought another unwanted guest into the palace.

Oliver's voice trembled with concern. "Help me get her to the chair."

Henri rushed to his aid, and together they gently guided Queen Annabelle to a nearby chair. She blinked a few times, looking like she was trying to shake off the dizziness.

An employee scurried over with a glass of water, handing it to Oliver, who then gave it to the queen. "Drink some water, Mother."

Queen Annabelle took a small sip, then handed the glass back to him as the color slowly returned to her face. "Let's not make a big fuss over this." She started squirming in the chair. "I just got a little light-headed. It happens when you don't eat breakfast. I'm perfectly fine." She bought her hands to her hair, checking to make sure everything was in place.

"Why haven't you eaten anything?" Oliver asked.

"As I said—let's not make a fuss—I'm fine," she huffed, then stood right back up on her feet. Impressively, she did not wobble even a smidgeon as she adjusted her dress.

"I'm sorry to have startled you, Your Majesty," Sebastian said.

Queen Annabelle glanced his way. "It wasn't you. I barely recognized you. It's been a while, you know."

"Forty years, to be exact," Sebastian said. "Except when I have seen you on television, of course. And you haven't changed one bit."

Queen Annabelle blushed and actually cracked the tiniest of smiles. "Why are you here?"

Her tone was quite pleasant, which surprised me.

Sebastian hesitantly took a step in her direction. "I was hired by Grace to repair the weathered altar for the wedding. For some reason, I thought you would have known this."

"I did not." The queen glanced at me, and for the first time, it was not with a fiery glare that could burn holes in my eyes.

Had she hit her head?

I stepped forward, deciding to add my two cents. "Your Majesty, since the altar holds great historical significance, I thought it deserved expert attention, especially when I noticed it had been damaged from condensation. Sebastian's company is renowned for his craftsmanship. His online reviews speak for themselves."

"To be honest, I don't do the work with the wood myself any longer. I'm retiring soon," Sebastian said. "I do have a team of professionals I oversee and they do outstanding work. But I thought it would be rude to not come here and inspect the altar myself, especially considering we were old friends, Your Majesty."

Queen Annabelle nodded and did her own kind of inspecting, glancing at him from head to toe. "How thought-ful. It looks like the years have treated you kindly, too. And there is no need to be so formal."

"Thank you, Your Majesty," Sebastian said. "I mean, Annabelle."

We were watching their exchange like it was a soap opera. I wouldn't have believed it if I hadn't seen it with my own eyes, but Queen Annabelle appeared to be acting like a normal person. Even cordial, dare I say.

"I also wanted to express my condolences for the loss of King Henrik," Sebastian said. "He was the greatest king this country has ever seen. I sent flowers and a card."

The Queen looked surprised by that. "To be honest, it would have been impossible to read all the cards delivered to the palace, but I do appreciate the kind gesture."

"My pleasure—it's difficult losing someone you love," he said. "I'm a widower myself, after being married for thirty-eight years."

"I'm sorry for your loss," Queen Annabelle said.

"Life goes on . . ." Sebastian nodded. "Anyway, I won't take up any more of your time. It was such a pleasure to see you."

"And you as well," the queen said.

He turned to the door and—

"Sebastian," Queen Annabelle said. "If your schedule allows, perhaps we could have tea after you have finished with your work. Just to catch up."

That surprised everyone in the room.

He gave her a grateful smile. "I'd like that. Very much so."

Sebastian and I strolled through the royal grounds, toward the enclosed storage area where the altar was being kept. As we approached, a sudden chorus of voices called my name. I turned, then saw a group of people wielding cameras, all pointed directly at me.

In a spontaneous decision, I reached for Sebastian's arm, guiding him behind the building. "Better if we go this way, unless you're in the mood to go viral."

"Not particularly," he replied with a knowing smile. "Speaking of that, I saw you on the news. With Prince Oliver at Atomic Adventures."

I nodded. "They're always looking for a juicy story."

"I can certainly relate," Sebastian said, surprising me by opening up about his past. "It's no secret that I have the distinction of being the man the queen dated before she got married to King Henrik."

It had been quite surreal to see the usually unflappable

queen in a moment of uncertainty and weakness, but now it all made sense.

"You were in love with Queen Annabelle?" I asked.

Sebastian nodded, then shared a story that was both beautiful and heartbreaking. It was a revelation that left me genuinely surprised, how the course of someone's life could change in a heartbeat. Somehow, I related to him, navigating the complexities of relationships with a royal and the uncertainty that comes with them.

"Those were different times back then—a different story altogether," Sebastian said, as if sensing my surprise. "Maybe you'll have a more positive outcome than mine."

"Who said your story was over?" I countered. "Maybe there's an epilogue waiting for you."

Looking perplexed, Sebastian asked, "What do you mean?"

"Well . . . Queen Annabelle is single," I pointed out. "You're single. You just need to believe that there might be a chance between the two of you, and let the Universe sort out the details."

I couldn't help but smile at my newfound optimism, realizing I had unintentionally echoed Oliver's words almost verbatim. Maybe I was starting to believe that something special could happen between Oliver and me.

Sebastian glanced back at the palace, then a grin slowly formed on his face. "She did invite me to tea."

"Sounds like that is a wonderful place to start," I said.

He inspected the altar with a trained eye, assuring me

that the damage was minimal. He promised to send someone the next day to begin the restoration.

Sebastian and I returned to the palace and said our good-byes near the terrace. He headed inside, while I paused outside for a brief moment, taking a deep breath and hoping the rest of the day would be drama-free.

Then someone called my name.

Prince Theodore approached with an awkward shuffle, his hands fidgeting nervously. It had been a while since our last encounter, one fraught with tension over the tiara incident. I hoped this interaction would be different, perhaps more positive.

"I've been meaning to talk to you," Prince Theodore began, his voice wavering slightly, most likely from guilt, as he could scarcely look me in the eyes.

Before he could say anything else, Veronica joined us. "You have some nerve, Theo."

Prince Theodore visibly stiffened, well aware of Veronica's resentment, considering it was her tiara he had taken.

"Perfect timing," he said. "I was just about to apologize to Grace for my foolishness, but I owe you an apology as well."

Veronica's eyes narrowed, and she crossed her arms, waiting . . .

He sighed. "I'm sorry for taking the tiara and for—"

"Why did you do it?" Veronica asked, sounding like she would not make it so easy to forgive him. "What could have possibly possessed you to do such a thing?"

Theodore glanced around nervously, then leaned in and

confessed, "Because I am one-hundred percent against your marriage."

Veronica and I glanced at each other, each taken aback.

What on earth could he have against her?

Did he think she wasn't good enough for Oliver or his family?

Impossible. It must have been something else.

Veronica asked, "Not that we need your approval, but why don't you want us to marry?"

Prince Theodore hesitated, choosing his words carefully. "Multiple reasons, actually. For one, I don't believe in arranged marriages. I think they are absolutely ridiculous. People should only marry for love."

"Well, I agree with you there," I said. "But what does taking the tiara have to do with that?"

Prince Theodore sighed. "Mother is superstitious, and I thought if I created some problems, she would consider it an omen and call off the wedding. I was trying to help my brother."

I tilted my head. "What else have you done?"

Prince Theodore blinked. "Pardon me?"

"You specifically said you wanted to create *some* problems," I said, using air quotes. "What else have you done besides steal the tiara?"

Prince Theodore opened his mouth and closed it.

"Theo?" Veronica said. "There's something else, isn't there? Tell us. Immediately."

Prince Theodore ran his hand through his hair and tapped his foot on the cement before he finally confessed. "I created a fake back-up list of guests, then put them in Grace's file, knowing she would start inviting them whenever someone sent back an RSVP that said they could not attend. They were people I knew Mother didn't want to be there."

I just stared at him.

"I also swapped the doves for peacocks," Prince Theodore said.

Now, I wasn't blinking at all.

My muscles were completely frozen.

"Then I changed the candle order for the wedding ceremony from lavender to black licorice," he added.

Veronica looked like she wanted to remove his head, but opted for poking him in the chest. "I don't think I have ever been more livid with anyone in my entire life. You're a cruel human being, Theo."

"Wait a minute . . . I wasn't doing it to be cruel," he stammered. "I was only trying to disrupt things, and it simply got out of hand. I'm not proud of my behavior. I thought they were harmless mishaps, and I certainly did not take into consideration the repercussions that would fall on Grace. For that, I am truly sorry. I hope you both will forgive me. Especially you, Grace."

It was a lot to take in.

Prince Theo did sound sincere, which helped.

As for Veronica, she wasn't having it.

"Apology not accepted," she said. "Please leave."

Prince Theodore opened his mouth and—

"Leave!" Veronica said, pointing back to the palace.

With that, Theodore turned and walked away, leaving me and Veronica contemplating his words and actions.

Veronica sighed. "I'm so sorry you had to go through that, Grace. Theo has had a chip on his shoulder for a while now. He's always been cold to me, especially since our marriage was announced. He just can't stand being second in line to the throne. It is killing him. Honestly, I feel sorry for the man. I'm going to inform the queen of his behavior, so you are cleared of any wrongdoing. I can't stand injustice."

I nodded, watching him go back inside the palace. "I don't appreciate what he did, at all, but his apology seemed sincere. Also, remind me to never get on your bad side." I shook my head in amusement.

Veronica let out a laugh and slid her arm through mine, her voice a conspiratorial whisper, "I like to scare men now and then—to let them know who's in charge. Not like Queen Annabelle, of course. But enough about Theo. I just had a chat with Oliver, and he came up with a brilliant idea for you and me to have a little brainstorming session."

"Sounds like fun," I replied with enthusiasm. "What are we brainstorming?"

Veronica grinned mischievously. "How to nix the wedding."

"Sign me up," I responded a bit too eagerly, doing my best not to think of Oliver's kiss in the Tunnel of Love.

"Perfect," she said. "Oliver mentioned to me that in your past career, you were a strategic business manager and consultant, specializing in profitable collaborations."

"Yup." I nodded. "That was me."

"Well, that's exactly what we need—a collaboration," she said. "I have a master's degree in agricultural science from the University of Copenhagen. Queen Annabelle wants the arranged marriage because Verdana desperately needs the alliance between our two countries to ensure vital grain shipments for the future. Oliver is certain you and I can come up with an even better plan, thus eliminating the need for us to get married."

I grinned. "Oliver is a genius. We can definitely do this."

And so, that was exactly what we did for the next ten hours. We collaborated seamlessly, did our research, and generated ideas until we had a solid plan. A dozen phone calls later, we wrapped up, feeling proud of our accomplishment and confident our plan was foolproof. The next step was to present the idea to Queen Annabelle for her approval, then put all the pieces of the puzzle together to make the plan a reality. Hopefully, we could do that the next day.

As for the moment, I was ready to collapse.

I finished my nighttime routine—teeth brushed, face washed, and pajamas on. Just as I snuggled into the warmth of my cozy bed, my phone buzzed, and a familiar name illuminated the screen, spreading a smile across my face.

Oliver: Are you awake?

Me: I'm just settling into bed.

Oliver: Don't do that.

Me: Why not?

Oliver: Veronica told me you didn't eat much today.

Oliver: I am preparing something for you.

Me: Seriously?

Oliver: I don't joke about food.

Oliver: Come to the kitchen.

Me: Your mother will kill me.

Oliver: She's usually sleeping by now. She's an early riser. And since when are you afraid of Mother?

Me: I'm in my pajamas.

Oliver: Even better. I bet you look cute in them.

Me: Is the Prince of Verdana flirting with me?

Oliver: It appears so. How am I doing?

Me: Not bad.

Oliver: I'll have to work on that.

Oliver: Now, get your adorable self to the kitchen.

Me: I have no idea where it's located.

Oliver: How could you not know?

Me: There are seventy rooms in the palace.

Oliver: Seventy-seven to be exact.

Me: Even worse.

Oliver: Please come. Head toward the dining room, but then keep going and enter the second door on your left. Follow the smell from there. And put some Chapstick on your lips. Yes, that was a cryptic flirt.

That made me smile as I slipped back out of bed. Even though I was exhausted, the promise of food and another kiss from Oliver certainly got my attention. I threw my robe over my pajamas and headed out of my room. Navigating through the royal palace, I eventually stumbled upon the colossal kitchen. Oliver was standing by the stove, diligently mixing something in a pot.

"This kitchen is humongous!" I said, doing a three-sixty and looking around.

"This is actually the smallest of the two kitchens," he said. "The other one is three times the size and is used for large events and celebrations."

Oliver dipped a spoon into the pot, then lifted it toward me. "Careful, it's hot. Blow on it."

"This looks and smells amazing," I complimented, the delightful aroma wafting through the air. I leaned closer, then blew on it.

His charming smile widened. Then he pulled the spoon away before I could take a bite. "Still hot." His eyes danced with amusement. "Blow a little more."

I shook my head in amusement. "Sounds like you are the one who is overheating." I held his wrist so he could not pull the spoon away and sampled the macaroni and cheese. "Wow. That's good."

Oliver nodded proudly. "Glad you like it. I had to toss the first batch in the garbage." He chuckled. "It had a little too much salt."

We sat down to eat and indulged in the delicious meal.

"Veronica told me you came up with the perfect plan," Oliver said.

I nodded and wiped my mouth. "I think it's pretty solid. I would be surprised if Queen Annabelle did not approve of it. Veronica is amazing. She knows a great deal about agriculture. It blew my mind."

"She said the same about you," Oliver responded. "That your strategic planning and analysis skills were fantastic. You make a good team."

"*We* make a good team," I said.

Oliver arched an eyebrow. "Miss Fullerton, are you flirting with me?"

"It appears so," I smirked. "How am I doing?

He nodded. "Not bad."

"I'll have to work on that," I said.

"You don't have to work on a thing," Oliver said, pulling me closer for a kiss. "You are perfect to me."

I tried not to blush as we finished our meal. Then Oliver suggested a walk under the stars. The night was enchanting, and we strolled hand in hand under the moonlight.

"Hey, how are the Tuscany Twins and Aunt Honey doing at Atomic Adventures?" I inquired, genuinely interested. "Any updates from them?"

"I talked to Aunt Honey earlier today," Oliver said. "They're having a blast and extended their stay another day. Enzo's apparently obsessed with that log ride and keeps dragging her back on it."

A chuckle escaped me. "Those two are a riot—the age difference doesn't seem to matter at all. Some things are just meant to be."

Oliver nodded, a playful glint in his eyes. "Aunt Honey thought the same about us, by the way. She asked how we're doing."

Curious, I prodded, "And what did you tell her?"

"I told her we're doing great," he confessed, sincerity in

his voice. "And that I can't get you out of my head when we're apart. She thought that was a good sign."

"Because it is," I admitted, feeling a warmth between us with each honest word. "I feel the same way."

"Speaking of us . . ." Oliver pulled me to a stop. "I have a question for you, if you don't mind."

"Okay . . ." I turned to him, having no idea what he was going to ask. "Go for it."

He looked at me with a hint of seriousness, appearing to be searching for the right words. "Under the right circumstances, if the wedding were canceled, and if you had a job you truly loved, would you ever . . ."

Okay, don't leave me hanging, Oliver.

I tilted my head to the side. "Would I ever what?"

"Would you ever consider living here in Verdana?" he asked.

I hesitated for a moment, surprised by the question, but also delighted that he'd brought it up. The truth was, I had thought about it.

On more than a few occasions . . .

As hard as I tried, I could not stop the smile from forming on my face.

I nodded. "I believe I would."

Oliver's face lit up with joy. "I was hoping you'd say that." He drew me closer, until our lips met in a sweet, lingering kiss. We pulled apart when he both heard approaching echoes of laughter.

In a rush, Oliver seized my hand and whisked me behind a dense row of bushes.

"Who do you think it is?" I whispered.

"Call me crazy, but it sounds like Mother," he replied in a hushed tone.

Panic crept in. "Oh, no . . ."

The voices of Queen Annabelle and Sebastian grew nearer, obviously sharing the same idea of a moonlit stroll. Had they spent the entire day together? My mind raced as their voices approached.

"You are quite rambunctious for your age," Queen Annabelle said. "Do you really think I enjoy your mouth on me like that?"

Excuse me? Did I hear that correctly?

What exactly were the queen and Sebastian doing?

My eyes widened, and I turned to Oliver.

He just shrugged and tried to get a better look over the bushes.

"Oh, for heaven's sake—quit biting me and just go pee," the queen added, her voice carrying a light-hearted tone. "Not you, Sebastian."

A shared laugh rippled through the air between them, and I couldn't help but find their interaction heartwarming. The light-hearted tone and jovial laughter from the queen was a shock to my system.

Oliver suppressed a laugh, covering his mouth with his hand.

I also fought back laughter, peeking in their direction as they basked in the moonlight. Queen Annabelle was walking Freddie, confirming Dante's insight that she loved the dog.

"I don't remember the last time I heard her laugh like that," Oliver whispered, his surprise evident. "It's all thanks to you."

As we listened to their conversation, it became clear that our secret rendezvous might have unintended consequences. Oliver pulled me closer, neither of us moving. My nose was itching and I prayed I would not sneeze. They were now directly on the other side of the tall hedges.

"I really didn't expect this," Sebastian said. "My only intention was to inspect the altar, and to hopefully say hello to you. But now, here I am, having spent most of the day and evening with the Queen of Verdana. I can't tell you how wonderful it has been to see you."

"Do you really see me as the queen after all we've been through?" she asked.

Sebastian's reply was sincere. "It's a surreal feeling that is very hard to describe, knowing you are the queen. When I saw you on television, I always wondered what my life would have been like if we had married."

"I've thought the same thing, but you know I grew to love King Henrik with all my heart," Queen Annabelle admitted.

"Of course—just as I loved my wife dearly," Sebastian replied. "I do find something quite odd, though. Or maybe fascinating would be the right word."

"What is that?" the queen asked.

"If the rumors about Grace and Prince Oliver are true, but he's going to marry Princess Veronica, it's almost as if history would repeat itself all over again," Sebastian said.

"Yes—I suppose you're right," admitted Queen Annabelle.

Sebastian's revelation lingered in the air, casting a shadow over us that was far greater than that of the moon. Was it wishful thinking that the queen would actually approve our future plan for Verdana? Was I merely caught up in a romantic reverie, or was there really a fairy tale waiting to unfold for me?

Sensing the uncertainty surrounding us, Oliver gently lifted my chin with his finger, locking eyes with me after Queen Annabelle and Sebastian had drifted away from us.

"Remember what I told you before," Oliver reassured me. "I believe in you. I believe in us. This is going to work."

I certainly hoped he was right.

Because I was falling for him.

The promise of our love story felt both enchanting and elusive, leaving me to wonder if my heart's desires were on the road to fulfillment or destined to remain a wistful dream.

Chapter Nineteen

PRINCE OLIVER

An air of both anticipation and tension enveloped the conference room, each passing moment intensifying the weight of the impending emergency meeting with Mother. In my heart, I had faith in the plan devised by Grace and Veronica. It was a sentiment that transcended personal gain. Their strategy promised not only to benefit me but also to usher in positive change and security for the people of Verdana.

"Mother will join us any minute now," I said, glancing at Veronica, Adriana, Theo, and Grace who were seated in front of me at the long conference table. Dante stood nearby, against the wall, ready to take any notes. There was an empty chair at the head of the table for Mother.

"This meeting is pivotal, as you all know," I added. "Grace and Veronica pored over the details of their brilliant plan for over ten hours yesterday, laying the foundation for a coalition that is absolutely genius."

"Nevertheless, dealing with Mother always introduces an element of unpredictability," Adriana said.

"That is an understatement," I said with a chuckle. "That is why we must do everything in our power to ensure Mother recognizes the merit in this proposal. The sole objective is to convince her to call off the wedding. We cannot afford to let her leave this room without doing so."

"It's going to happen," Veronica chimed in with complete confidence in her voice. "Speaking of the Queen, I think I hear her coming."

"It's showtime," I said.

Henri opened the door, allowing Mother to enter the conference room with Freddie comfortably cradled in her arms. She scanned the surroundings, then honed in on Grace, her gaze narrowing with a disapproving edge.

"Why is *she* here?" Mother questioned. "I explicitly expressed my desire for the two of you to be nowhere near each other."

"Grace is the reason this meeting is even happening," I explained.

"Grace is the reason for the turmoil in my life," Mother said. "Everything was sailing smoothly until she arrived in Verdana like a hurricane, destroying everything in its path."

An uneasy feeling crept over me as the atmosphere became charged with tension. We were losing control of the meeting before it even started. I needed to step in before the two of them dropped to the floor and wrestled.

"This meeting is important to all of us, Mother," I said. "Please have a seat. We won't take much of your time."

Mother glanced at Grace. "Are you sure Grace will feel comfortable in the same room as a dictator?"

"Enough, Mother!" Adriana said, pushing out her chair and standing. "We are all quite tired of you blaming Grace for everything that does not go according to your plan. She has done nothing wrong. In fact, Grace is absolutely wonderful. And just so you know, she is not the person responsible for all the so-called destruction you continue to speak of."

"Then who is?" Mother asked.

Adriana pointed to Theo. "Your son is the mastermind behind all the chaos you've been lamenting about."

Mother gasped. "I don't believe it."

Theo, under the spotlight, fumbled for words, and his audible gulp reverberated through the room.

"It's the truth," Adriana continued, unfazed. "Stealing the tiara was only a small part of it. Theo also concocted a fabricated list of wedding guests to invite that would make you cringe, and slyly inserted them into Grace's file so she would invite them all."

Mother's breathing seemed more pronounced as she glared at Theo.

"But wait, there's more . . ." Adriana held up a finger. "Those peacocks in your garden and the black licorice candles for the wedding? All courtesy of your loving son, Theo." She pointed accusingly at him. "*He* has been the pain in your backside, Mother. Not Grace."

"Yes, it was me," Theo promptly said. "I'm not proud. I've apologized to Veronica and Grace, and explained my reasons, though not everyone has been receptive to my apologies."

Veronica huffed. "How about you let me shave your head and we'll call it even?"

Theo reached up to touch his perfect hair and swallowed hard.

"Why would you do this?" Mother asked him. "I don't understand."

"Because I do not approve of this wedding," Theo said.

"And now you have the truth," Adriana said. "Please stop being so cruel to Grace."

"If anything, you should be thanking her," I said.

Mother stared at me. "Thanking her for what?"

"You seemed to have forgotten the tremendous amount of donations she helped bring in for the gala," I said. "And through the kindness of her heart, she brought you this beautiful dog and gave it Father's middle name." I gestured to Freddie. "Because of Grace, you reconnected with Sebastian after all these years. These are all delightful strokes of good fortune that will only enhance your life. And do not deny it, because it was clearly evident on your stroll through the garden last night."

Okay, maybe I shouldn't have added that last part.

Mother stopped stroking Freddie, and her eyes went wide. "How would you know about that?"

"It doesn't matter how I know, because there was nothing wrong with what you were doing," I said, looking to change the subject. "You deserve to be happy. We all do."

After a moment of reflection, Mother cleared her throat,

her gaze softening. She opened her mouth and closed it, the pause hanging in the air as she grappled with the words that seemed to elude her.

Finally, she nodded and said, "In that case, I need to take back many of my words. Apparently, I was in the wrong, but how would I know my son was sabotaging his brother's wedding?"

The conference room was quiet.

Was Mother being vulnerable for once?

I could not believe she'd just admitted that.

She glanced over at Grace and blinked a few times, nodding. "Grace, please accept my apology. I admit my actions were far from royal-worthy, and knowing the truth, I must admit I'm not proud of how I have treated you. Thank you for Freddie. I didn't properly express my gratitude for such a delightful companion. You can all see I've become quite attached to this adorable dog. He's a source of joy and entertainment for me, no doubt."

Grace smiled. "Apology accepted. And you're welcome. Freddie seems to be attached to you as well, which makes me happy. That was my hope when I got him for you."

Mother nodded. "Well then, I'm glad we got that cleared up." She glared at Theo. "You and I have a long conversation pending." She turned, as if she were about to leave.

"Mother—we haven't finished here," I said. "We called this meeting because Grace and Veronica have been working on a very important project together. They need to share their findings with you. It's very important. Please, take a seat."

Mother raised an eyebrow, her attention briefly diverted by Freddie's playful squirming in her arms as she sat down. "Well, let's make it quick. I have a full calendar, and I wanted to plan something special and private tomorrow for the one-year anniversary of your father's passing. Maybe we could do an early dinner on the terrace, just the family, and then take a walk to his favorite spot on the property."

"That sounds perfect," Adriana said.

"I would love that," Theo added.

"Great—we can work out the details later," I said. "Let's get back to the main reason we are here, Grace and Veronica's project. Are you ladies ready?"

They both nodded.

I leaned closer to Grace and whispered, "You're up. Knock it out of the park."

Grace smiled and joined Veronica at the front of the conference room.

"Thank you for your time, Your Majesty," Veronica said, then clicked the remote to start the PowerPoint presentation.

The first frame displayed an image of a vibrant Earth globe encircled by golden wheat stalks, bearing the words "The International Grain Coalition" in bold. Below that, the slogan read, "From Fields to Tables, Together We Flourish." Veronica advanced the presentation to bullet points that conveyed the essence of their proposal.

"Your Majesty," Grace began, "we present to you the International Grain Coalition. Imagine, a collaborative effort among multiple European nations, working together to ensure food security for all."

Mother blinked twice. "What does this have to do with the wedding?"

"You will find out in a moment," I said, trying to be patient with her. "Let's continue, since you are pressed for time, Mother."

She gave me a suspicious look but didn't reply.

"As you can see," Veronica continued, advancing the slide, "forming this coalition would diversify our grain sources, reducing the risk that any single nation's instability could threaten our food supply." She clicked the remote, revealing a world map dotted with various country flags in Europe. "We've already reached out to the ministers of agriculture in these key European nations, including Spain, Italy, and France. They are open to exploring the idea further and expressed their enthusiasm about the possibility."

The next slide showcased economic and political benefits.

"A diversified network means you're not putting all your eggs, or more accurately, wheat, and rice, in one basket," Grace said. "It's not just about food security. It's about nations standing tall together. It could be compared to a version of the European Union, but one that is solely focused on food. Your economies become interconnected and resilient to external pressures. A rising tide lifts all boats, so the coalition could also jointly plan and distribute their excess capacities to be shared with under-privileged nations. It's people helping people, Your Majesty, sharing and trading their natural resources, just like many years ago. A win-win situation for all."

They had certainly done their homework and covered every aspect of the alliance that Mother had hoped for. I really didn't see how she could say no to such a plan that would benefit everyone involved.

"Oh, and there's one more perk that I'm sure will make you smile," Grace revealed, casting a smile in my direction. "After crunching the numbers a few times, I'm confident that the money saved from the alliance could fund the creation of a new Royal Academy of Arts. Verdana has been longing for such a cultural gem for far too long."

I felt a lump forming in my throat as her words sank in. "That would be incredible. Do you genuinely think it's achievable?"

She had not mentioned that to me before, and it was a wonderful surprise.

Grace nodded, her expression unwavering. "I do."

Her thoughtfulness left me speechless.

This was beyond my expectations; she just kept surpassing them, leaving me utterly touched by her considerate actions.

Ten minutes later, and with a final click of the remote to return to the first page of their presentation with the image of the globe, Veronica wrapped it up by saying, "This International Grain Coalition isn't just a pact; it's a promise to foster collaboration, ensure food stability, and strengthen the bonds between our kingdoms. We've done the research,

Your Majesty. We've talked to advisors. We can make this happen. All we need is your blessing."

All heads in the conference room turned toward Mother. She sat there thinking as she stroked Freddie's head.

"Well?" I said. "What do you think?"

"You're doing this because you want me to cancel the wedding," Mother said confidently, then glanced at Grace suspiciously.

"Yes," I said. "But the people of Verdana will benefit tremendously. You have always argued that our marriage was critical to cement an alliance that would ensure vital grain shipments continued to sustain Verdana for decades to come. Veronica and Grace have crafted the perfect plan, surpassing even the potential benefits of an alliance with Veronica's country. And, more importantly, we don't have to get married to see it come to fruition."

Mother continued to contemplate, taking far too much time, which heightened my concern. How could she not see the wisdom and benefit in this alternative?

"I agree the plan has merit," Mother finally said. "And I can see the bride is just as much against it as the groom, but we can't just cancel the wedding. We have almost a thousand people who will be in attendance, people coming from all over the world. Dignitaries, royals, celebrities, news outlets documenting every moment. Imagine what the people would say if we just canceled the wedding at the last minute."

"Imagine what they would say if we got a divorce a year later," I countered.

Mother blinked twice. "Pardon me?"

"Actually, I would give it six months at the most," Veronica said with fantastic timing as she turned to Mother. "I love Oliver like a brother. The thing is, I believe I can find true love, without sacrificing my country or yours."

I pointed to Veronica. "You see there? We agree ours would not be a happy marriage at all."

Like a well-timed choreography, Adriana jumped in to say, "Theo and I agree, Mother. It's time to move into modern times and discard the antiquated practice of arranged marriages. The happiness and compatibility of individuals should take precedence over outdated traditions, and that includes for me. You've been pushing me toward Prince Ivan, but he simply doesn't align with my preferences. In fact, while we're candidly discussing relationships, I might as well mention that I already have a date with a Greek gentleman who is outside the royal spectrum."

"Demetrio?" Grace inquired.

Adriana nodded with a smile. "Yes."

"Who is Demetrio?" Mother asked, sitting up. "You're not referring to the fashion designer, are you?"

Adriana nodded and seized the opportunity to strengthen her case. "Yes. Demetrio is a successful and accomplished individual in his own right. This goes to show that even in matters of the heart, individuals should have the freedom to choose based on personal compatibility and shared values, rather than being confined to predetermined alliances."

"I agree," I said. "It's time for us, as a royal family, to embrace the idea that true fulfillment comes from genuine connections, not merely the titles or status of our potential partners."

Mother absorbed this, and for the first time, I sensed a shift in her thoughts. Perhaps, just perhaps, genuine happiness could prevail over tradition.

After what felt like an eternity, she finally broke the silence.

"Very well," Mother said, her voice tinged with a hint of uncertainty as she continued to absentmindedly stroke Freddie.

Mother would make an excellent poker player. She was a master at keeping her emotions veiled behind a composed facade. I contained my excitement until I was given the clarification I needed because her response was vague.

I leaned forward in my chair. "Very well, *what?*"

With a sigh, Mother conceded, "I hope I don't regret this, but we can cancel the wedding."

"Yes!" I said, pumping my first in the air as a surge of relief washed over me. "Thank you. You won't regret it." I was over the moon, and smiled at Grace, then Veronica, happy to know I could move on with my life.

"Grace, you'll need to get the message out to everyone on the attendee list ASAP," Mother instructed. "Then contact the vendors to let them know their services will no longer be required. There is no need for elaborate excuses. Just apologize for the inconvenience. We'll issue a press release to cover the details. Oliver will ensure you're paid in full, and then you'll be free to return to the United States. Once again, I apologize." She pushed her chair out and stood. "Now, there is something else that requires my attention, but I believe we've covered everything related to this matter."

Little did Mother know we were far from wrapping up this topic. An imminent challenge loomed ahead for me, one that I deemed monumental, given her persistent expectations for me to wed someone of noble lineage. How would Mother respond when I told her that the only person I would even consider for marriage was Grace?

Chapter Twenty

GRACE

The last twenty-four hours had been a chaotic blur, contacting attendees and vendors until late in the night, followed by going through the wedding files, multiple times, to make sure nothing was missed. I was sure there were no loose ends and nobody sabotaging my work. The only thing left was the press release the palace would send out, but at least that part was not on me.

The wedding had been officially canceled!

I finally emerged from my room, ready for some much-needed relaxation with Oliver. I walked through the opulent halls of the palace toward the pool, my thoughts consumed by him and our potential future together. I was eager to find out exactly where our relationship stood.

I stopped beside the display case that featured the Fabergé egg, when the man of my thoughts and dreams walked toward me, clad in a white robe and flip-flops.

He had a mischievous grin playing on his lips as he

glanced at the turquoise cover-up sarong I had over my matching bikini.

"What's with that big smile on your face?" I asked.

"That happens when I think of you, of course," he replied, his eyes twinkling with playful charm. He glanced around, then leaned in to plant a kiss on my lips.

"Stop," I whispered, even though I really didn't want him to. "I have gotten into enough trouble for one lifetime."

"I can't make any promises once I get you in the pool," Oliver said with a chuckle as we walked in that direction.

We didn't get far before I asked, "Do you hear that rumbling sound?"

Oliver stopped, his head cocked to the side as he listened intently. "Call me crazy, but that sounds like my brother's motorcycle."

"You mean Prince Augustus?" I asked.

He nodded. "Family and friends call him August. It's odd, though, because the last I heard, he was on a motorcycle journey across South America." The mysterious rumbling sound deepened, and Oliver ushered me into the nearby tea room to peer out the window.

A tall man clad in black leather dismounted a sleek motorcycle, then removed his helmet, revealing hair almost identical to Oliver's. As he gracefully slid off his leather jacket and laid it across the handlebars, I caught the contours of his muscles through the snug black T-shirt. I couldn't help but marvel at the family resemblance, although he was built bigger than Oliver, with wider shoulders and a very impressive frame.

"That's him," Oliver said, then turned to me. "Get ready for some entertainment. Mother and August don't exactly see eye to eye on anything."

"More family drama?" I teased. "It's like this is some royal reality show."

"You have no idea," he replied, a wry smile playing on his lips, then gestured back to the hall. "Time for a dip."

The colossal Olympic-sized outdoor swimming pool at the heart of the royal palace was a sanctuary of luxury. It was surrounded by marble columns and adorned with intricate mosaics and tall, lush palm trees, just like in the old Roman Empire movies.

An employee had already prepared for our arrival, placing two inviting margaritas on a table nestled among a long row of plush lounge chairs.

I untied my sarong, and Oliver wasted no time, tracing the contours of my figure with his gaze. I swallowed hard, a blend of nerves and excitement, as I took a sip of the perfectly chilled margarita.

"To being unemployed," I declared with a laugh, raising my glass.

Oliver chuckled and took a step closer, clinking my glass. "Don't you worry about that. You are simply in between jobs. Besides, I came up with a couple of promising ideas for employment that I think you'll like. We can chat about that later."

"I look forward to hearing about them," I said. "It is kind of weird, though. You brought me all the way to Europe to plan a wedding that's not happening anymore, for which I was paid a ridiculous amount of money." I couldn't resist probing, seeking reassurance amidst the uncertainty. "And yet, you still believe in us?"

"Now, more than ever," he said without hesitation. "And there will be plenty of time to discuss that later in the day as well, when we have more privacy. Let's put on some sunscreen and get it in the water. It's time to play and have some fun."

"Sounds good," I said.

Oliver untied his robe and dropped it on the chair. I couldn't help but admire every inch of him, from the chiseled chest to the toned arms, down to those solid navy blue swim trunks that accentuated his muscular legs.

I grabbed a bottle of sunscreen, feeling the warmth of the sun on my skin as I squeezed the lotion onto my hands. The air was charged with unspoken chemistry between us as we applied the sunscreen in silence, occasionally stealing furtive glances at each other.

A moment later, Oliver's voice broke through my thoughts. "Let me get your back."

"Oh . . . okay." I gulped, feeling a mixture of nervous anticipation and exhilaration of having his hands on my body.

With a deep breath, I turned around, attempting to steady my breath as his hands touched my shoulders, slowly and intently. Closing my eyes, I savored the sensation of his touch, reveling in the electrifying connection that seemed to spark between us with each inch of my skin his hands covered. Oliver's hands slid down the middle of my back, lower and lower.

Keep doing that. Don't stop.

But then I worried I was enjoying it way too much, and my nerves took over when I blurted out, "What did you do last night while I was working? Did you miss me a little?"

"I think you know the answer to that question," he said. "As for what I did, I was putting the finishing touches on your portrait. I am almost done."

"How could you do that without me?" I asked.

"It wasn't difficult at all," Oliver said. "I have memorized every inch of you." He guided me back around until I was facing him again.

"And what was your favorite part?" I asked with a flirty smile.

Oliver glanced at my mouth. "That's easy—your lips. Although, I am thinking I have some new favorite parts."

I wanted to grab the man and kiss him right there, but I knew it wasn't the place, especially if Queen Annabella came out. There would be plenty of time for that later. At least, I hoped there would be.

"Let me get your back," I said, although I wondered if it was such a good idea to have my hands on his body.

I squirted sunscreen into my hand as he turned around, exposing his broad shoulders and back. Starting behind his neck, I moved with deliberate strokes, tracing the firmness of his muscles, enjoying the softness of his skin. The intimacy of the moment made me wonder if he'd mind if I continued this tactile exploration of his body for a few hours. My hands slid over his skin, from the middle of his back to his sides, lingering near the top of his waist-hugging trunks.

"All good," I managed to say, placing the sunscreen on the table before I self-combusted. "We need to get into the water now. I'm ready to cool off a little bit."

Oliver chuckled. "I agree."

We both stepped into the pool and worked our way further out, until the water was just above our waists.

"Do you come out here often?" I asked.

"Not as much as I would like," he said. "I usually do laps."

"Me, too," I said. "And no, I don't want to race, if you're thinking of another bet. Judging by the muscles in your legs, I won't stand a chance."

"Your mind reading skills are quite impressive," Oliver said. "It's a little scary."

"Be very afraid," I said. "Now, if you want to see who can hold their breath underwater the longest, I will take that bet. If I win, you'll share the video of you doing the 'Macarena' with the world."

He shook his head, amused. "Okay, Miss Predictable. I will take that bet. But if you lose, you owe me a ten-minute kiss."

"Sounds like I win either way," I smirked, diving underwater.

Seconds later, Oliver plunged under the water in front of me, his eyes wide open.

I wiggled my fingers at him.

He waved back with a closed-mouth grin.

I fixated on his determined gaze, vowing silently to emerge victorious as my competitive spirit kicked in. His features remained resolute, bubbles escaping from his nose as he maintained his submerged stance. I focused on his regal features, his jawline, his eyes, anything to distract myself from the seconds ticking away under water.

It felt like an eternity, and I was losing hope. Luckily, just when the pressure in my chest reached its peak, Oliver jumped up and broke the surface of the water. I prepared to claim my victory, however, before I could make a move to go back up, his powerful hands reached for me, grabbed me by the waist, and pulled me out of the water and against his body. I found myself pressed against him, water droplets trailing down our faces. I was breathless, not just from the challenge, but from the proximity that took me by surprise.

"You win," he said, his playful eyes flickering with a hint of something more before his lips met mine in a kiss that defied the playfulness of our contest.

His mouth moved against mine with a passion that caught me off guard, igniting a fire within that mirrored the heat of the sun on my back. Our wet bodies slid against each other, with every touch, every movement, every dance of our tongues almost too much for me to handle.

Unfortunately, just like that, the kiss ended.

"There y'all are!" Aunt Honey said, startling us both. "Looks like someone is having way too much fun without me."

We glanced in her direction, both of us out of breath.

Aunt Honey pulled off her beach cover-up, set it on the lounge chair, and stepped into the water.

There was one big problem, though.

If Aunt Honey was there, that only meant one thing . . .

Like clockwork, Enzo and Renzo strolled into the pool area.

"Cousin Oliver!" Renzo called. "And beautiful Grace!"

"What a pleasant surprise!" Enzo said. "Great minds think alike!"

They both slipped off their robes simultaneously to reveal lean, bronzed bodies, both wearing matching Speedos with the colors of the Italian flag.

Enzo entered the water first and moved straight toward Aunt Honey. "What a vision of beauty you are. I could kiss you all day."

"What a coincidence—my calendar is wide open, sugar," she said, fanning her face as he moved in and planted his lips on hers.

I leaned closer to Oliver and whispered, "A lot has certainly transpired between those two since we saw them at Atomic Adventures."

"You're not kidding," Oliver said. "So much for privacy."

"Looks like our party is just getting started!" Renzo said.

Veronica and Adriana approached two of the lounge chairs. Prince Theodore was the last to join us, pulling off his shirt and parking himself on one of the lounge chairs next to mine.

"And by the way—you cheated," I said, even though I didn't mind one bit. "You lost the bet, therefore you shouldn't have been kissing me. What do you have to say for yourself?"

Oliver scratched the side of his head. "I guess I misunderstood the stakes." He laughed.

"Uh-huh . . ." I pointed toward our things on the lounge chairs. "Go post the video."

"I don't have my phone with me," Oliver said.

"Then go get it," I said, playfully pushing him back toward the edge of the pool. "A bet is a bet."

"And my word is my word," he said, leading me back out of the water.

While Oliver went to get his phone, I dried off and relaxed on my lounge chair, taking a sip of my margarita.

"I would be happy to move if you are uncomfortable with my presence," Prince Theodore said as he intently watched Veronica walk along the pool's edge in her teal bathing suit.

I smiled. "Relax. Life is short, and besides, I have already forgiven you."

He nodded, thinking. "You are a good person, Miss Fullerton."

"Please, call me Grace," I said good-naturedly.

"Thank you, Grace. And please call me Theo. It seems my brother has taken quite a liking to you and I hope that means you'll be around a lot more," Theodore replied.

Theodore's gaze didn't pull away from Princess Veronica.

He was watching her like a hawk.

There was something in his eyes that told a story . . .

It didn't take long before the realization hit me.

"How long have you been in love with Princess Veronica?" I asked.

Theodore craned his neck in my direction, blinking rapidly. "Pardon me?"

How had I not noticed this before?

His grumpy behavior appeared to have nothing to do with being second in line to the throne, but with the fact that Oliver was going to marry the woman he loved. Now it all made sense!

"You love her," I whispered. "Princess Veronica . . ."

A few seconds later, he nodded, then watched Veronica dip into the water. "Not that I can do anything about it. Even now, with the wedding called off, I am far too young for her, plus her parents would never approve. Besides, I am not the only one in love with her."

What was he talking about?

I followed his gaze toward the far end of the pool.

Prince Augustus stood there.

And he was eyeing Veronica in the water.

Wait, both brothers were in love with Veronica? But then Oliver had been the chosen one to marry her? Had August returned because he knew Veronica was single and available again?

Talk about a soap opera . . .

Still dressed in his leather motorcycle pants and black T-shirt, August walked toward Adriana and gave her a warm embrace.

"I'm happy you're back, big brother," she said with a big smile. "I missed you."

"Cousin August!" Renzo called out. "Good to see you!"

"Come join us," Enzo said.

One person did not look as eager to see August.

Princess Veronica.

She glared at him, then ducked her head under water in the pool, and began swimming laps. What was going on there? More drama, I could only imagine.

The employee returned with a tray of margaritas, placing them on the tables in between the lounge chairs. The camouflaged speakers around the perimeter suddenly played upbeat European dance music.

"This place certainly got lively in a hurry," Oliver said as he returned with the phone in his hand. "You'll be happy to know that I posted the video." He scrolled on his phone, and turned the screen, in order for me to see it.

"Uh-huh . . . and how do I know that's really live on social media?" I asked.

"Check on your phone or just give it a little time," Oliver said. "When you hear Mother screaming my name at the top of her lungs, then you'll know we have another viral video among us." He chuckled.

"Well, get ready for the world to fall head over heels for you after they get a glimpse of this," I teased with a playful grin. "This will humanize you and make you even more likable."

Oliver folded his arms, feigning offense. "Hold on, I thought I was already Mr. Likable."

I leaned in, pretending to scrutinize him. "Not bad at all."

Just then, August strolled over and enveloped Theodore and Oliver in a hug. It seemed like the trio had a solid camaraderie going on.

Oliver quirked an eyebrow at August. "What brings you back? I thought you were busy riding across South America."

August nodded with a triumphant grin. "I finished that amazing journey last week. Eight thousand miles. I had been visiting a friend in Cypress the last few days and came back since Mother called me yesterday and told me she was going to honor Father with a special dinner this evening. Either way, I had to return, since I would not miss the impending wedding festivities."

"I guess you haven't heard," Oliver said. "The wedding has been called off."

August, slightly taken aback, turned to look at Veronica in the water before facing Oliver again. "I had no idea."

There went my theory of August rushing back because Veronica was back on the market. Why hadn't he asked why the wedding was canceled?

Interesting . . .

"Pardon my manners," Oliver apologized. "August, meet Grace."

"Ah, the wedding planner extraordinaire!" August greeted me with a twinkle in his eye. "You're quite a celebrity in our country already. Delighted to finally make your acquaintance, Grace."

"The pleasure is mine, Your Highness," I said, wobbling through an awkward curtsy. "I swear, I'll nail it, eventually."

"No pressure at all," August assured with a grin. "Feel free to drop the formality. Call me August."

I nodded, relieved. "Sounds good."

"You certainly are entertaining," August said. "I saw the video of you and Oliver at the gala, and the other one at Atomic Ventures. Never a dull moment."

I laughed. "That is an understatement."

"Cousin August!" Renzo called out. "Please come in. The water is amazing!"

Oliver gestured toward the pool. "Looks like a wardrobe change is in order."

August shrugged nonchalantly. "I've got a much easier solution." He peeled off his T-shirt and then unzipped his leather pants.

My eyes widened.

The man was not the least bit shy.

Oliver had mentioned that August was a free spirit, but was he really about to strip down to his birthday suit in front of everyone? My margarita became my new best friend as the show began. August pulled his pants off, revealing black, square-cut briefs underneath. The man was like a Greek God, a tower of muscles. I continued to watch with admiration as he folded his clothes and neatly placed them on the lounge chair. Then he walked to the edge of the pool with Theodore, and dove into the water.

He was attractive—any woman with decent vision could see that. But those devilishly handsome looks would only get him so far. Oliver, on the other hand, was the complete package. Smart. Funny. Generous. And gorgeous as well. August was like candy to the eyes, but he was no comparison to the man I loved.

I froze, analyzing my thoughts.

Wait a minute . . .

The realization hit me like a ton of bricks.

I love Oliver.

My mouth dropped open.

"Okay—I think you're drooling," Oliver said with a chuckle as he grabbed his margarita. "And just so you know, I'm not offended or jealous. It's a common response when women meet August. I had become accustomed to it many years ago, since we were both teenagers."

I shook my head, taking a long sip of my margarita, attempting to gather my thoughts. "It's not that. Yes, he's gorgeous, but I was just hit with a stunning revelation that caught me off guard. I'm simply trying to process it."

"What's going on? Can I do anything to help?" he asked, his brows furrowing.

I let out a snort, unable to contain my frustration. "You've already done enough, Mr. Trouble-Maker. You're the reason I find myself in this predicament."

His confusion deepened. "What did I do? I don't get it."

Looking into his eyes, I blurted it out without thinking, "I love you."

Oliver's eyes widened, and for a moment, he remained silent. I didn't expect him to reciprocate immediately, but a simple acknowledgment would have sufficed. Something that showed he appreciated those three words that came from my mouth. Instead, he stood there like a statue, leaving me hanging. This was rather embarrassing, to say the least.

From my perspective, it was also a terrible sign.

A sudden clearing of the throat startled me.

I swung around, and it was my turn to freeze.

Oh no . . .

Queen Annabelle.

And she had just overheard me declaring my love to her son.

There was only one thing I wished for at that moment.

That the ground would open up and swallow me whole.

Chapter Twenty-One

PRINCE OLIVER

Nothing could have rivaled the joy of hearing Grace confess her love to me. It was an unexpected revelation that set my heart racing. However, the euphoria was smothered by the sudden presence of Mother, who now seemed to be on the verge of fainting again.

My mind raced, desperately trying to map out a route through this delicate situation. The declaration of my own love for Grace would have to wait for a more romantic setting and moment, hopefully private.

"Your Majesty," Henri interjected at the most opportune moment.

I mentally applauded him for the interruption.

Mother swiveled on her heels to face him. "Yes?"

"Miss DuPont is waiting for you in the sitting room," Henri said.

"Thank you, Henri," Mother replied. "Let her know I will be there shortly. Please offer her tea."

Henri nodded and turned back toward the palace.

I breathed a silent sigh of relief, but had to ask, "When did Miss DuPont return from France?" I thought it would be best to redirect the conversation away from the topic of love.

"This morning," Mother responded. "I contacted her a few days ago and asked her to return when we were having a few issues, but she hadn't been informed about the wedding being canceled. Not a problem. I'll use the time to discuss the annual parade with her."

"I'm *so* glad she's here! I have something of hers I found with the wedding files. I'll go get it." Grace wrapped herself in her sarong and scurried away before either of us could utter a word.

"Not even a cheetah could have escaped faster," Mother commented, observing Grace's swift retreat. "It appears as though we need to talk."

"Pardon me, Your Majesty," Dante interjected.

I could kiss him.

His timing was impeccable.

"Yes?" Mother said.

Dante gestured to me. "If I may have a word with Prince Oliver."

"How can I help you?" I asked.

Please, take your time . . .

"Edward and Conrad from Verdana Construction have been urgently trying to reach you," he said. "They would like to speak with you at your earliest convenience. Today, if possible."

"Thank you—I'll be in touch with them shortly," I said. Dante left, and I picked up my phone from the table. "I need to make this phone call, Mother."

"What business do you have with Verdana Construction?" Mother asked.

I was hoping she would ask.

It was much better talking about my plans that were not related to matters of the heart. The best thing I could do was be honest with Mother, to be crystal clear that there was no way I would abandon this project now that Grace had planted the seed of possibility in my head.

"Conrad is the general manager with Verdana Construction—Edward is the lead architect," I said. "We're going to discuss construction of the new Royal Academy of Arts, timeframe, design, budget, and so on."

"Don't you think you are acting prematurely on this?" Mother asked. "It would be wise to wait until the coalition is in place before moving forward."

"I agree—I'm not signing anything just yet," I said. "I merely want to get the ball rolling and see what we are working with. You can't fault me for being excited about the project." I grinned. "I'd be happy to discuss it with you after dinner. I really need to make this call."

Mother eyed me suspiciously. "Very well."

Disappointment lingered as my pool time with Grace was abruptly cut short. The knowledge of her love for me only heightened the desire to be with her. I found myself yearning to tell her that I loved her in return, but that would have to be after dinner.

After showering and dressing, I walked toward my office to do a video conference with Verdana Construction. Unfortunately, I did not get far, as Henri stopped me near the billiards room.

"Your Highness," he said. "Her Majesty would like to speak to you immediately on the terrace."

"Did she give a reason?" I asked, hoping that I could delay the conversation with her until after dinner.

"I'm sorry—she did not," Henri said. "Only that it was urgent."

I nodded. "Thank you."

I made my way toward the terrace, wondering what could be so important that it could not wait until we were at the dinner table. At least, I knew it had nothing to do with the wedding, since that was finally behind me. Was it the "Macarena" video that I had posted online? Had it already gone viral? That must be it.

Stepping onto the terrace, I was immediately engulfed by a sea of beautiful orchids, their delicate, colorful petals reaching out in all directions, everywhere I looked. My brow furrowed in bewilderment. Were they part of the memorial for Father? Why were there so many?

A lightbulb flickered to life in my thoughts, then the pieces immediately fell into place. These were the orchids that Grace had brought back from Romania, the ones that were supposed to be in our garden shade house, slowly adapting to our climate for the wedding. I had completely forgotten about them. But why were they on the terrace? And why was Miss DuPont still here, and talking with Mother, both with serious looks on their faces?

"Welcome back, Miss DuPont," I greeted her, attempting to appear calm. "How was France and your grandfather's one hundredth birthday party?"

Miss DuPont hesitated with her response to me. "Hello, Your Highness. The trip and his party were both wonderful. Thank you for asking."

Maintaining composure, I said, "I'm so glad to hear—"

Mother cut through the pleasantries. "I know the truth, Oliver. All of it."

I swallowed hard as a particular conversation came to mind.

Words Miss DuPont had said before going away . . .

Please be aware that if I am questioned directly by Queen Annabelle about this particular matter, I will be forced to tell the truth.

Had Miss DuPont told Mother of my initial plans to sabotage my wedding? Would it even matter, now that the wedding had been canceled?

Miss DuPont stood next to Mother with a worried look etched across her face. My gut warned me that it still mattered, and that I might be walking into a minefield, especially when Grace entered the terrace from the opposite end and walked toward us.

Mother wasted no time dismantling the facade. "I cannot believe you had Grace cancel the order with the florist for magenta peonies and then sent her on a ridiculous trip to

Romania to bring back one hundred and twenty-five Adana Orchids we did not want or need."

"What?" Grace exclaimed, staring at me in disbelief. "Why would you do that? You told me you wanted to honor your father at the wedding with these orchids. That's why I had the gardener move them here to the terrace for your dinner this evening. I wanted to do something special for you and your family. You told me they were his favorite flowers."

"King Henric's favorite flower was the violet delphinium," Mother revealed. "The truth is, Oliver wanted you to fail. His only goal was to cause problems with the wedding planning because he wanted me to believe the marriage was cursed, so I would cancel it. He sent Miss DuPont to France under the guise of celebrating her grandfather's birthday. Then he hired you, knowing you would make a mess of things, based on your awful reputation."

Grace's mouth gaped, her eyes shifting between Mother and me, searching for any sign of denial.

"Is this true?" she asked.

I could not lie. Especially since I had given Miss DuPont my word that I would take full responsibility if this conversation ever came up in the future with Mother.

I hesitated, then blew out a frustrated breath. "Yes, but—"

Grace held up her hand. "So . . . I was just a pawn in your little game?"

I shook my head. "Of course not. I just—"

"How could you do this to me?" Her voice quivered

with a pain that cut through the air. "I thought you were the only one who actually believed in me, in my talent and in my abilities. You lied to me and played with my feelings. What kind of man are you?"

Her words hit me like a barrage of arrows, each one sinking deeper into my heart. Grace's eyes, once filled with warmth and trust, now reflected a devastating mix of hurt and betrayal. She blinked rapidly, taking a step back, as if physical distance could shield her from the emotional turmoil that I had inflicted on her.

I scrambled to find the right words to explain. "Grace, you have to understand. Things are different between us now. My plan was conceived before I met you."

"It doesn't matter when you thought of it!" she said. "You could have told me the truth when Theodore was outed. How could you not be honest with me? The fact is, you came up with a deceitful plan and did not even consider the consequences of hurting someone."

I sighed. "Please let me—"

"This is beyond cruel," Grace continued. "You're no better than your brother. I already forgave him and understood his reasons. You have no excuses, Your Highness."

This was even worse than I thought.

Grace was back to addressing me formally.

My heart was breaking into tiny pieces.

She turned and walked away.

"Grace—wait!" I pleaded, as my heart pounded in my chest.

She ignored my plea and disappeared inside the palace.

I turned to Mother, frustration bubbling to the surface. "Why did you say those things? You ruined everything."

"Me?" she said unapologetically. "I only told the truth, Oliver. Nothing more. And she was right. You should have told her the truth long ago, before I canceled the wedding."

"But why was it even necessary to bring this up in the first place?" I demanded, my patience shattered. "There is no wedding! It didn't matter anymore!"

The realization of the depth of my mistake hit me, and a sense of desperation fueled my steps as I rushed after Grace, praying that I could salvage what was left of the love that had slipped through my fingers.

"Where are you going?" Mother called out, her tone indifferent.

I turned around to look at her. "To stop the woman I love from walking out of my life forever."

Chapter Twenty-Two

GRACE

With every ring and ping of my phone, I wished for a miracle that would erase the memory and the pain of Oliver's deception. What had I been thinking? How could I have been so foolish as to imagine a life with the future King of Verdana? It was as if I had convinced myself I could bridge the gap between our two very different worlds, until reality had delivered a cruel royal awakening.

Oliver had been outside my room several times in the last few hours, knocking on my door, begging me to open up and hear him out. There was nothing to talk about.

What I needed at the moment was someone to pull me out of this darkness and misery. I reached for my phone to call Cristina, my go-to person and the keeper of positivity in my life. If she couldn't give me a glimmer of hope, nobody could.

"Grace!" she answered. "How's everything going over

there? You've been so quiet. I didn't know if that was good or bad."

I took a deep breath, attempting to steady my quivering voice. "It's over, Cristina. Oliver played me like a puppet. I'm a fool. My heart's a war zone."

"Wait a minute—slow down," Cristina said. "I thought everything was going so well! What about your chemistry? And that amazing kiss you texted me about? What happened?"

I couldn't hold back the sob that escaped my throat. "It was more than one kiss, but they meant nothing to him, *obviously*. Oliver used me. He never believed in us. He hired me under false pretenses to ruin his wedding. His feelings were nothing but physical attraction, *obviously*."

I poured out the details of Oliver's deception, from sending Miss DuPont away so he could hire me, to the unnecessary trip to Romania to track down those orchids, and the cruel manipulation. Cristina listened in stunned silence, absorbing the pain in my words. After I finished, there was a heavy sigh on the other end of the phone.

"I find this so hard to believe," Cristina said, her voice gentler now. "From everything I've read online, he seemed so genuine and kind. Are you sure this isn't just some misunderstanding?"

"He admitted it, Cristina," I said. "Then he tried to make excuses, but I didn't want to listen to more lies."

"Maybe you should hear what he has to say," she said. "Sometimes there is a very logical explanation for the baffling things people do. Try to imagine why he acted that way, then see if there is even the slightest possibility that you might have done the same thing if you had been in his shoes. Maybe that would make it easier to forgive him, or lessen the pain you're feeling."

"I understand he wanted to get out of the wedding, and really, I don't blame him one bit," I said. "But lying and manipulating to make it happen make it hard to forgive. I thought he was different. I thought he was the one! Now, my life is over."

"I don't think I've ever heard you like this," she said. "Not even when that bride from hell announced she was suing you."

"I've accepted the fact that I'm going to be depressed for the rest of my life," I said.

"Not true," Cristina said. "Grace, you're strong! You'll bounce back! We'll get through this together, you'll see."

Her words were appreciated, but they provided little solace.

After a few seconds of silence, Cristina asked, "What are you going to do now?"

Becoming a nun to escape the wreckage of my love life briefly crossed my mind, but the idea of monotony and wearing the same clothes every day was a big turnoff. There was only one logical choice.

I wiped away a tear and said, "I need to get away from this place and Oliver. I'm going to catch the next flight back to the US. I'm coming home, where I really belong."

Oliver had initially arranged in my contract for my return on his private jet, but I needed to take a commercial flight, for my honor and dignity. The last-minute flight would be very expensive, but at least I could afford it now.

"I'm going to check flights right now," I added, opening my laptop and searching for the first available flight, no matter how many layovers there were. "It looks like the next flight back leaves at nine in the morning, with a three-hour layover in Paris. That's it. I'm going to book it."

"Are you sure this is the right thing to do?" Cristina asked. "Maybe you should talk with Oliver."

"I just can't—it hurts too much," I said. "I need some space to think, to re-evaluate my life, and decide what I want to do next."

"Okay then, I won't push it any further," Cristina said. "Send me the details and I'll pick you up at the airport. And I'm sorry you had to go through this, Grace. You know I love you."

"Love you too," I said.

After we ended the call, I immediately booked the flight, then began packing my belongings. Memories of the good times with Prince Oliver, the laughter shared with his wild Italian cousins Enzo and Renzo, the fun energy of his Aunt Honey, and even the enjoyable moments with Princess Adriana and Princess Veronica flooded my mind. Deep in thought, I packed my suitcase, each item a bittersweet reminder of a love that had crumbled.

Henri had knocked on the door and had left food outside on a tray for me. I tried eating the pasta with shrimp, but it was as bland as my appetite for love.

After a restless night with very little sleep, I snuck out

of my room at six in the morning. I winced every time the suitcase wheels ran over the tiles in the floor, the clacking sound bouncing off the walls. I just needed to make it outside without waking up anybody, especially Oliver.

Fortunately, I made it outside, but ran into Henri, who was guiding Freddie along the lawn, trying to get the dog to do his business.

"Good morning, Miss Grace," he said. "I was not aware you were leaving today."

"I have a flight at nine, but wanted to get to the airport early," I said. "I didn't want to wake anybody, so I called a taxi."

"I understand," he said, moving closer with Freddie. "I hope your stay in Verdana was pleasant."

Preferring not to delve into the drama and heartbreak, I replied, "It was very memorable." That was a loaded statement, open to interpretation.

"I'm glad to hear it," Henri said.

I crouched to pet Freddie along the length of his long Corgi body. "Be a good boy, Freddie. Don't you ruin any more dresses in the palace."

As if he had sensed my distress, Freddie leaned closer and licked me on the cheek. I scratched him on the top of the head, fighting back the emotion in front of Henri, even as my eyes welled up with tears.

"And take care of the queen," I added. "She needs you." I stood, wondering if I should have said that last part out loud, but it was the truth.

I said goodbye to Henri and walked toward the security

gate, turning around to glance at the palace one last time. Who knew how long it would take for my heart to get over this? Only time would tell.

Outside the palace gates, I walked toward the waiting taxi, ready to leave the Verdana chapter of my life behind me for good. In the backseat on the way to the airport, I pulled out my phone and glanced at the viral video Cristina had shared with me of Oliver doing the "Macarena."

Just my luck . . .

I won the bet, but lost the love of my life.

Chapter Twenty-Three

PRINCE OLIVER

Dante and I ran side-by-side in the palace gym, our treadmills humming in unison, while August grunted on the leg press machine behind us. It was still quite early in the morning, and my plan was to wrap up my workout in ten minutes, head for a quick shower and change, and then position myself directly outside Grace's door.

Sooner or later, she'd have to come out to eat.

I couldn't shake the memory of that devastated look on Grace's face. Her feelings of betrayal weighed heavily on my conscience. I now knew I should have found a different way to call off the wedding, or at least should have told her sooner what I'd done, but who could have predicted our developing feelings for each other? The plan had been to get out of one marriage, not find another one, but there I was, completely unafraid to make a future with Grace, because it *felt* right. And what was gutting me most was the fact that I hadn't been able to declare my love for her, to her. She utterly believed our relationship was a farce.

If only she would listen . . .

Grace was the love of my life.

I was determined to wait patiently outside her door all day, seizing any chance to make amends and make sure she understood the depth of my feelings. I needed to express my remorse and proclaim my love for her, even if I had to repeat it a thousand times for her to believe me.

"What do you think, Oliver?" Dante asked, stopping his treadmill and getting off.

I swiped my forehead with the towel and glanced over at him, confused. "What do I think about what?"

He chuckled. "He's not even listening to us."

"Not even a little," August said.

I had been so deep in my thoughts about Grace, I hadn't heard a single word of their conversation since they started talking about August's trip through South America, and how he got the inspiration after watching the movie *The Motorcycle Diaries*. Whatever they'd said after that was a complete blur.

August finished his set on the leg machine, then got up and walked over to my side, leaning against the treadmill. "We were saying we should all shave our heads and join a monastery. Good times for everyone, don't you think?"

I sighed. "I prefer my hair to fall out the natural way. From stress."

"It's your loss," August said with a grin. "Seriously,

brother, I was asking if I could be involved in the planning for the new Royal Academy of Arts, in some way."

"Of course—I'd like that very much," I said, pressing the stop button on my treadmill and getting off. "I was counting on Grace to play a significant role. I even had the perfect job in mind for her. I just hope it's not too late and I can convince her to stay in Verdana."

"She has refused to talk to you?" August inquired.

I wiped the back of my neck with a towel. "Yes. I knocked on her door multiple times, left voice messages, and sent texts. I slid a handwritten letter underneath her door, opening up my heart to her and telling her how much I loved her, but she pushed the envelope right back out, unopened. I had Henri deliver dinner to her room, but she didn't even touch it. I even went outside and tried climbing up the side of the wall to her terrace, like they do in the movies, but I lost my grip and fell into Mother's prized rose bushes."

August glanced at the scratches and thorn marks on my arms and winced. "Whoever said love can be a little prickly wasn't lying. You've got the battle scars to prove it."

"It's nothing compared to the pain I have caused her," I said. "I shouldn't be surprised she wants nothing to do with me. I ended up spending most of the night in my art studio, listening to music, and putting the finishing touches on her portrait."

"Opera classics?" August guessed.

I nodded. "Mostly, yes. But when 'Time to Say Good-bye' by Pavarotti started playing, I nearly lost control of my emotions and decided it would be best to retire to my suite. It just kills me to think I might lose her over this."

"You won't lose her," Dante assured me.

"How can you be so sure?" I asked.

"Because I have never known you to give up on something when you believe in it so strongly," he replied.

I agreed with a nod. "It hurts beyond words, but the worst thing is knowing that she's suffering because of me. She needs to know I love her."

"Then don't give up." August leaned toward me and clapped me on the back. "Find a way to look her in the eyes and tell her how you feel. It doesn't have to be romantic or the perfect place. Just tell her. You have nothing else to lose."

"He's right," Dante added. "Show her how much she means to you, and make it big. Even a public declaration, if you have to. You owe her that much."

I gave them both a grateful smile and a nod, then ran out of the gym.

After a quick shower and change, I headed straight to Grace's room and settled on the floor next to her door. There was complete silence inside, so she was still asleep. I was prepared to wait, no matter how long it would take.

A few minutes later, Henri walked by and paused in front of me, wearing a curious expression. "Is everything all right, Your Highness?"

I nodded and kept my voice low. "I'm waiting for Grace to wake up. What time will her breakfast be delivered? I need to speak with her."

"I'm sorry to inform you, Your Highness, but Miss Grace is not here," Henri revealed.

"What?!" I jumped to my feet, cursing myself for not spending the entire night in front of her door. "Where could she have gone so early?"

"She mentioned she was on her way to the airport, Your Highness," he disclosed. "Her flight back to America departs at nine."

My heart nearly stopped.

How had I not seen that coming? The only thing Grace wanted was to distance herself from me and my lies, and who could really blame her? I deserved it, but that didn't mean I wasn't going to try to stop her. The thought of a life without Grace made my heart ache.

"This is a nightmare," I muttered, checking my watch. "I don't have much time."

"Is there anything I can do, Your Highness?" Henri offered.

"Yes—please prepare the helicopter," I instructed urgently. "I need to get to the airport before that plane takes off."

Chapter Twenty-Four

GRACE

My flight was scheduled to board in ten minutes, and all I could think about was getting on that plane and escaping the remnants of a relationship that had turned into a dumpster fire. The sooner I got home, the better.

Then, out of the blue, fate decided to kick me while I was down.

I glanced up at the departure display at the gate, only to witness the status of my flight change from "On Time" to "Delayed."

I stared at the dreaded D word in disbelief.

It made no sense.

The plane was there.

The passengers had disembarked ages ago.

What could possibly be causing this delay?

Determined to unravel the mystery, I approached the airline counter. The employee wore a grin so exuberant it could have powered a small country.

"Good morning!" she said. "How may I help you on this beautiful day?"

"Good morning," I replied, though my heart wasn't in it. "Any idea why the flight is delayed? I thought we were just getting ready to board."

"I don't have a clue!" she chirped. "I'm sure it won't be much longer. You hang in there. I'll try to get an update and make an announcement soon." Another radiant smile followed.

I mumbled my thanks.

Then she squinted at me and tilted her head. "You know, you look somewhat familiar. In fact, now that I think about it, you are the spitting image of that woman who's rumored to be Prince Oliver's new girlfriend."

I stammered. "I'm definitely not his girlfriend."

That didn't stop her from continuing the conversation.

"He's so dreamy," she said. "Imagine if you *were* his girlfriend."

I'm trying to forget.

"They do make a cute couple, that's for sure!" she added. "They looked like they were having so much fun on that log ride at Atomic Adventures. I'm sure more than a few people have told you that you look like her."

I felt a flush of discomfort. "Not really."

The employee laughed, brushing off her comment. "Well, you look like her. Can you imagine going out with Prince Oliver? Oh, my goodness." She fanned her face. "Talk about a fantasy."

I was eager to escape this conversation and the unsettling reminder of my own romantic disaster. All I wanted was to bid Verdana farewell and move on with my life.

I managed a weak smile, the awkwardness lingering. "Yeah, that's a fantasy, all right. Anyway, thank you for your time."

And please dial down your happiness a notch.

"You bet!" she said. "That's what I'm here for!"

Back at my seat, I found a couple taking up not only my spot but the one beside it too. And, just my luck, they were deep into a full-blown make-out session. The airport love-birds seemed completely unaware of my irritation. Their limbs were all intertwined, and they whispered sweet noth-ings as if they were the stars of their own romantic comedy, making my annoyance skyrocket.

It hit a little too close to home, reminding me of the times Oliver and I shared those same kinds of kisses. That's when I heard a voice over the airport intercom system, and it sent a jolt through me.

"Attention! Your attention, please!" the man said. "Would Grace Fullerton please report to the Verdana Airlines VIP Lounge immediately."

My eyes shot up to the ceiling in disbelief.

It was Oliver.

His voice echoed through the airport.

"Once again, Miss Grace Fullerton, please report to the Verdana Airlines VIP Lounge immediately to receive an apology, a confession, and your personalized gift."

A hushed murmur around me suggested others recognized the voice too, speculating he was a movie star or someone famous.

Oliver's voice continued, "Come on, Grace, don't keep all these lovely people waiting. You deserve to know the truth."

My shock deepened. Oliver was not just present in the airport, but he seemed to be orchestrating this flight delay. My mind raced with the possibilities of what he had planned as I contemplated the inconvenience this might cause hundreds of passengers.

"That's Prince Oliver!" a woman said.

Someone also nearby said, "She'd better get over there now!"

"Get going, Grace!" another man called out.

Reality hit me with a mix of surprise and intrigue. I couldn't just sit there and ignore what was going on. I tried my best to look casual as I made my way back up to the counter.

"There she is again!" the woman said.

"Could you please tell me where the Verdana Airlines VIP Lounge is?" I whispered.

The employee's eyes went wide as she beamed proudly. "I had a feeling it was you! This is *so* exciting. Don't keep the prince waiting!" She pointed past the burger cafe by the next gate. "Walk just past the restaurant, and it will be on your right. Look for the bright blue sign. Actually, forget that. I will personally take you there myself. Nobody will be allowed to board until Prince Oliver says so, anyway." Before I could say a word, she came around the counter, grabbed me by the hand, and pulled me toward the lounge. "This is so exciting! Love is in the air! I'm Freya, by the way. It is such an honor to meet you."

"You, too. I'm Grace."

"Yes, you are! What fun!" she replied. "This only happens in the movies."

I tried to act casual as we speed-walked to the VIP lounge, but there was no discounting the fact that everyone was gawking and glaring, and were as equally animated as Freya. I was sure I looked hideous from all the crying, but my heart told me to give Oliver a chance to explain and make it right. The truth was, I didn't want to leave Verdana, but I also didn't want to be a fool.

Freya guided me to the door of the lounge, where Mr. Stoic was standing outside on watch, turning away women who said they were me.

"Okay—you've got this, Grace," she said, squeezing my hand like a close friend I had known forever. "Men do dumb things, just remember that. It's in their genes." Then she practically shoved me in the door and closed it behind me.

I swallowed hard as I took a few steps into the lounge and saw Oliver standing there patiently, next to Dante, and an easel covered in red silk.

Oliver was dressed in a dark blue suit, white shirt, with a red tie.

Dante took a few steps toward me and nodded. "Miss Grace. It's good to see you." Then he walked past me and out the door.

The entire VIP lounge was empty, except for me and Oliver.

I could feel my nerves intensify as he approached me.

Let him talk.

Give him a chance.

Please, please, please don't cry now.

"Grace," he said, his voice carrying a mix of urgency and vulnerability. "The thought of you not being in my life is the absolute worst feeling in the world, without a doubt." He took another step closer, his gaze never leaving mine. "I couldn't let you go without trying to make things right. Please, give me a chance to explain."

I nodded as my throat tightened with a mixture of emotions.

Oliver took a deep breath, his eyes searching mine. "I made a terrible mistake. I didn't take into consideration how my decision would affect you. I let my pride and responsibilities and ego get in the way of what is right for my life. I thought being a prince meant following a certain path, and that I could never stray from it, but I've realized that the only path I want to follow is the one that leads me straight to you."

I wanted to believe him.

"You hurt me," I said.

"I know, and I can't apologize enough," Oliver said. "And honestly, I feel conflicted about the entire situation. What I did was wrong, absolutely, but if I hadn't done it, I wouldn't have ever met you. And you mean the world to me."

Tears welled up in my eyes, and I blinked them back. "Why should I believe you, Oliver? How do I know what you're saying is sincere?"

"I'm speaking from the heart, Grace." He pulled an envelope from his jacket pocket. "This is the three-page letter that I wrote to you, the one I slid under your door that you didn't open. You don't have to read it at this moment, but everything in there is also from the heart and one hundred percent true. And keep in mind I'm not even close to finished with this apology."

Oliver set the envelope on the table next to two documents. They were contracts, both printed on official Verdana Royalty letterhead. He gestured to the first contract and slid it toward me on the table.

The entire document was just two sentences.

I promise, Grace, never to lie to you again.
This is my solemn vow.

He pulled a pen from his pocket and signed it in front of me.

There was sincerity in his eyes that I hadn't seen before.

Then he slid the second contract toward me.

It was a job offer.

I gasped. "President of the Verdana Royal Academy of Arts?"

"Yes," Oliver said. "Your experience as a high-level strategic business manager and consultant makes you the perfect candidate for this job. Now, you can get back to what you're truly passionate about, but this time in a positive environment, and for a good cause." He grabbed my hands. "You're talented and brilliant, and I want the world to see that."

I was speechless.

"And that's not all," Oliver said, a mischievous glint in his eyes.

He took a few steps toward the easel, then slid the silk off, revealing the breathtaking painting of me in my purple dress. My breath hitched in my throat when I saw Oliver standing beside me in the portrait. I took in the beauty of the painting, but what captivated even more was the adoration and kindness in Oliver's eyes.

"This is how I want us to be, Grace," Oliver said. "Side-by-side, a team, facing whatever comes our way." He gestured to the tiara he'd painted on my head. "And the tiara is because you deserve to be treated like a princess. When I picture my future, I see you there, always and forever."

A surge of emotions filled me from my head to my toes.

I felt a tear escape down my cheek.

"Oliver, this is beautiful," I whispered.

He leaned in, his eyes searching mine. "Grace, I love you. More than anything. I should have told you immediately about my feelings when you confessed your love for me, even if my mother was standing there. Will you forgive me?"

I took a deep breath and nodded enthusiastically. "Of course, I forgive you."

Relief washed over his face, and he pulled me into a tight embrace. "You don't know how much this means to me." Then he leaned down and kissed me on the lips, the emotion almost too much for me to handle. "I love you, Grace. Always and forever."

I smiled. "I love you, too."

"That is music to my ears when you say that." He pulled me even closer, and a playful twinkle lit up his eyes. "We'd better alert the airline, so they can get going without further delay. Oh, and I guess I am going to owe you another apology shortly."

Furrowing my eyebrows, I asked, "Why is that?"

Oliver gestured toward the exit. "Because you and I are going to walk out that door together, as a couple, hand in hand, which will only mean one thing." His grin widened. "We're about to go viral again."

I smirked. "I wouldn't have it any other way."

Epilogue

PRINCE OLIVER

Three Months Later . . .

While Grace believed our trip to Corfu, Greece was solely for her birthday celebration, there was a hidden agenda.

The real reason was my impending proposal.

Proposing to a woman when you know she will say yes doesn't make it any easier. I was a bundle of nerves because I wanted every detail to be flawless. To make it even more special for Grace, I had even flown in her best friend, Cristina, for the occasion. I envisioned an evening filled with fun and romance, hopefully something that Grace would always remember.

The guest list was as lively as the location—Mother and Sebastian, Enzo, Renzo, Aunt Honey, Dante, Adriana with her new boyfriend Demetrio, Theo, August, Veronica, and of course, Cristina.

Cousin Renzo's expansive fifteen-bedroom beachfront estate provided the ideal backdrop in an exclusive area of Corfu.

After a sumptuous steak and lobster feast in the dining room, we migrated outside to the patio, eagerly anticipating the Mediterranean sunset. The crowning glory awaited us, a grand birthday cake. Double chocolate fudge, Grace's favorite. The plan was for me to pop the question after the birthday song and candle-blowing ritual.

Grace and Mother were chatting over by the water fountain, both smiling. It warmed my heart to see that they were on agreeable terms after such a rocky and tumultuous start. In fact, Grace and Mother now took biweekly walks around the palace property, just the two of them, something I wouldn't have predicted in a million years. Sebastian's return had a profound effect on Mother, creating a remarkable transformation from a bitter heart to one filled with sweetness and light. She was like her old self again, especially with the addition of Freddie to her life.

Dante, ever the conspirator, leaned in. "Do you have the ring?"

I patted my pocket for what felt like the umpteenth time and nodded. "Got it. Here comes the birthday girl. Act naturally."

Grace stopped in front of us with a beaming smile. "What are you two whispering about?"

I played it cool. "Guy things."

"I'm not so sure I would categorize it as whispering," Dante said with a shrug. "I have always been a big proponent of projecting my voice, if you must know. I'm sure you'll notice when we sing happy birthday to you."

"I can't wait to hear it," Grace said, then glanced over at Veronica. "August and Veronica are playing the avoidance game again. What happened between them? She looks like she despises him."

"He broke her heart, but this is not the time to talk about that," I replied. "We're celebrating your birthday."

Renzo approached, looking starry-eyed. "I think I've found my soulmate!"

I chuckled. "Who's the lucky girl this time?"

"Cristina," Renzo confessed, glancing at Grace's best friend with such adoration. "Please tell me she's single, or my heart will be in perpetual despair."

Grace winked. "As a matter of fact, she's very much available."

"*Mamma mia*—this is fantastic news!" Renzo exclaimed. "Excuse me while I prepare my finest wooing tactics."

"Go for it," I encouraged, then turned to Grace after he walked away. "Do you think Cristina would fall for a guy like Renzo?"

"Without batting an eyelash," Grace assured. "She's got a soft spot for romantic Italian men."

"Here comes the cake, Your Highness," Dante said.

This is the moment I've been waiting for.

I attempted to steady my breathing.

The candles were lit, and everyone gathered around the

cake and sang to the woman who was minutes away from becoming my fiancée.

Dante's voice indeed was heard over everyone else's.

Grace smiled and even winked at him.

After she blew out the candles, everyone cheered, then Cristina asked, "Did you remember to make a wish?"

Grace nodded and glanced at me with the biggest smile. "I sure did. And it was a *very* good one."

I moved toward Grace, ready to propose.

Out of nowhere, Mother stepped in front of me and said, "As long as we are celebrating, I guess this would be a good time to tell you that Sebastian and I are getting married."

Paralysis set in. I was left standing there, dumbfounded. Congratulations, hugs, and kisses showered Mother and Sebastian, stealing the spotlight, but I refused to let this unexpected turn of events spoil my plans.

Then Enzo raised Aunt Honey's hand, revealing yet another diamond ring. "My wish came true as well! We are getting married! Which means I'll need to start taking extra vitamins and supplements to keep up with your boundless energy, my wild enchantress."

"You got that right, my Italian sugar plum!" Aunt Honey said.

Enzo dipped her and kissed her passionately.

The cheers erupted once again—this time with laughter.

I felt a sense of impending doom.

Was this a conspiracy against my proposal?

I was on the brink of cardiac arrest as the engagements kept rolling in. My carefully orchestrated surprise proposal was slipping away. Dante shot me a sympathetic look, but there was no time to dwell on it.

Unfortunately, the announcements kept coming . . .

Next, Theo revealed that he was moving to Cambridge, Massachusetts to get his undergraduate degree in aerospace engineering at MIT.

I was happy for him but drowning in a sea of well-wishes. I wondered if my moment to propose would ever come.

"What about you, Cousin Oliver?" Enzo said. "How are things going with the new Royal Academy of Arts? I do not remember what you do there."

I pasted on my best smile and answered, "Hopefully, we'll be breaking ground on new construction within the next few months. Grace and I are at the helm as president and director. Together, we're overseeing the institution's overall artistic and administrative direction, including exhibitions and programs. I'm absolutely loving it."

"Me, too." Grace hooked her arm around mine and smiled. "It's something very near and dear to our hearts."

My chance had arrived, and I seized it with determination.

Nothing is going to stop me now.

I cleared my throat. "Speaking of my heart . . . there is someone here who has stolen mine, and that is you, Grace."

I pulled out the diamond ring and dropped down to one knee.

Grace's hands flew over her mouth.

The backyard fell silent, amplifying the intensity of the moment.

"Grace, you are the love of my life," I continued. "From the moment I met you, you have captivated me with every little thing you do. Nothing would make me happier than to spend the rest of my life with you by my side."

As I held her hand, the warmth of her touch resonated with the emotions swirling within me. A soft smile played on her lips, and I continued, my gaze unwavering. "Every sunrise, every sunset, every high, every low, I want to experience them with you," I said. "And so, I ask you this with all the love from the bottom of my heart, will you marry me?"

A tear slipped down her cheek as she nodded. "Yes."

Joy surged through me as I gently slid the ring onto her finger. Rising to my feet, I closed the space between us, our lips meeting in a kiss. Cheers erupted around us, but in that magical moment, I had no desire for the kiss to end.

"Cousin Oliver, you might want to find a room," Renzo teased. "The house has many. Take your pick."

Grace and I broke away from our kiss, laughter bubbling up as we realized we might have gotten a bit carried away.

"That was an impressive kiss, I must say," Enzo playfully chimed in, then he turned to Aunt Honey. "Looks like we have some competition."

Grinning from ear to ear, I proudly announced, "We're getting married!" My proclamation was met with a chorus of congratulations and warm embraces.

"My wish came true," Grace said, holding up her hand to admire the ring.

"Mine as well," I said with a grin.

This marked the beginning of a lifetime of love, laughter, and shared dreams. I could not wait to marry Grace.

"Congratulations," Cristina said, hugging Grace. "You're not thinking of planning your own wedding, are you?"

Grace snorted. "No way." She turned to me. "I assume we will be hiring Miss DuPont, right?"

I nodded. "If you're okay with that."

"Definitely," Grace said.

Cristina hugged me as well. "Congratulations. And thank you for flying me here for this on your jet. It means a lot."

"It's my pleasure," I said.

"The timing of this could not be more perfect," Mother said with energy I haven't seen in years. "Because I have another announcement to make. I was going to wait, but since today is a day of good news, why not now?" She glanced at Sebastian, then back at the rest of us. "I am abdicating the throne."

A collective gasp filled the backyard.

"What?" I said.

"When?" Theo asked, his surprise mirroring mine.

"After Oliver's wedding, of course!" Mother said, looking at me. "I'm ready to enjoy other things in life with Sebastian. And Oliver, I'm certain you will be a king we can all be proud of."

"This day keeps getting better!" Enzo said, then pulled Aunt Honey close and kissed her passionately.

Clearing my throat, I interrupted the jubilation. "I'm sorry, but I don't want to be king."

All eyes turned to me, registering a mixture of shock and confusion.

"Oliver—where is this coming from?" Mother asked.

"I want to dedicate my time to the Royal Academy of Arts," I answered. "Nothing would give me more joy." I glanced at Grace. "Are you okay with this?"

She nodded with a smile. "Of course. Whatever makes you happy."

"Who is going to be king then?" Aunt Honey asked.

"I will," August said, stepping forward. "I'm giving up my vagabond lifestyle and returning to Verdana to play a larger role in the Monarchy. It's time. And I will be solely focused on giving the people of Verdana a better life. It would be my honor to be king."

"I can't think of anyone better suited for the position," I said. "Even better than I could ever be. Believe me, this was meant to be."

August hugged me. "Thank you, I appreciate that. And nothing would give me greater pleasure. As long as we have Mother's support on this, of course."

Mother glanced at us both, before smiling and saying, "You have my full support. And I'm sure your father would be very proud."

Glasses were passed around with dessert wine.

Aunt Honey raised hers first. "To love!"

"To love!" everyone said, clinking glasses.

"It looks like it's settled then," Mother said. "The future of Verdana will be in good hands. There's only one item left on the agenda that would make everything complete."

"What's that?" I asked.

"Nothing that should be too complicated," Mother said. "Now that August is going to be king, we need to find him a suitable wife."

All eyes slowly turned toward Veronica.

THE END

Thank you for reading ROYAL CRUSH!

I hope you enjoyed Prince Oliver and Grace's story. Ready for more fun? Get the next book in the series, ROYAL TWIST, August and Veronica's story. You can find it on Amazon here:

https://bookgoodies.com/a/B0CLH65NLC

Subscribe to my newsletter to receive updates, sales and new release alerts, and behind the scenes fun! Plus, get a FREE copy of my super-fun romantic comedy, *Happy to be Stuck with You.*

http://www.richamooi.com/newsletter.

You can also browse my entire list of 22 romantic comedies on Amazon:

Author.to/AmazonRichAmooi

Find me on social media here!

https://www.facebook.com/author.richamooi/

https://www.instagram.com/richamooi

https://www.tiktok.com/@romcomrich

Acknowledgments

Dear RomCom Lover,

It takes more than a few people to publish a book, so I want to send out a big THANK YOU to everyone who helped make *ROYAL CRUSH* possible.

A hundred million kisses and an enormous thanks to my Spanish Princess, my wife, my angel, Silvi Martin. I am the luckiest man in the world. I LOVE YOU SO MUCH!

Thanks to Sherry Stevenson, Robert Roffey, Deb Julienne, Lori Pfister, Sue Trainer, Paula Bothwell, Sue Traynor, Tracie Banister, Elena Johnson, and Emma St. Clair. YOU ROCK!

To my wonderful readers, thank you for your support and telling everyone about my books! I love your emails, as well as your comments and interaction on Facebook and Instagram. You motivate me to write faster! Don't be shy. Send an email to me at rich@richamooi.com to say hello. I personally respond to all emails and would love to hear from you.

Until next time . . .

Stay Safe. Be Happy. Love Always.

Hugs from San Diego, California.

Rich

About the Author

Rich Amooi is a Taleflick Discovery Winner, a three-time Readers' Favorite Gold Medal Recipient, Holt Medallion Finalist, and the bestselling author of 22 romantic comedies.

A former radio personality and wedding DJ, Rich now writes romantic comedies full-time in San Diego, California, and is happily married to a Spanish Princess. He believes in silliness, infinite possibilities, donuts, gratitude, laughter, and happily ever after.

Connect with Rich!
www.richamooi.com
rich@richamooi.com

facebook.com/author.richamooi

instagram.com/richamooi

tiktok.com/@romcomrich

goodreads.com/richamooi

Made in the USA
Las Vegas, NV
12 January 2024

84260425R00192